Beth Shriver's fresh voice and satisfying Amish romance will keep you turning pages to the very end.

—Jennifer Beckstrand
Author, *Huckleberry Summer*

a novel
Clara's Wish
An Amish Christmas Romance

Beth Shriver

Most Charisma House Book Group products are available at special quantity discounts for bulk purchase for sales promotions, premiums, fund-raising, and educational needs. For details, write Charisma House Book Group, 600 Rinehart Road, Lake Mary, Florida 32746, or telephone (407) 333-0600.

Clara's Wish by Beth Shriver
Published by Realms
Charisma Media/Charisma House Book Group
600 Rinehart Road
Lake Mary, Florida 32746
www.charismahouse.com

Although this story is depicted from the town of Lititz, Pennsylvania, and the surrounding area, the characters created are fictitious. The traditions are similar to the Amish ways, but because all groups are different with dialogue, rules, and culture, they may vary from what your conception may be.

Cover design by Bill Johnson
Design Director: Justin Evans

Visit the author's website at www.BethShriverWriter.com.

Library of Congress Cataloging-in-Publication Data:
Shriver, Beth.
Clara's wish / Beth Shriver. -- First edition.
pages cm
"An Amish Christmas romance."
Summary: "In this Amish Christmas romance, Lizzy Ryder

discovers that this holiday season could be her best friend's last. Will she find the comfort and love she desperately needs?"-- Provided by publisher.
ISBN 978-1-62136-597-6 (softcover) -- ISBN 978-1-62136-598-3 (ebook)
1. Amish--Fiction. 2. Female friendship--Fiction. 3. Christmas stories. I. Title.
PS3619.H7746C58 2014
813'.6--dc23
2014026975

First edition

14 15 16 17 18 — 987654321
Printed in the United States of America

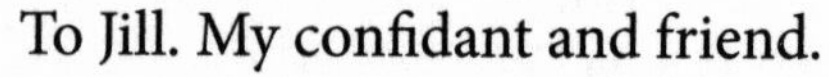
To Jill. My confidant and friend.

Chapter One

Come home. Clara *needs you.*

That was all the letter said.

Home was the last place Zack Schrock wanted to be, but the letter was about his sister, Clara, so he'd made plans to leave straightaway. Questions flew through his mind. It had to be something bad for Lizzy to be the one to write to him. He didn't particularly like Lizzy, but she was friends with Clara, so he tolerated her.

Clara was the only one in the community who kept in touch with him, and that was only by letters. Guilt washed over him now as he thought of how few times he had written back. He'd lived in the city long enough now to pick up a phone, something the community frowned upon. It had been interesting and exciting when he first arrived in the city, and people there appreciated his different ways. But soon he began to morph into them, and now Lizzy's letter was calling him back to the community.

Her community, not his. He'd washed his hands of that place years ago, and he had no plans to go back to their way of life. Not that they'd let him.

Dried prairie grass bent in the breeze as the cold Pennsylvania wind whistled through the window of his rental car. He looked over his shoulder as he neared the town of Lititz and patted the duffle bag by his side. He'd found himself watching out for cops ever since he left Philadelphia. Maybe now he could begin to relax a bit.

One question plagued him: Why would Lizzy write instead of Clara? Something was very wrong, and it made the drive seem twice as long as it was. His mind raced, but all that came through loud and clear was that Clara was ill.

She'd fought off illness when she was young. *Lord, please don't let it be that again.* For Clara to be that ill again would make all of his troubles seem small, although he did have some bad choices catching up with him.

But if something happened to Clara, he didn't know what he'd do. He was in a bad place and knew he needed to change his ways, but God understood, didn't He? Surely He wouldn't let Clara die.

The glow of the small town under the gray sky did little to keep the foreboding from creeping up inside him. He couldn't remember the last time he'd been home, but he did remember his last conversation with his father, confirming his decision to leave. His two younger brothers, Eli and Jonas, might not even recognize him. If it wasn't for Clara, he wouldn't be there at all.

Clara had told him she wanted to make a visit, travel to the city, and spend some time there with him for a short while, but her true intentions were revealed when she told him she really wanted him to come home to stay. He wondered now whether she'd known something back then about what Lizzy was telling him.

"It's been long enough you were away from your own flesh and blood, Zack Schrock." Clara's voice was sharp like their mother's, impossible to ignore, and easily swayed

him. She had tried to get him to agree to come home for Christmas. He'd had no intention of going.

He had come as far as his car would take him. Now he was on empty, and he would have to go in and pay cash at a gas station. A strange noise in the engine had started up a few miles back, so for once in a very long time, he was glad he was back in this small town of Lititz, Pennsylvania.

Zack had to be cautious and take situations into his own hands. Because of his boss, he couldn't do things the easy way, but Clara must need help, so Zack would do what he had to.

He filled up and put some oil in the car. Then he got behind the wheel again and scanned the area. He was close, and the last few miles created anxiety as he thought of entering a place that didn't want him. The horse and buggy trotting along going the other direction told him how close he was. The exhaust from his car and the constant bouncing irritated him, and he wished for the shiny black Mercedes he drove in the city.

A cough from the exhaust forced him forward, encouraging him to pick up the pace, but the way his car was sputtering, he couldn't.

"Won't be too long now," he muttered.

There would be no comfort for him once he got there.

Chapter Two

LIZZY RYDER TAPPED her finger on the counter of the small community store, waiting for the store owner to cut the blue material for the dress she planned to make. Lizzy's *mamm* had told her the color would bring out her blue eyes, unlike the black she usually wore. She'd sold her jams and jellies to a horde of people at the farmers market to pay for the material. Every one of them agreed her preserves were the tastiest around. "Can you hurry, Lloyd?"

Lloyd stopped and stood straight. "What's the rush? You don't want me to make a mistake and cut it wrong, do ya?" He tapped his bifocals down to the tip of his nose and took slow clips as he made his way to the bottom. "This is mighty fine fabric you got here. What's the occasion?"

"Clara was going to make me a dress, so I decided to make it myself."

Neither of them needed to say more. Clara wasn't able to follow through with her promise—or much of anything lately. She hadn't been herself for some time now, often out of breath, feeling nauseous and with no appetite. The one thing Clara held fast to was fixing Lizzy up with a beau. Lizzy would let Clara play matchmaker, but only because it was Clara. Everyone loved Clara.

Lloyd stopped cutting, irritating her to no end. She had to have time to get this dress made, and quick.

"Well, I'm looking forward to seeing her healthy again, she's a sweetheart." He took a breath to continue, but Lizzy had heard enough. She didn't like to talk about her friend's condition; it was out of her control, and Lizzy *always* had to be in control.

"*Jah*, she will be. What time do you have, Lloyd?" She gathered the cut material for him to wrap it up.

The older man turned to the cuckoo clock on his desk behind the counter. "Heading toward dinnertime already. You better skedaddle." He handed her the material, now neatly wrapped and bagged.

She backed toward the door. "You'll be sure to tell me when the spindles of thread come in, won't you, Lloyd?"

He stared past her and pursed his lower lip. "Well, I'll be."

She turned around and looked at the open door. Her jaw started to drop, but she pulled herself together and broke the silence. "Zack. You came."

He looked down at her with those same dark eyes that she remembered so clearly, like looking into a dark well and trying to come up out of it. If any of the stories about him were true, he was in deep trouble.

"If it isn't little Lizzy Ryder. You of all people are the first one I run into." His mouth tipped to one side, and her heart stopped.

"What are you doing here?" It wasn't quite how she wanted it to come out, but she'd been put off balance by the golden flecks in his eyes or perhaps the way he held himself so straight and tall. *I can't believe I don't remember that.*

He slowly turned his head, his eyes narrowed slightly as

he took her in. Lizzy worried for a moment she had been too jaded and tried to start over.

"I mean, it's good to see you again."

He hadn't blinked, kept his eyes on her, and stood stock-still with his hat in his hands.

Still has the bad manners, though.

"I don't have time for small talk." He shifted his gaze back to Lloyd. "Lloyd, good to see you."

Lloyd's eyes were wide, unmoving at the moment. "I didn't expect to see you, Zack." Lloyd stood up as straight as his old back would let him. "Your family know you're here?"

Lizzy bet he was scanning Zack for something else, like a festering wound or black eye. But Zack didn't look like he was feeling ill—his sun-kissed face gave him a healthy ruddiness.

Zack's jaw tightened as he turned his attention back to Lizzy. "Is my sister in a bad way?"

Lizzy and Lloyd looked at each other, but neither spoke.

"Where is she?" The last word lifted into a higher pitch, but it was the look on his face that caught her attention—a mix of anger, desperation, and sorrow.

He turned and headed out the door, his boots hitting the wooden, wraparound porch double-time. Lizzy rushed out behind him, but his long stride kept her three steps behind. He walked to a car. The thought of Zack driving was strange to her. She studied the machine, wondering how it had gotten him there in one piece.

He looked from the car to her. "It's all they had at the car rental. Is she home or at the doc's?"

Lizzy tried to guess but honestly didn't know whether Clara was getting remedies or asleep in bed. "At the doc's."

"Why didn't you tell me she was sick?"

"I believe I just did."

Zack's brows lifted.

He'd grown into a man since she'd seen him last. She wondered whether he'd matured in other ways as well. He was always in some sort of mischief, right up until the time he left. She remembered his mother sobbing for days after he'd gone.

"Are you coming or do you plan to just stand there?" Zack's brass voice brought her back to the moment. He put his hat on his head and started walking. Lizzy took quick steps, passed him, and didn't stop until she was at the doctor's *haus* at the edge of the community.

Clara was lying on a small couch. Her eyes fluttered and then closed again. "Zack?" Her voice was soft as an angel's. She'd never had much strength, but now she couldn't seem to even keep her eyes open, as if it was too much work to say more than a single word. Zack looked scared.

"Zack." Doc came in from the back room with his black bag. "I didn't know you were back."

"Temporarily." Zack took off his felt hat and squeezed it with a grave expression.

Lizzy wondered whether he knew something more that he wasn't telling them, or whether the distrust of everyone here had raised the tension. He had to sense it.

"Is she in a bad way, Doc?" Zack watched Clara's chest rise and fall in shallow breaths.

"*Jah*, I believe she is." Doc nodded to confirm what he'd said.

"What have you been treating her with?"

Lizzy remembered back to when they were younger. The bishop had given Zack's *mamm* a hard time for taking

Clara to the hospital for treatments. Lizzy was hoping they had become more lenient since then.

"We'll have to get her upstairs where she'll be more comfortable. Then I'll need to give her some more treatments and watch her for a while."

Zack lifted Clara and carried her to a cheerful bedroom upstairs. Lizzy followed close behind, but stayed outside pacing in the hallway as Doc got Clara settled in bed.

Zack looked long at Clara, as if staring at her would bring her out of the deep sleep she appeared to be in. Doc left the room with slow steps, nodding at Lizzy as he passed. She wished Doc would tell them Clara was going to be all right, that she'd pull through whatever ailed her. But the expression on his face remained grave.

Lizzy walked into the room and sat down, noticing Zack's worried expression as he sank down into a chair. When he bowed his head, she thought she heard him whisper a prayer.

Chapter Three

"Zack!" Lizzy's shrill voice brought him back. He'd closed his eyes for one second to clear his head but he managed to doze off instead. With Lizzy practically screaming in his ear, he didn't look up right away, so he wouldn't say something he'd regret.

The last person Zack hoped to see when he came home was Lizzy. He'd have some explaining to do with his *mamm*, and he'd have to get to know his younger *bruders* again after being away for a while, but dealing with Lizzy even topped trying to making things right with his *daed*, as unpleasant as that would be. Zack remembered how sassy Lizzy was and how she always got her way, at least when a cluster of guys was around.

He sat up and opened his eyes, hoping to see his sister, but the doctor had asked them to wait downstairs while he gave her a treatment. "Did Doc say anything more about Clara?" He rubbed his face. Too much time on the road with little to eat had depleted his energy.

"*Jah,* he said no change. She's sleeping again. I asked you a question before you nodded off. How can *you* sleep?"

His irritation flared up by reflex, but he was too tired to make anything of it. He should have expected this from Lizzy. He leaned back into the hard wood bench they sat on together and tried not to look over at her. He didn't want to be persuaded by those bright-blue eyes. He could honestly say he'd never seen anyone as pretty—or as ornery.

"What do you want?" The words slipped out before he could stop them. His tone was sharp, and he shook his head when he sensed it. He knew by the way her head slowly turned to him that she didn't appreciate his short response. Then the sounds of footsteps caught their attention. Thankfully, the doctor's timing was going to spare Zack a tongue-thrashing. He could go toe to toe with her, but not tonight.

He lifted himself a bit when he realized he'd been sitting on the edge of her dress and pulled away from the hem when she stood. She looked back and frowned at him.

I'll probably hear about my tone and her dress.

He looked at the doctor. "How is she?"

The doc scratched the back of his gray, balding head. He had only herbal medicines, of which Zack was skeptical, but he had no choice except to go along for now.

The doc looked from Lizzy to Zack. "She's not well. Whatever this illness is, it has taken its toll on her. She was awake just long enough to drink some of the herbal tea."

"What else can we do for her, Doc?" Lizzy seemed almost as upset as Zack was. He'd seen Lizzy when she was this troubled before, but it was usually something about herself.

"I'll make up some remedies and keep her here until morning and then see how she is." He placed a wrinkled hand on Zack's shoulder. "I'm sorry, Zack. But I'm glad you're here for her and your family." His tone didn't quite match his words, but at least he didn't tar and feather him and send him out of town, whether he wanted to or not.

Lizzy's bottom lip quivered, and she sucked in a breath.

"Everybody loves Clara. We'll all pitch in and take care of her." It was rare for her to show any feelings.

"You're right about that, Lizzy. I'm sure she'll have lots of special care."

Doc's words were softer with her, smooth and assuring. Zack had expected to be treated differently, but not to this degree. They were assuming a lot about him without knowing the facts, but it would be futile to try and convince them otherwise. Besides, he was here for Clara.

"I take it you haven't been home to see your parents." It was a statement. The doctor knew the answer. It seemed Zack couldn't do anything right anyway, so why try to correct another situation?

"No, I figured they were at the auction, so I came straight here. Scares me to see her like that." Putting it mildly, but he didn't want to be too dramatic. He'd just never seen Clara quite so vulnerable, even during her previous illness. She was the rock, the peacemaker, always with a smile, no matter what the situation. Until now.

Lizzy was frowning when Zack looked over at her. "The Schrocks are at the mud sales, Doc, remember?"

"Quite right. I'd forgotten." The doc looked over at Zack again. "I want to get some liquids in her, and then she needs some rest." He didn't seem as alarmed as Zack thought he should be. But then he'd been practicing medicine a long time. Even though he hadn't been in the habit of praying much lately, Zack knew whatever was going to happen was in God's hands; fretting about it wouldn't help anything.

"I'm going to see my sister." Zack turned on a heel and walked down the hallway toward the stairs. Doc took care of the families, but when something was too much for him to treat, he'd send them off to the city, which was where Zack wanted Clara to go. Zack had been in the "world" long enough to have taken their ways as his own. Although he didn't spend much time with God, he prayed now that this would work out as it should.

"Well, then, I'm coming with you." She stood behind him, bristling. Maybe mad at him or just upset about Clara, probably both. He glanced over at her. The last thing he needed was her on his case.

The *click-clack* of her boots grew closer, and soon she was by his side. How those short legs caught up with his he didn't know, but her determination didn't surprise him.

He took the steps two at a time, until they got to Clara's room. Lizzy gasped. Clara's skin was pale, and her chest barely moved, making it appear she wasn't breathing well. Lizzy took her cold hand, but her eyes didn't open. Zack moved closer and touched Clara's other hand. It felt frail, as if it could snap like a tree limb.

"She doesn't look like Clara." Lizzy seemed to be talking to herself. After a minute that felt much longer, Lizzy let go of her hand and bumped into Zack. "Sorry, I wasn't paying attention."

Whoa. An apology? That won't last. "Are you all right?"

"*Jah*, I'm fine." And just that quick, the old Lizzy was back.

Clara's eyes fluttered as if she was trying to find the strength to open them and respond to him. He said her name but saw little reaction.

"Clara needs sleep, so her body can heal itself." Lizzy glanced at Zack, who was ignoring Lizzy's suggestions.

"I wonder if she should be at a hospital."

"Don't you believe in our remedies anymore?" Lizzy

asked. He'd expected Lizzy to be offended by the idea, but he was tired and wanted the best for his sister. Now that he thought about the many miles he'd traveled to be here with Clara, he wished he had stopped at a clinic somewhere that had "real medicine." But that was hindsight. There was no point trying to change what had already been done.

Chapter Four

LIZZY WATCHED AS Zack sank slowly into a chair next to Clara's bedside. He let his hands hang down between his legs, head dropped and eyes shut.

Is he praying again?

She'd never known him to do more than just what was expected in the community, sometimes defiantly, so what was this about? Must be the prayer one sends to a distant god they hold on to in a crisis. Maybe that was what God was doing with him—making Zack run back to Him. But then she could never see that really happening. If he was pleading to God, it would be over once Clara had recovered. And she *would* get better. That much Lizzy was sure of.

"I'll get her some more water."

Clara had hardly taken a sip from the cup next to her bed, but the doctor would be making up something that would do more than soothe her parched lips.

Zack didn't respond, so Lizzy slipped out and went down the hall to see about what she could do to help Clara. The doc had gotten a little slower in his old age, and she wondered whether he was on top of things. She wanted the best for Clara, even if it meant pestering him a bit. She knew people thought of her that way—as a nag—but from her position, she thought it a plus to get things done and done right. Sometimes people were just too nice, too polite.

Lizzy reasoned you couldn't get things done that way and took advantage of her ability to make things happen.

She glanced into a room down the hall where the doctor made his remedies and examined patients. It was a bedroom of his oldest son, who'd moved into a house of his own. Doc now used it to store what he needed and to keep the patients close if they needed time to stay there. Lizzy walked in and watched him add a pinch of this and a little of that until he was satisfied and gave it all a good shake.

"What helps with what Clara has?"

Doc startled and looked up at her through round glasses. "Ginseng for overall wellness, and willow to ease any pain she has." His brows lifted as he looked up at her. "Not to worry. She's in *gut* hands."

"*Jah*, I've been keeping the Lord real busy with my prayer requests. He's probably wondering why I haven't called on Him in the last five minutes." She felt better just hearing herself saying those words. It made God feel more real, or something like that.

Lizzy remembered Zack telling her before he left that the mention of God and His everlasting goodness didn't work for him anymore. He'd grown away from his Christian upbringing. Too many condemning hypocrites for Zack to take seriously.

And now the only person Zack honestly cares about is seriously ill.

Doc stopped grinding the rest of the herbs of different colors in a granite bowl and responded with a slight flush in his cheeks. "I thought I already told you."

"I don't remember you telling me anything, Doc." She wasn't exactly sure what else to say.

The older man seemed to be losing his touch due to age and perhaps the pressure to change his old ways.

"I'll warm this up, and you can take it to her straightaway."

His hand shook a little, and when he took the baggy and squeezed the water through the tea bag, she noticed his breathing was labored.

"Here, let me take it for you." She dipped the bag in a mug and let the herbs steep in the boiling water. When she turned to the doctor, she saw him rubbing his hands together, and when he stopped, his hands shook. "Are you all right, Doc?"

"*Jah*, course I am. Just a little tired is all. Now, go on and take that to Clara." His brows drew together with irritation, and he began cleaning up the room. She was glad to leave his presence.

Old grump.

Lizzy balanced the mug on the small tray and decided Clara needed crackers or something to help settle her stomach. She tried to be as cheerful as possible, even though she didn't feel that way. Now Lizzy was worried about Clara *and* the doctor.

Maybe she'd talk to Zack about it, if he'd listen. He seemed to think she wasn't good enough for him. Maybe all of those English women caught his eye, and she was too plain for him now. But what did it matter? She got enough attention in the community.

When she looked at Clara, she was sound asleep after hours of discomfort. "What's this?" Lizzy whispered.

Zack gave her a weak smile. "The same thing I'm gonna be doing. Sleeping."

Lizzy put down the tray, went over to Clara, and brushed

a stray hair away from her cheek. "She's not as clammy as she was earlier. That's a good sign, don't you think?"

"Yeah, but let's not get our hopes up just yet. There was something really wrong when I first got here." Dark circles under his eyes and his gravelly voice told her he too was exhausted, more than she'd realized until this point. She was always so annoyed with him that she began to wonder if it had become a habit without any real cause. They had been apart for a long time. Maybe things had changed.

"You don't think the doctor's remedies work, do you." Lizzy didn't ask; she made a statement because it was obvious. And when he didn't reply, the annoyance came right back to her. "Fine. If you don't want to explain yourself, no need. We never did agree on anything. Why would we now?" She paused, waiting for him to reply, but he was silent.

She couldn't think of a single person who made her this angry this quickly. It was maddening. She whirled around to give him a piece of her mind, but when she turned to him, she found him with his head against the wall, mouth open, sound asleep.

Well, all right, then…but when he wakes up, he's getting an earful.

Chapter Five

ZACK COUGHED AND opened his eyes. He blinked twice and looked around him. Lizzy paced the floor, looked out into the hall, and continued walking again. Cradling his face in his hands, Zack hoped to wake up to see Clara doing fine, that whatever the problem had been, it was gone, and he could see his sister in good health before he left this place.

His mind raced, thinking over everything, wondering what Clara ate, where she'd gone, and what she did to get her in this situation. A moan caused him to jump up out of his chair, bumping into Lizzy as she rushed to Clara's beside. The doc hurried in with his bag in hand.

"What is it, Doc?" Lizzy asked before Zack had a chance to speak, another irritation that caused him to shoot a condescending stare her way. She didn't know well enough to leave things be and let him take care of his sister. With their *mamm* and *daed* away at the mud sales, it was just the three of them to care for Clara, which at the moment he appreciated.

"I can't make heads or tails of it." A ruddy color suffused Doc's forehead and spread down to his neck as he examined Clara.

Zack felt sure the doc had run out of ideas and concoctions. Now was the time to take action. "Clara, can you hear me?"

Her eyes fluttered. She opened them and said his name. "Zack, you're here." The corners of her mouth turned upward before she shut her eyes again.

"I'm taking her to the hospital." That was all that needed to be said, and Zack waited for the rebuff.

"You've hardly given Doc a chance, Zack." Lizzy flipped her *kapp* strings behind her and stared at him with those flaming blue eyes.

"I can't believe you're willing to let her stay here just to save face with the doc, instead of taking her to a hospital where there are more options. The doc just said he couldn't figure out what's wrong." Zack paused, letting it soak in. He knew Lizzy cared deeply about Clara, but she was his kin, not hers, so he'd call the shots. He watched her contemplate what to do, one of the few times she didn't have an immediate response to use against him.

"When you put it that way, there's nothing else to say." She crossed her arms over her chest and frowned at him. "Well, if you're going to do something, get to it."

Zack was taken aback just for a second. He'd never heard her give in before on anything. "All right, then. I'll run get my car and take her to Lancaster Regional."

Lizzy shook her head. "Heart of Lancaster is closer."

"I didn't know there was a new one." Zack was unsure which hospital would draw any attention to him. As far as he knew, they were there to treat the patient, not do background checks on family members, but they might need information from him that he couldn't give. Not yet. "I'm not gonna argue. I'll take her there. We'll keep in touch, Doc."

"I should hope so." Doc's voice betrayed his irritation. "I

still think she would do better right here, but if you're set on taking her to the hospital, I'm washing my hands of it."

Zack told Lizzy, "You might want to stay here in case family starts coming back." He paused, hoping she would get his meaning. Not only did he not want her at the hospital, due to the information he might have to reveal; he also wanted someone here who could convey the information in a proficient way, unlike the way the doc seemed to.

Lizzy's eyes lifted and locked on to his. "I am going wherever Clara goes, although I have to say I'm not happy about this either. I doubt Clara would want to go to a hospital."

There was no reasoning with her.

I should have known better.

He had some choice words to say but stuffed them down his throat for another time. "Fine, but you'll have to ride in my car."

"*Gut.*" She sauntered over without another word and began gathering up her shawl, re-pinning a lock of hair. She turned on a heel and walked to him. "We should tell your *mamm* and *daed*." She patted Doc on the back.

Zack held out his hand and pumped Doc's, something he hadn't done for quite a while. "Thanks, Doc. I know you've done everything you can."

"I'll be praying for her. And for you." Doc smiled weakly and walked back to his little herbal pharmacy, catering to his left side as he made his way.

Zack watched Clara's chest move quickly now. He didn't know which to worry about more—when she was breathing like she was now, or when she barely moved at all.

"What's happening?" Her parched lips and pale cheeks

didn't fit the healthy, vibrant person he knew and loved. *I'm doing the right thing.*

"Clara, I'm taking you to a hospital."

It took him no time to run back to the store where he'd parked his car. Then, with no great effort, he picked Clara up and carried her downstairs. Lizzy was close behind him with a blanket and a few toiletries. He had to admit those weren't things he would have thought of and gave her a little credit.

He laid Clara to the backseat with blankets beneath and around her and then opened the driver's door. Then suddenly the darkness set in as he remembered the previous illness.

God, don't let it be that. Not that again.

What will it take for Clara to be healthy? Why is this happening again?

He didn't want to go any further with his questions. He'd wait to hear the truth from a doctor rather than try to make sense of it on his own. The surprising thing was Lizzy hadn't voiced a lot of her own assumptions, for which he was grateful. At the moment he was just trying to get Clara comfortable and in the capable hands of a doctor as soon as he could—a real, board-certified doctor.

He was about to get in and start the car when Lizzy's parents pulled up in their buggy. Zack stayed the course and occupied himself making sure Clara was settled. He knew it might appear rude, but he had his priorities and that wouldn't change. He listened to their voices, her dad's growing higher, and then footfalls coming closer to the door. He took in a breath and waited to see what their responses would be.

"Zack Schrock?" Ray Ryder stared at Zack. This was

only the beginning, and what a way to start—with Lizzy's *mamm* and *daed*. A lot of others would be shocked and surprised that he was back, just like Lloyd was. His mother would cry and his brothers would take his dad's lead as to how to treat him. He wasn't looking forward to any of it.

None of that mattered at the moment. Clara needed him.

"Ray." Zack straightened and held his hand out when Lizzy's *daed* walked closer.

Ray looked down at Zack's hand and then to Lizzy. "What's going on here?"

Zack answered. "Clara's not well. I'm going to take her to the hospital, and Lizzy is going to stay here with Doc." Now he had two people mad at him, but he didn't care; he'd deal with them later. Ray's frosty gaze told of his reproach. Zack found he had no patience for it.

He was almost positive he was doing the right thing, but he knew the Amish ways, especially if the bishop got involved.

"I'm going with Zack, *Daed*. I want to be with Clara." Lizzy stood by the passenger side of the car, not moving.

"You'll do no such thing. Not without our permission." Ray looked at Zack's car and peered through the window at Clara. Then he turned to where Lizzy stood with her arms crossed over her chest. Zack didn't so much as look in her direction as he took one step toward the car door. He'd almost made it when he heard the *click-clack* of her boots and someone else's beside him.

"Lizzy, you're going home with me." Ray was close behind her but couldn't keep up with her small, quick strides.

"This isn't about him, *Daed*. It's about Clara."

When Ray looked at Lizzy, his frown doubled across his forehead. "You aren't to travel by car, and especially not with him." He nodded toward Zack.

Zack had expected this, but it was still awkward. He was almost in the car when Lizzy leaned against the door. They were too close, so he slipped into his seat. He didn't need to be part of this feud between Lizzy and her dad; in fact, he thought there must be more to this than just him.

Lizzy climbed in, shut the door, and locked it. "You know what my *daed*'s like. It's no excuse, but I want to say I'm sorry, all the same."

Lizzy's reaction to her dad's response took Zack off guard. Lizzy was one of the few people he thought would understand him.

"I appreciate that, Lizzy, but you should go with your dad."

"That's for me to decide." She looked forward and waited.

Zack prayed the car would start. The engine rumbled to life as Ray walked away with long, angry strides.

"You shouldn't go against your dad's request, Lizzy." He knew she could be ornery at times, but not to her dad. That just wasn't done—not in his parents' home or in most others he'd seen while growing up. When she didn't move, he tried again. "Don't put me in the middle of this. I have enough to deal with coming here."

"I need you right now to make this happen." She fastened her seat belt and then looked forward. "Go, before they get to their buggy."

Zack stopped and stared, not sure of what she'd just said. "Are you saying you want me to help you?" Even if it was true, she had to have another motive, so he waited and listened until he caught it. His bet was on Lizzy getting her way to stay with Clara. He didn't want that to happen—too much drama and bossing him around.

"You're not leaving without me." She slowly turned her head to look at him but wasn't quite as insistent as he'd expected.

He let out a breath, knowing Clara would want her there. "Fine, as long as you don't get me in trouble."

Once they were on their way, he was prepared for the thoughts and suggestions Lizzy would surely be giving him. To his surprise she kept her eyes on the road or glancing behind to check on Clara. It was then he realized how much she cared about his sister. She was a tough one to figure, but he was realizing she might care for his sister as much as he did...almost.

"You and my sister are close." He didn't look away from the road.

"She's like a sister to me." Lizzy's voice was almost a whisper. She kept her eyes forward, almost as if hiding the emotions on her face. But at a glance he could see right through her, and what he saw surprised him. Blotchy pink covered her cheeks.

"I remember you spending a lot of time together making mud pies and selling lemonade along with Mom's oatmeal cookies."

She smiled slightly, just enough for him to see the whites of her teeth. "*Jah*, and we still cook up a storm when we're together."

Zack leaned back in the seat and relaxed a little. Lizzy was telling him about her scripture cake as thoughts of Clara stirred. It was as if she wanted to be in on the conversation with them. "Your dad is going to be mad about you leaving."

"He and my brother are overbearing. You'd think I was a child." She made a move as if to cross her arms but stopped.

He paused over his next thought, sensing it could easily be reworded into something in her favor, but he couldn't quite think of how to phrase it. "That's what dads do, right? Watch over their children, especially a young woman like you."

"What is that supposed to mean?" She turned her head to glare at him straight on, so he looked forward, avoiding eye contact.

"Just that you have your own mind about you is all." He tried to downplay the comment, but didn't know whether it came out that way.

Lizzy opened her mouth to give him what he expected was a correction, but she smiled instead, as if she approved what he'd said. Before she could speak, a *thunk* from the engine distracted them. She looked nervous. "What is that noise?"

Zack shook his head. "It's this car. It started acting up about halfway here."

"What does 'acting up' mean, exactly?" Lizzy looked behind her. "*Ach*, no."

"What now?" Zack wished he hadn't asked; he could only take so much at one time.

"My brother is following us." She studied the dashboard, though he doubted she knew what anything was. "Going this slow, you might as well pull over. He won't quit until I go home with him." She leaned back against the headrest and closed her eyes.

Zack turned his attention back to the road. He'd been planning on going into the nearby town to find a place to stay, but now he didn't know whether the car would make it.

He looked in the rearview mirror and could barely

make out the black buggy and bay-colored horse so far away. “If I stop, the car might, too, and I might not be able to start it again. So what do you want me to do?”

“You mean to tell me I went through all this to get in a car that doesn’t work?” She groaned.

“How much farther do you want to go?” He couldn’t hide his frustration and didn’t like not knowing where he was going.

“Just keep going. Luke can’t make it all the way to the hospital at this time of night.” Lizzy didn’t keep her eyes on the road, talking faster than he could keep up and drive this half-dead car. “It’s not getting any louder.”

“Yeah.”

“And Luke is gone.”

“Uh huh.”

“So everything’s all right.”

“No, not until we get there. I’ll be going ten miles under the limit once we hit the highway.”

He was reaching his boiling point. He knew that if she didn’t get out of his car or quit talking, one of the two, he’d be leaving her on the side of the road. Let her brother take her home.

Cars honked as he merged on to the highway at such a slow speed. Lizzy turned to him and started to speak, but he ignored her and sighed in relief when he saw the tall hospital building right off the road. He let out a long breath and turned to see Clara and then Lizzy. Clara started to move, and Lizzy was stock-still with arms crossed. He was in enough trouble without worrying about her. He’d have some explaining to do to with his dad, the bishop.

Chapter Six

BEEP . . . BEEP . . .

The shrill sounds of the hospital kept Lizzy on alert. Every noise, smell, or response from staff made her tighten. How could Clara's condition suddenly go from bad to worse? *Jah,* she was obviously uncomfortable, but it didn't seem like anything more than a bad case of the flu or bad reaction to something.

"Do you think it's food poisoning?"

Zack scoffed, lifted his head, and turned to her. "No, it's not that."

"Then what?"

She watched him look from her to Clara's room and tried not to be upset with his condescending tone. "I wish the doctor would come out so I could talk to him."

Even a nurse would do.

Lizzy tapped her toe on the eggshell-colored Formica floor, entranced by the repeated sound.

"Stop, please." Zack's voice was loud enough that a man and his wife looked over. Zack slid his hand over his face and stood abruptly.

Lizzy felt her cheeks warm, embarrassed he would react in such a way for everyone to hear. She understood he was upset, but everyone else didn't need to put up with his pain.

Maybe some fresh air would cool her down and give her some strength to deal with Zack.

But it's not about Zack; it's about Clara.

They just happened to be caught up together in the same awful experience. Clara was fragile, which only made it more worrisome, but she had a strong mind and faith. That would have to pull her out of this mess.

Zack sat down next to her before she could stand. She knew it was him by the way he let out a long breath and paused before he spoke. It was if he was always figuring what to say before he spoke, making each word count. It about made her crazy, because she liked to get things done and send the next word rolling off her tongue before anyone else got a chance.

"You here to apologize?" She didn't want to look at him, not yet. It was too distracting.

"Not exactly, but that's not what I need to talk to you about."

She almost chuckled. He never needed anything. That was half his problem, why he wouldn't stay in their community. Too many rules, not enough excitement.

They probably all had some excuse for leaving.

But most came back, except the real lone wolves like Zack. Something had happened to get him to come home, and it wasn't just Clara. She couldn't help but look at his knee—the one he catered to. He was a good-size man, strong and able to fend off anyone who might give him trouble, and there'd always been trouble as far as she could remember.

"I need you to listen to me." He moved closer and looked around. "I can't be Clara's next of kin. You have to do it."

Lizzy frowned. "That makes no sense—"

He held up a hand. "Keep your voice down." He glanced at the security guard by the door, who looked toward him.

Lizzy became more intrigued than irritated. She could see it in his eyes—fear. Whatever it was, she was actually seeing him in a way she never had before. "Why are you acting like this? Does it have anything to do with Clara?"

He shook his head. "I don't want her involved, or you."

Lizzy blinked twice at his words. She knew it wasn't anything sentimental but took it that way, all the same. "Involved in what?"

"I can't talk about it now. Just be her friend and go over the paperwork." He patted his pocket—something Amish didn't have—and brought out a bulge of cash held together with a silver clip. "Use whatever you need to pay the bill. No pending balance; pay it all off."

"The community will take care of it. You don't need to pay it all."

"I don't want the money." He looked down at it and lifted his lips in disgust. "It's blood money. It's this or I'll find someone else to give it to."

Lizzy sucked in air at his words. She didn't know exactly what he was doing, but she did know what he was referring to, and it wasn't good. So why was he using her for this? "You're going to get me in trouble, Zack."

"No, I'm keeping you and Clara from exactly that. Just do as I say." He spoke with confidence, but his eyes were pleading for her to listen and follow his request. "When you pay cash, things go quickly. Understand?"

She couldn't imagine how much this would cost or where he'd gotten the money. Maybe it was better she didn't know. After all, it was for Clara. "I hope you know what you're doing." She glanced at him and then clutched the money against her chest. "I'll do it for her."

He let out a long breath and gave her a nod of thanks. His shoulders relaxed and his eyes seemed to soften. Whatever this burden was, it had a strong hold on him. Why she was trusting him she wasn't sure, but in her mind, it had little to do with him.

Lizzy stood. "I want to get this over with. Where do I go?"

"The sign that says registration. I'll be here if you need me."

It felt awkward to be handling such a large amount of money. She'd put some in her purse that didn't hold more than a few dollars, a handkerchief, and a napkin with a snack of pumpkin bread, in case her blood sugar dipped.

She stood by the door until a dark-skinned lady motioned for her to come in.

"What can I help you with?" She adjusted her computer screen and waited for Lizzy to sit down in a green chair.

"I would like to pay for whatever costs are involved with my friend Clara Schrock's medical expenses." She said it firmly so there would be no misunderstanding. It wasn't all that strange with other Amish paying this way.

"Yes, ma'am. I can do that for you."

The clerk asked numerous questions, some that Zack would have been able to answer, so Lizzy did the best she could. Fortunately they were a simple people without much to store up. "Is there any other family with Clara?"

Lizzy hesitated. "*Nee*, just me right now." Putting it that way, it wasn't a lie. She still felt a bit guilty, but she also felt the need to protect Zack. He was Clara's *bruder*, after all.

When she came out of the office, Zack wasn't in the

chairs they had been sitting in, and as she scanned the large waiting room, she didn't see him anywhere. She let out a sigh, disappointed and a little annoyed. Then she thought of the danger he had exposed himself to just by staying as long as he did. She leaned back into the chair and noticed a nurse stop and talk to another nurse and then wave Lizzy over. "Are you with Clara Schrock?"

"*Jah*, how is she?" Lizzy followed the nurse's quick steps down the hall.

"Better, but she's been through a lot. She's exhausted, so try to keep it short. This is Clara's room. The doctor will be in shortly." She cleaned up torn pieces of paper, and plastic tips of what looked like medicine were in a container with a hole in the top.

Lizzy wondered what all had happened in this room over what seemed like such a long time, but now that she oriented herself, maybe it hadn't taken as long as she thought. The waiting just felt longer.

Clara's head rolled over to the side, and she smiled.

Lizzy couldn't get to her soon enough when she held out her hand. Then she paused, wanting to hug her. In the end she settled on taking her hand. "You look so much better. What was it? What's wrong with you?"

"I can explain if you like."

Lizzy turned to see a handsome man with a stethoscope draped around his neck. "*Jah*, please." He hadn't asked for their relation, but maybe the dialect and Amish clothes explained enough.

"I'm Doctor Kauffman." The doctor leaned against a cabinet with a sink and shelves and then set his clipboard down next to him.

Lizzy was somewhat surprised his last name was Amish

but then thought maybe that was *gut*, considering the situation.

"Clara has pain in her stomach. There could be a number of different possibilities as to what is causing the discomfort. Is there anything else?"

Clara's cheeks turned pink and she looked away. "*Jah*, bloating, all the time, seems like."

"Don't be shy, Clara. The more information we can gather, the better we'll be able to treat you. Anything else like vomiting, or blood in the stool, trouble swallowing, or weight loss?"

"*Jah*, you've lost some weight." Lizzy looked down at Clara, wondering why she wasn't offering more information.

Must be her lack of strength.

"Loss of appetite is another sign. You're dehydrated, as well. Anything else?" He was awfully thorough, and Clara needed to rest, but he was the doctor, so Lizzy held her tongue.

"There is a sore spot on my belly, but it's hardly anything." She automatically touched her stomach.

"Let me take a look." He rubbed the stethoscope and looked straight ahead for what seemed much too long. Then he hung the stethoscope over his neck and pressed around the area where Clara touched.

"Could be nothing at all, but I'm going to order an X-ray."

"How long before you'll know what's wrong?" Lizzy asked.

"It all depends on what the X-ray shows."

"What are the possibilities?" Clara's voice almost made Lizzy cry. It was weak and cracked with each word.

"Gravity can move things around, causing them to migrate, slowly penetrating into one area while the body tries to eliminate it, until there is enough to cause the body to go into overload."

"What do we do now?" Zack's deep voice made Lizzy jump, causing them to all look at him.

Clara reached for him. Dull, dark bags under her eyes took away the big, blue color. He stood by her bed, placing a large hand on her forehead and over her eyes, and bent over to kiss her cheek as if no one else was in the room. The relief seemed to drain from his face as he took her all in.

A strange sort of jealousy crept into Lizzy's mind. She could only wish for that kind of love and care from a man. Maybe there was no one of interest, like she always said, or maybe it was her. As she watched this act of endearment, she wondered whether maybe she'd been too hasty.

"We need to get her strength up. Then we'll reevaluate. We should see a change in the incoherence and disorientation now that she's had an IV." The doctor gave Clara one last look and left the room.

The quiet made Lizzy squirm a little.

"It's been a long time since we were all together." Leave it to Clara to think of that to break the silence.

"It was a year ago," Zack answered. "Right around Christmas." She wondered if he had ways of keeping tabs on things back home. But he would always have the memories of being home.

Lizzy wondered what he'd thought when he heard about this incident. She was surprised he didn't come running home on one of those planes. But then there would be a price to pay coming back, to the bishop, minister, and deacons. Zack wasn't one to confess to anyone concerning his comings and goings. Maybe that was part of his problem.

We must all confess, especially Zack.

His voice startled her. "Clara and I were filling up buckets of snow to make snow ice cream. It was Christmas Eve, and we wanted something for the little ones to do that evening."

"I remember." Clara's voice wavered. Zack filled up a cup of water and handed it to her. She moved forward. "Is there anything else you remember?"

"*Jah*, your pecan pie." He grinned, and that made them smile too. It occurred to Lizzy that he missed the cooking he grew up with.

"Hmm." Clara grunted with pain as she adjusted herself against the pillow.

"You must be hurting, and traveling in a car isn't something you're used to."

Lizzy could see him putting it all together.

"*Nee*, it's a rare thing for me."

"Anything else we can do for you?" Zack seemed content with the doctor's explanation, and Lizzy had to admit the doctor seemed thorough, but she'd stand by Doc back home just as much.

Clara shook her head. "Just you. I'm glad you came, but I wish it was when I was feeling better."

"You didn't know I was coming?" Zack turned and stared at Lizzy.

"*Nee*. When Lizzy told me, I wasn't surprised. I knew you'd come back to us someday. *Mamm* and *Daed* will be so glad to see you, and so will Jonas and Eli."

His eyes narrowed. "I guess we owe our thanks to Lizzy."

Lizzy had never seen the color in Zack's face until this moment and could only hope he didn't take her letter as trickery. But then again, maybe it was.

Chapter Seven

ZACK WAS STEAMED, madder than ever that he hadn't realized the true reason he'd come back here. He would have come faster and prepared for a longer trip. He'd have to let his job know he needed more time, which would enable him to think over some things he'd been considering for a while now.

And then there was Lizzy. He was enamored with her growing up. He'd hoped things had changed, but unfortunately they'd been coming back bit by bit from the moment he laid eyes on her. His reasons for coming back were twofold, and one of those two was seeing Lizzy.

Clara blinked. Then blinked again. Zack's heart flipped as her eyes opened. Her gaunt features seemed as if they would melt away with any move she might make. He reached out to touch her cheek, just to know she wouldn't disappear into a puddle on the linoleum hospital floor.

"I've been waiting for you to wake up." His attempt at humor seemed only to confuse her. He took her hand. "You've been asleep for quite a while."

"I have?" Her voice was only a whisper. She cleared her throat, and he swallowed as if to moisten her throat for her.

He knelt down next to her. "Do you remember where you are?"

She glanced around the room and frowned. "*Jah*..."

She tried to say more but choked instead. Zack grabbed a cup of water from the steel tray by her bed and handed it to her. She took a small sip and coughed. When she covered her lips, he handed her a napkin from the table.

"Take slow drinks."

She took another drink with better success.

"You had me scared for a while. I'm glad you got some sleep."

She slowly moved her head to get a better look at him, but her neck was stiff, so she shifted her eyes instead. "*Nee*, not much really. Bits and pieces of people talking. Lights went off and on, and people's faces faded and came back. It feels like I've been gone for a long time." Her throat caught, and she held out a jittery hand to take the plastic cup.

"Not that long, it just seems like it." He shook his head. "I should have brought you in earlier."

They both knew that couldn't happen, but it made him feel better to say it, no matter how guilty he felt.

"*Gott* always knows the perfect timing." She paused. "What's making me so miserable?"

He pulled up his chair and rested his arms on the bedrail, watching her eyes widen. "Do you remember the doctor asking about your symptoms?"

She answered. "*Jah*." She looked down and laid a hand on her belly. "Just like this one." Her eyebrows drew together as she stared at him. "My stomach?"

He knew she wasn't thinking right and gave her a minute to calm down before she heard the rest. "You have a lump that they need to biopsy."

She pressed her hand over her mouth and stared at him,

saying nothing as a tear ran down her cheek. "What's wrong with me?"

"Something about your stomach. That's why it hurt you in the car when we were driving here." He touched her cheek and caught the tear that rolled down. "The doctor is very thorough. He'll figure out what's bothering you."

"Why the long faces?" Lizzy's presence filled the room, a characteristic Zack remembered about her from before he'd left the community. She could be annoying as all get-out but could also light up the place.

She embraced Clara. "How are you feeling? Are you hungry? Does it hurt? Do you need some painkillers?" She put a hand behind Clara, fluffed her pillow, and then raised the bed so she could sit more upright.

"Slow down." Zack made motions with his hands flat, pushing down. Lizzy seemed so anxious, and another emotion…concern, maybe. It was as if the hard side of her had turned away, and she was all about Clara.

Lizzy eyed him and put a hand on his arm. "Can I talk to you privately?"

"Sure. What about?"

"Step outside the room with me for a moment." She marched ahead of him and then turned to face him in the hall. "Clara may be your sister, but she's as close to me as a sister ever could be, and I'm not going to hold back because of you and your quiet ways about things." She took a deep breath and crossed her arms over her chest, waiting for him to refute her.

Instead of being defensive as she no doubt expected, Zack bent his head and waited for her to finish. Then he looked up. "She might be your friend, but she's my sister, and I'll decide what happens until my folks step in."

"Fine."

He walked past her and into the room.

"Have you seen *Mamm* and *Daed* since they made it back?" Clara's voice was stronger, but it still sounded like gravel when she talked. "They'll be happy to see you."

Zack scoffed. "I doubt it. The only reason I'm here is to support you. Nothing else matters." In fact, he hoped to avoid seeing his parents. He expected they would come after the day's work was done.

"Time for your meds." The small but robust nurse held out a paper cup for Clara. She cleaned up and then looked at Zack. "And no visitors after nine."

Zack nodded his response.

"I'll take good care of her, along with the rest of the community." Lizzy said.

"Actually..." Zack stopped. He must feel much the same as Lizzy did, but this was an emotional moment for all of them. "She is my sister, and I will make sure she's cared for."

The look in Lizzy's eyes made him pause. He didn't usually put up a fight, but this meant enough to him to make a stand. She'd have to give a little on his account.

"She's like a sister to me too, Zack."

They stared at each other, silently repeating the conversation they'd just had in the hall. Zack dropped his head, wondering yet again why Lizzy had to be so stubborn.

"When you two are done, I'd like some water." Clara always knew how to handle them. There was something about the way she said things that arrested poor attitudes and stopped conflict in its tracks.

We shouldn't have bothered her with our battle over who will be her caretaker.

It didn't matter anyway. Lizzy could be with her more than he could. It was just that simple. Dressing and helping with anything a young woman needed would fall to her.

Lizzy was at her side with a cup before he could come out of his thoughts. "Well, that was quick."

"What were you thinking about?" she asked.

He stared at her. Although he would get some resistance from her, he also realized her help would be indispensable. He shook his head.

Clara reached out for Lizzy with a shaky hand. "It was good you were the first person I saw when I woke up. Were you two here alone?"

Clara would be the one who was more interested in her and Zack than she was in her own health. She had to be the most unselfish person Zack knew.

"*Jah*, don't tell the deacon." Lizzy forced a smile.

"I never thought that was what made my back hurt." Clara looked down at her side as if she could see the pain. "It is strange that this would happen when Zack finally decided to come home." She looked at him. "Are you going to stay?"

Lizzy wiggled in her seat. "I'd like to know too." Her eyes were downcast, as if she was uncomfortable. "What kept you away so long?"

In spite of himself, Zack wanted to see her reaction when he answered.

His mind went wild with what he'd been through and what had taken place. Living in the flesh only brought bad and sinful things, according to the Amish. He was sure they were dying to know what he'd done. Clever as she was at prying news out of people, she had picked the perfect moment to ask.

"I've done some things that are against your ways." That was vague, though not as vague as he wanted to be. But even a piece of what had happened to him might be enough.

"*Ach*, what could be so bad?" Lizzy pushed him a little further.

"Depends who you're talking to." Zack wouldn't take the bait. He didn't trust her.

Clara frowned. "It's only for him to share if he chooses to."

Lizzy hadn't stopped staring at him, but he'd been in much worse situations. She was obviously growing weary of the lack of information. "I'm sure Zack has nothing to hide."

Neither of them knew that with what Zack had done, it would not go well for him when he met with the bishop.

Chapter Eight

JACK TOOK IN the cool air as he stood in front of the hospital entrance. He shrugged his shoulders as he watched Lizzy walk toward him. Her expression was placid, unreadable. That scared him more than if he knew what was on her mind. "Morning."

She frowned. "Did you stay here all night?"

He nodded.

She stopped in front of him and tucked her hands under her arms for warmth. "Have you seen your family yet?"

He really didn't want to talk about it. He turned around to go back into the hospital. He would rather stay there than go to the community, but he knew he would end up right where he didn't want to be. He wouldn't leave until Clara was healed, and there was no telling how long that would be.

"Briefly." He said it loud enough for her to hear, with a tone that explained his position. He wouldn't let her talk him into saying anything more. "They left early this morning to do chores."

When she walked right past him without saying a word, he was taken off guard, so he squeezed into the revolving door with her. When she turned and scowled up at him, he grinned, knowing she didn't like him being that close.

He kept his eye on her as they stepped out of the turning door together without tripping over each other. He almost saw a small smile when he had to jump to keep from getting his foot stuck.

"You could have gotten hurt." She whipped her head around but kept her back to him. He was beginning to think something besides him was bothering her.

He scoffed. "Heaven forbid you have a little fun for a change."

"What was fun about it?"

"You almost smiled when my foot got caught." One side of her mouth lifted, but she stopped herself from smiling. He caught up and bumped into her with a mild tap, like they used to do. "You worried about Clara?"

"*Jah,* you should be too." Curls of her blond hair stuck out, and her *kapp* hung loosely to the side, pinned up as if she'd been in a hurry getting there.

"What, you think I'm not taking this seriously?"

"As a matter of fact, *jah.*" They entered the elevator when two other people exited.

"Only you would accuse me of not taking care of things right with my sister. You've got some nerve, Lizzy." He shook his head in frustration.

"If everything was all right, they would be letting her go home." She looked away, but he caught the rosy color covering her face, the one thing she couldn't hide. He knew she was worried—sad too, maybe—but she wouldn't show that side of her, just the angry part, to keep him at arm's length.

The elevator came to a stop and then went up another floor. He pushed two buttons, making the car stop, and started talking to her before they got to Clara's floor. "It's not right that you're taking this out on me, so I'm going to ignore your rude behavior. Just remember I'm not the bad guy here. It's whatever ails her that should get the blame, not me."

The elevator buzzed, so Lizzy moved his hand away. Then it lurched, went a few inches, and stopped midway between two floors. "Don't tell me we're stuck." Her eyes widened as she looked from him to the bright light that told them the car was jammed on the ninth floor.

"I'm afraid so. Relax, we'll be out of here in no time." He had no idea, but the pink glow on her skin told him to play it down for her sake. He'd been stuck in an elevator crammed with other people in Philly for over an hour. He was just glad it was only him and Lizzy in this tin box. But he didn't look forward to the conversation. She was mad at him for something that was out of his control, as usual.

"Easy for you to say, living in the city with all these machines to depend on." She crossed her arms over her chest and kept her eyes on the glowing light with the number nine.

"Horses can break down just as easy. Or have you forgotten the time we were up to our ankles in mud to keep it out of a mud hole?" He grinned, remembering she'd had to hold up her dress to stay out of the sludge and ended up falling backward into the sloppy mess.

"I'm still mad at you for laughing when I couldn't get up."

"You weren't mad then. As a matter of fact, you laughed right along with me." Remembering those days, back when they got along, made his heart beat one extra time. He couldn't remember how often he'd thought about their time together and realized how much he missed it. And then Lizzy blossomed, and every guy around wanted her attention. Things had changed when he left on *Rumspringa* and didn't come back. But he missed it back here, although no one would ever know that.

She leaned against the metal door and took her time to respond. "I haven't let myself remember those things. Once you left, things changed."

What does she mean by that?

The elevator shook and low voices were audible above them. They both looked up, and Zack hollered to them.

"You all right in there?" A man's voice boomed in reply.

"Yeah, how long is this gonna take?" Zack covered Lizzy's ears so he could yell loudly enough for them to hear, and she actually let him. He brushed his hand against her cheek, feeling the softness.

"Don't know right yet." Shuffling noises above them ended the conversation, so he leaned against the door next to Lizzy.

"Looks like we might be here for a while." Whether she wanted to be or not, she was stuck with him. Funny thing was, though, he wasn't dreading it like he thought he would and realized the reason was because she was quieter than usual.

She tapped her hand on her side and her face was as pale as fresh milk. Now they could hear voices that seemed to come from above the door, perhaps on the next floor up. "How long does it take to fix one of these?" she asked.

"Are you in a hurry?" The sarcasm came through without thought. He'd always had a zinger to shoot right back at her. Zack wasn't a kid anymore, and neither was she. He realized from the tear slipping down her cheek that he'd have to make an effort not to talk off the cuff. To his surprise, she didn't have anything to say back to him.

He reached out and touched her shoulder. "I'm sorry, that was rude of me."

She shrugged his hand away. "I don't like this machine, and I want to see Clara."

He felt like a jerk. It wasn't like him to pick on someone, but he and Lizzy had a history together, one they'd obviously grown out of. He wasn't sure where to go from there and suspected she wasn't either.

She stared over at him. "Is this her floor above us?"

"Yeah, why?" He could see her thinking a mile a minute.

"Then why aren't we talking to them?"

He turned and placed his hands on her shoulders. "It may take a while. They're locating the malfunction in the motors and switches."

She frowned. "How do you know all that?"

"I used to work on them." He shrugged. She didn't need to know he was making it up to console her. "They're not going to let this box move until they know what's wrong, but most of the time it's nothing major, so don't worry."

She let out a breath, but then she gave him another look and raised her eyebrows. "Box?"

"Do you hear that?" He tilted his head, and she nodded. "Once they connect the wiring that cools the panels and electric motors, we'll be out of here."

"Where did you learn this?" She shook her head slightly.

"From working in the city."

"With elevators?" She looked up and around, taking in the information.

"I read the blueprints to decide what equipment and material is needed for installation or repair."

"So you're the boss?"

"Sort of. It doesn't work that way. I have a lot of jobs."

"Did you have to go to school to learn how to do these things?" She kept her eyes steady on his, seemingly more interested in his work than he'd expected.

"I had some courses of training for that kind of work." He hoped it would distract her until the elevator started working again. If she knew everything he did, she'd get dizzy just hearing about it. The longer he could keep her mind off the broken machine, the better. He'd never seen her so scared.

"Can this thing fall?" The color of her fair skin seemed to soften. Maybe the distraction of talking actually helped.

"It's rare. Compared to the old units, there is a secondary wire that takes over if they need to use it, which hardly ever happens."

Her eyes widened when the elevator made a noise like metal hitting metal. "Did something happen?"

"The noises are the techs, nothing to worry about." He didn't think about this being a problem, but he should have. He knew she was scared of heights, especially on an elevator, something she rarely used.

"I didn't ask what you did in the city."

"That's not surprising." People here probably couldn't understand the urge to make a life after leaving the community, or that one could actually making a living out there.

A jolt made Lizzy grab her chest and move closer to him. "I don't know how much longer I can do this." She looked him in the eyes. "Did I tell you I'm afraid of heights?"

He groaned, thinking his choice of topics wasn't a good one. As he watched Lizzy brace herself for another jolt, he decided he liked her better when she was a little scared. Her dependence on him alone was enough to make him want to forget the other side of her, so full of sharp comments and brittle looks. But he knew better than to think that as soon as they got out of here, she would give him the time of day.

Lizzy shut her eyes and then opened them. "What's holding us up?"

"Cables, thick and very strong. Thankfully, that's not the problem. You shouldn't worry, really. It's a malfunction that is being taken care of."

"Seems like we've been here for a long time." Still pale as a ghost, she leaned against the steel panel behind her as if for stability. "Do you make money there?"

He frowned at her question, common in the outside world but uncommon to the Amish, who would speak well of an employer paying well for an Amish man doing a day's work in the field. "I'm not complaining."

"But that's not where you got the money for the hospital bill." She asked like she already knew the answer, and he wished she would stop questioning him. So he just shook his head, mentally kicking himself for telling her as much as he had. There was no other way to get her to pay the bill, though, and that he didn't regret.

"Are you going to tell me why that was 'blood money,' as you called it?" The elevator hiccupped, and she took in a heavy breath. He appreciated the diversion.

He took her hand and squeezed. She was claustrophobic *and* afraid of heights? "You're all right. They're just making some adjustments."

Her face was so white, he started to worry she might pass out. "Take some deep breaths." He drew air in through his mouth and let it out. She followed his lead, and they were soon in sync.

"In and out," he encouraged her. Finally some color started to show on her cheeks.

"What floor are we on?" she asked, but didn't open her eyes. "I don't remember."

"It doesn't matter. We'll be out of here and in Clara's room soon." He watched her chest lift and lower quickly. "Maybe they'll release her, and we can take her home."

"That would be nice. Did the doctor tell you that?"

The lights flashed. *Whoosh.* Cool air filled the elevator. Lizzy let out a long sigh. Zack did too.

Chapter Nine

The elevator whined. The sound seemed unnaturally loud after the time they'd spent in that "box," as Zack put it. Lizzy wondered how he'd learned so much about machines he'd never seen before. Regardless, she was touched by the gentle way he'd explained everything to her.

When the doors opened, she let out a long breath.

"Are you all right?"

"*Jah, danke.*" But she wasn't all right. Being stuck in that machine took away her courage and her pride. He seemed genuinely concerned, which made her think that maybe she should let down her guard a little.

But not too much.

They walked in silence to the third door on the right, where Clara lay in bed with the doctor standing by her side. "I'm so glad you're here, both of you." She hugged them and said a little something to Zack. He pulled away and shook his head.

"How is she?" Zack asked before Lizzy had a chance to.

"The gastroenterologist's endoscope found a tumor on her stomach. It could be benign." Dr. Kauffman spoke without lifting his eyes from the chart he held. His eyes shifted back and forth, reading.

Lizzy's patience began to wane. She opened her mouth, but Zack quickly held up a finger. She pressed her lips tightly together with irritation and looked over to Zack. He shrugged it away.

"I've scheduled a biopsy." He glanced at Zack, skipped over Lizzy, and then to Clara. She knew the hospital rules, but she had spent more time with Clara over the last few years than Zack had, and Zack didn't need to give her that look when he knew she wanted to be a part of the decisions.

Clara gave the doctor a pale smile. "I feel fine, Doctor." She nodded as if urging him to let her leave, but he didn't seem the kind of doctor to be persuaded. This doctor worked with many of the Amish due to his history with them and knew they shared the cost of medical bills. His kind effort would be appreciated, but with Zack paying the bill, questions would be asked.

"If that's what she needs, then that's what we'll do." The words came out before Lizzy could stop them. "That is, if your folks agree."

"They've agreed with whatever I suggest." The doctor studied Lizzy for a moment. "You are not related to Clara, correct?"

Lizzy didn't like the way he said it, as if putting her in her place. "*Nee*, but in our community, we're one body, so in that case, we're sisters."

"Yes, I'm fully aware of the Amish ways."

Her eyes didn't leave his; she needed him to know how involved she was in Clara's well-being. Lizzy knew she might seem overzealous about their friendship, but there was just something about Clara that gave her strength and security. She understood Lizzy with all of her flaws and loved her just the same—unlike Zack, who was staring her down. She must have said something he didn't agree with, but she didn't care. She was feeling emotional and didn't want him to keep her from doing what she thought was best for Clara.

Lizzy swallowed hard and lifted her head as she watched the doctor leave the room. She felt the need to keep herself intact in front of Zack. She didn't deal well with appearing helpless. When her eyes met his, he tipped one side of his lips and took steps closer to Clara.

Lizzy sat down in a stiff hospital chair and pulled out a book. "Would you like me to read to you, Clara?"

Zack leaned against the wall by Clara and crossed his arms over his chest. He didn't move as she read. Clara closed her eyes, appearing to sleep, but each time Lizzy stopped reading, Zack would ask if she was awake. Lizzy could feel his eyes on her as she spoke, and when she glanced up at them, he turned away.

After she finished, she laid the book on the small table next to the bed.

Zack kissed Clara on the cheek. "I've got to go, but I'll be back later."

"My mysterious brother," Clara replied. "How did you know our family was coming?"

"I know *Daed*'s ways." He kissed her forehead and headed for the door, where he hesitated and turned back to them.

"You're right about the family." Clara pulled the sheet up to her shoulders and shivered. "*Daed* is always on a schedule, even picking the best day to start harvesting. And he's always right."

Lizzy's stomach growled, reminding her she hadn't eaten since breakfast. "*Jah*, I've heard as much. He's like the weathermen the English watch on television."

Zack cleared his throat and addressed Lizzy. "Do you have a ride back?"

"*Nee*, but I'm all right."

"I'm gonna grab something to eat in the cafeteria if you change your mind." He waved and walked away.

"Why don't you go on with Zack? I need a couple winks before the family comes by." Her complexion was somewhat better than the night they'd brought her there, and she was eating a bit of bland food.

Her suggestion surprised Lizzy, making her wonder if there was something more to Zack's offer. She should be home, tending to her household duties, but she didn't want to leave until Clara's family got there. "I wish I could take you home with us. Did they say when you would be discharged?"

"It can't be very long. I feel much better." Clara raised a hand, and they embraced. "Go on now, and let me get my beauty sleep." She grinned and carefully eased down onto the pillow behind her.

"All right, I know when I'm not wanted." Lizzy enjoyed the banter between them, as if nothing had ever happened. But the discomfort was still there. She could see Clara wince when she tried to do too much.

Lizzy's boots squeaked as she passed by the hospital rooms where patients with IV drips and bandages lay in beds similar to Clara's. The smell of rubbing alcohol wafting through the air made her appreciate the better smells of home. She said a quiet prayer as she walked into the elevator.

Reading the signs, she followed the arrows to the cafeteria. Zack was reading a paper, with two coffee cups and Danishes on the table. Her eyebrows rose in surprise, and she walked over to him and sat down. "You were expecting me?"

"Yeah, I could hear your stomach growl." He handed her the sugar and a container with cream.

She felt the heat rise in her cheeks.

"Don't be so surprised."

"Well, I am."

"Why?" He blew on his coffee and waited for her answer as she took a bite of Danish.

"Because you usually seem annoyed with me." She had a much longer list, but since he was feeling generous today, she thought she should let it wait.

He grunted. "Interesting...I thought it was the other way around."

Lizzy shrugged and took a sip of her coffee, trying not to appear fazed by this conversation but feeling quite the opposite. She was almost enjoying his company, but she knew better than to think it would last and guarded herself accordingly.

He nodded. "It would make Clara happy if we got along."

"Is that why you're doing all of this?" She looked at the spread on the small table and waited to hear his answer.

"Clara is our first priority."

She squelched a surge of envy. He had a perfectly good reason to say that, so where did that feeling come from? "*Jah*, she is."

Zack looked over her head, wiped his hands, and stood. "My cue to leave." He nodded. She turned to see what he was referring to. His *bruder*, Jonas, looked up at the same time she did and then saw Zack. It all took only a couple of seconds, and then Jonas walked away, hand in hand with a young Amish girl.

"Aren't you going to talk to them?" Lizzy couldn't stand the look on Zack's face as his *bruder* turned away. She wanted them to communicate somehow. Just a simple "hallo" would be better than nothing. And who was the girl he was with? Lizzy didn't recognize her. It was all she could do not to intervene.

Zack let out a breath and pushed his chair in place. "I'm not here for him, or anyone else, for that matter."

"You're not going to see your family while you're here?" She frowned, unable to understand how he could come this far and not at least make the effort. She and her *daed* were at odds at times, but not like this.

"I'm here to see my sister, that's it. Understand?" He shoved the chair so hard, his cup went flying across the table. Splatters of the black liquid darkened her dress. She stood, and he grabbed a handful of napkins. He reached over to blot the moisture but stopped when he realized what he was doing.

"Sorry, I'm working on my temper." He sopped up the remaining coffee, avoiding her stare.

"You've always had a temper," she barked at him. He was one who settled situations physically. She remembered his *mamm* telling him to use his words and not his fists, but it obviously still wasn't working.

"Yeah, but I've never tried to tame it."

Lizzy was surprised to hear him say that and couldn't hide it. "Well, it's good you're trying. If that's what that was."

He cracked a smile and glanced up at her while he wiped his hands. "Thanks for the encouragement." His large, brown eyes bore into hers for only a brief second, but she didn't miss the connection. Even though he aggravated her to no end, she saw a good side of him that was new to her. He was being exposed and losing his temper. The emotions he must have felt about his *bruder* showed a different side of him.

"Tell your *bruder* hallo if you see him. Unless you're going back to the community."

"I don't know how long the car is drivable. I don't mind taking the chance it'll stall on me, but I wouldn't want anyone else to. Besides... you, a young Amish girl, with an *Englischer,* an ex-Amish..." He was stone-faced, his usual state. The Zack she liked disappeared. "You wouldn't want to be seen with me. People might talk."

She was silent for a moment due to his sarcasm. "I didn't know it bothered you so much, being in a big, fancy city. I figured you were glad to get rid of us."

He scoffed. "I think it was the other way around."

She couldn't figure where that came from. It was his decision to go or ask for forgiveness for his...

She stood abruptly without looking him in the eye. "I'm going to catch the bus."

He shook his head. "Don't put me in that position. I plan to stay here as long as Clara does." "I didn't ask for a ride. I'm used to taking the bus." Lizzy knew he was avoiding going back to the community, but he might have to face his past sooner than he thought. "The doctor said if the biopsy was normal, she might be able to go home."

He frowned. "They won't have the results until tomorrow, at the earliest."

She pointed to where her attention had shifted to his younger *bruder,* Eli. He walked through the hospital door and stood and stared at Zack. The look in his brother's eyes said it all—disappointment, anger, sadness—much of what Zack probably felt.

"I'm sorry, Zack." Lizzy didn't know where the words came from, and now she wanted to take them back. Zack didn't seem to want pity, especially from her.

Chapter Ten

SQUEAK, SQUEAK.

Zack tried to find where the noise came from. He struggled to open his eyes. No matter how hard he tried, they seemed stuck together. He jolted forward off his chair, tugged his eyes open, and looked around to see a gurney go past him. He wiped his hand over his face. Sweat covered his forehead as the anxiety grew.

A dream, more like a nightmare. That's all. Not the hospital in my head. I'm in the one with Clara. Not Mercy General with Sandra.

"Zack, are you okay?" Clara's nurse brought his heartbeat up another notch.

"Yeah, I'm fine." He let out a long breath and stood. "How's Clara?"

"The results are in." Her small smile gave him hope the diagnosis was good.

"I could use some good news about now. Do you think they'll discharge her?" As much as he wanted her out of this place, he also dreaded going back to the community. He couldn't even imagine what all had been said about him over the time he was gone, even though Amish weren't to speak of those who were shunned. The longer he was away, the more he felt they were hypocrites. But then he was probably one too. After all he'd done, he had no room to talk.

"Did you hear me?" The nurse tipped her head to the side, waiting for his answer.

"Sorry. I'm a little distracted."

She put her hand on his arm and blinked her brown eyes. "Don't apologize. You've been through a lot." Another nurse walked by and frowned.

He didn't want this sweet little nurse to get the wrong idea. He gently moved his arm away and led the way to Clara's room. "Thanks for looking after her." When he smiled at the nurse, she lit up and waved a hand.

"Morning, beautiful." Zack stopped and stared at Clara. "You look great. Color's back in your cheeks."

"Oh, Zack." She waved him over and whispered, "Why are you sweating?" She put a hand to his chest. "Your heart's beating like a drum."

"It's nothing, I'm fine."

"Sounds like anxiety." The nurse came closer to examine him. His ears pinged with each step she took closer to him. His patience was waning. Zack shut his eyes and counted to ten. "Clara, are you clear to leave?"

"I hope so, but you should stay a bit until you feel better." Clara ran a hand across his bangs. Her cool fingers felt like ice against his forehead.

"Do you have a temperature?" The nurse placed her hand over his. Zack jumped up and away from them. He clenched his hand in frustration.

"Zack!" Clara's soft plea was worse than a shout. Until he heard the voice of Jed Schrock.

The nurse turned and drew herself up straight. "Bishop Schrock. I'm so glad you're here. I'll call the doctor in." She flipped her black hair over her shoulder and darted for the door. Zack didn't share the gratitude the nurse had toward his *daed*, like most did. He made many visits to the hospital when needed.

Zack noted the gray hair and worn face lines around his mouth. He was balding much more in just the years since Zack had seen him. He wondered whether any of the stress had come from him.

"Hello, Bishop." The title seemed to fit their situation. He was a lost *Englischer* in an unwanted place, and his acceptance would come from the one in charge—his *daed*—who happened to be the bishop elected by the council. But what would it matter? He'd be gone soon enough.

"Hallo, son." His *daed*'s eyes glistened as he took him in. Zack felt sad and defensive at the same time. Was it purely disappointment or some understanding from his father? Zack was much like him at one time, someone others thought would play a part in their community, perhaps even a prominent part as his dad did.

When Zack nodded to his mother, her bottom lip quivered. He wanted to go to her and let her know he was still her son even if everyone around her thought differently. "I saw Eli and Jonas. They look well."

His mother lit up when he mentioned the boys. "*Jah*, Jonas will be married come fall." She hesitated, and his *daed* glanced over at her. Zack recognized the look he gave her, as if she was sharing too much information.

"Are you still on your own, Zack?" There was reservation in his tone. Zack was far past the usual age at which most married. He'd had his time with a woman, but after things went sour he hadn't wanted a relationship of any kind.

"Yes. It's best this way." He could sugarcoat it for his mother's sake, but there was too much baggage to know where to start. There were too many things that would upset her for him to share the information. Besides that, he didn't want to go through all those emotions.

"I'm sorry, son." Her face tightened as she attempted a smile.

"Don't be. I'm fine." He felt he was putting on a good front but knew better with his dad. He was one who could reach into your soul, pick out the muck and mire, and come out with forgiveness at hand. But only if it was followed by his rules and qualifications.

Silence took over the room.

"How long will you be staying?" His *daed*'s question sounded genuinely inviting. Zack wished he could give him an honest answer, but he only knew that he didn't want to go back to his job in Philly, not now that he realized what his boss has really been up to. For now, until Clara showed some progress, he would stay put. Where he would go after that, he wasn't sure. Although his dad was the bishop, that didn't mean he would get any special favors—probably less than another would. Jed Schrock was not a kind man, and no pushover.

"Good morning." Doctor Kauffman's loud voice diverted their conversation, causing them to all turn his way. "Bishop." He nodded to the bishop out of respect.

"Clara, the results are back from the biopsy." He rarely smiled, but Zack saw one spread across his face—a gesture of comforting. "How are you feeling?"

"A little bloated."

"No pain?"

She hesitated. "Not much."

"Your fever isn't decreasing." He held the clipboard against his chest. "There were cancer cells in the tumor.

But we caught it at a very early stage, so the chances of it spreading are small."

He tipped his head and stared at her, ignoring the responses in the room.

Zack's heart sank. He'd assumed too much, prayed too little, or both. He waited with bated breath to hear what the doctor had to offer in this situation.

"You have to be honest with me so I can treat you properly. We'll start chemotherapy, which will take from two days to seven weeks, depending on how the cancer responds to the treatment."

He turned to the room full of visitors. "She will need a lot of rest. Clara, the nurses will give you the details."

Zack felt he was in a whirling tornado after that quick overview. Doctor Kauffman didn't seem concerned, but then the man didn't show much emotion. His mind was churning with the worst scenarios. He had much more to say and ask, but all that came out was, "Is Clara going to be okay?"

"What caused this to happen to her, doc?" the bishop asked at the same time.

"We have state-of-the-art medicine here, Zack. She's in good hands." The doctor narrowed his eyes at the bishop. "I'd say it was most likely from the pesticides used on your crops."

Zack puckered his forehead and stared at his *daed*. "Do you use pesticides?"

He nodded in thought. "Could it be from something else? Our farmers are not to use pesticides."

Zack's brothers and Lizzy stood in the doorway along with Jonas's girl. "Is this a bad time?" Jonas looked around the room and stopped at the bishop. "No." Zack heard the doctor's words but wasn't sure what he should tell his brother. "The doctor was just saying there is a cure for what ails Clara. That is something to be grateful for, and we'll pray for perfect healing."

His dad and brothers stood silently, probably surprised at his response. Lizzy stared at him for a second and then joined in, clapping her hands in praise.

"*Jah*, our God is an awesome God," Jonas chimed in.

His dad, using his cane, walked to a chair and sat down with a broad smile on his round face.

The nurse came in and held a finger to her lips. "*Shhh*, you'll wake the whole floor with all this noise. And get me in trouble." Her hair slipped down onto her shoulder as her eyes caught Zack's. When he turned toward Lizzy, she was watching. He wondered whether she cared enough to say anything about the contact between them. Then he realized he didn't know why he was even thinking about either one of them.

The nurse walked over to Clara, smiling as she passed Zack. He wondered whether she'd be giving him the same attention if he was still Amish.

The nurse stood beside Clara, between her and Zack. "The chemo isn't what you should be thinking about. What's important is taking care of yourself. You're a giver at heart, but right now, it's about taking care of you. Eating well, your attitude, and faith are the things that will keep you going and help you get through much better."

"Good advice." Zack found himself nodding in agreement with how she was encouraging Clara. He hadn't given those things much thought, but it made sense and would give her a focus other than the chemo. "Thanks...I don't know your name."

"Ellen, and you're Zack."

He nodded but didn't want to have a conversation in a room full of people.

Now that the suspense of finding out what was wrong with Clara was over, Zack felt himself getting tired, and he didn't want to spend another night in the hospital waiting room or his car. "I've been staying in the waiting room. Is there someplace here at the hospital where visitors can get a couple winks?"

His *mamm* cleared her throat. "Zack, you're welcome to stay with us." Her soft voice made the offer a little more desirable, but he knew it would be awkward. He was a little surprised that no one in his family hesitated about the offer.

He made sure he said no before any of them rejected him.

"Okay. Tomorrow then." She seemed more determined the second time, so he didn't argue, just nodded with a small grin.

"There are strict visiting hours for this type of procedure. I'm sorry." Ellen placed a delicate hand on his arm. This was crossing a line he wasn't comfortable with, and he was sure it wasn't professional. But Ellen was awful cute, and even better, Lizzy was so irritated, he couldn't help but enjoy the fireworks.

Chapter Eleven

Leaving Clara at the hospital had Lizzy in a spin. The nurse told her it was best and said that Clara had a few long days ahead of her. Lizzy didn't like the words the doe-eyed, dark-haired nurse used as she explained. She made it seem Clara might be unavailable for weeks. If so, Lizzy wanted even more to be there.

She sighed, knowing she had her own responsibilities back home. A farm never stopped operating. When working with live animals, challenging weather conditions, and cooking three meals a day, not considering daily chores, planting, and harvesting, it wasn't realistic to think she could be away long.

"Looks like a storm is coming through." Jed squinted into the flakes as they hit the windshield of the bishop's buggy.

Lizzy looked up to the sky. The snow would be thick by the time she got back to the farm. That meant getting chores done would take even longer. One good thing about having a brother was that he did a lot of the outdoor chores on days like this. She and her sisters cooked with their *mamm*. Lizzy loved to bake, mainly because she loved sweets, but even more because it was her way of making people happy. There was something about dessert that made a person content.

Zack's *mamm*, Anna Mae, turned to meet gazes with

her. "You're awful quiet, Lizzy. Don't think too much. *Gott*'s got His hand in this."

Anna Mae had glanced at her a couple times, but Lizzy wasn't in the mood to talk. Zack's folks were good people, but when Zack left, they were humbled even more. Lizzy figured it was much harder to have a wayward child if you were in the position the bishop was in. Others shook their heads and whispered as he and his family passed them by.

"Penny for your thoughts." Eli sat next to her in his *daed*'s special-made buggy. The bishop's justification for the extravagance was that he could spend more time with the Lord, studying the Word, if he didn't have to walk. Not that he needed a reason; he seemed to care little about the opinions of others.

"Well, I'm thinking of Clara, of course." She admitted to herself that she was also thinking of Zack and what home in the city must be like. She pictured tall buildings and many people making their way down the busy streets. She imagined the houses big, like her family's, with room for friends, meals, and much talking afterward. For a moment she thought that it might be an interesting way of life.

"You look worried." Eli was a nice guy, but he was oblivious to his continuous chatter. He tried too hard to catch a girl's attention.

"*Nee*, Clara's strong. She'll pull through, whatever it is." Her demeanor was confident, maybe too much so. But then she could say that of him, as well. It was easier to deny anything but the positive.

"I bet it's strange for you to have Zack back here again." Eli seemed to be fishing for more information about the two of them. Maybe it did seem odd that they had been together alone, but at this point she didn't care.

"Only as much as it is for you, I'm sure."

He nodded once. "But it can be awkward."

She guessed it was difficult, more so than most due to the bishop's role in the community. But she wasn't all that sure of the rest of his family. Zack's brothers were younger. It was almost as if there were two separate families living in the same *haus*.

"It's hard to know what to say and do. He's my *bruder*, so I gotta stand by him, even though I think it's pretty selfish to up and leave your family like he did."

"But it's permitted to leave on *Rumspringa*." She felt the need to defend him, but didn't know why.

"And he's been baptized." He scoffed. "It's a little different when you're the bishop's kid too." His brows lifted.

"I suppose so. He's seen much worse among the community." Now she was defending him again. She'd told herself to stay out of their affairs, but that was hard to do when you lived in a community where everyone knew most everything about one another.

"Your stop is here." The bishop bellowed as loudly as he did on Sunday mornings when he gave a sermon. "*Danke* for taking care of Clara, Lizzy. She's had a lot of love these past couple of days."

"*Jah*, I'll go back once I get some things done around the *haus*." Lizzy hopped out of the buggy and waved. She wanted to go straight back to the hospital, but she knew Clara was in good hands. Zack would meet her every need

The wind snapped at her as she pulled the shawl tighter around her chest to keep the cold air at bay. Clara's health made Lizzy appreciate her own. She took for granted the strong mind and body *Gott* had given her. She prayed Clara would be thanking Him for the same very soon.

Taking the last few steps to her *haus* froze her down to her bones. Lizzy readied herself for a tongue-lashing from her *daed*. She had pushed the limits when she took off with Zack to go to the hospital. She opened the front door to the sound of her sisters bickering and hoped her *bruder* was home, but he usually knew better and made himself busy when meals became too dramatic.

Neither of her sisters seemed to notice as she hung up her shawl, took off her boots, and looked around the room. *Daed* sat at the table, having just finished his meal. "Your *bruder* just left."

Lizzy wrinkled her nose, wishing he was there to stop the girls from arguing and to keep her from getting involved. She usually had her opinion as well, but tonight her mind was on Clara.

"We'll have a conversation once the milking's done." Her *daed* showed no expression or emotion, maybe too tired to make the effort. Lizzy hoped for that rather than his anger regarding her ride in Zack's car.

"Adah, that's enough." *Daed* always seemed to pick out Adah when Katura was usually the cause of the problem.

"How is Clara?" Her *mamm* picked up a bowl of potatoes and handed it to her. Locks of gray hair sprouted from under her *kapp* as she continued to clear the table. *Mamm* served Lizzy a spoonful of broccoli salad, a slice of ham, and her own homemade cheese bread.

"She is the way you would expect her to be. Solid as a rock but probably scared inside." She didn't like the words coming out of her mouth. The thought of Clara being scared didn't fit.

Mamm sat down beside her. Her thin wrists and wrinkled skin made her appear older than she was. Her sisters were probably part of the reason for her aging, with their ongoing squabbles. "*Ach*, she's a strong soul." They paused, each in her own thoughts. "I heard the bishop paid a visit."

"*Jah*, I saw him there with Eli and Jonas." She knew what was coming, so she started in on her meal.

"*Jah*, I know Jonas will be married this fall." *Mamm* rested her knuckled hand against her cheek with her eyes on Lizzy.

Lizzy didn't want to fall into the trap of seeking a suitor—not again. She had promised Clara to really try and see whether the man she'd been referred to might prove promising. With everything that had happened in the meantime, it seemed that might not happen. And she didn't care one way or another at this point. There were just too many other things going on.

Her blue-eyed sister marched over to her *mamm*. "You know how Adah promised me she wouldn't flirt with Benjamin Fisher. But she is flirting. I know because I've been told, and I've seen her with my own two eyes."

Lizzy sat back in her chair watching as the three of them tried to work through the jealous fits and sharp tongues. She took one last bite of the broccoli, which was seasoned to perfection. The volume rose. *Mamm* stepped away, and Lizzy had had enough.

"Stop!" The room hushed as *Daed* stood, pushed the chair in, and whistled. "There'll be no more of this. One of our own is fighting a deadly disease, and here you two are squabbling over a suitor neither of you have. I demand peace in this *haus*. At least for Clara's sake."

A hush fell on the room. It amazed Lizzy how many people loved and cared for Clara. Not that others weren't taken care of when life held them back. But there was just something about Clara.

"Sorry, *Daed*." Lizzy's apology was meant for more than what was happening at the moment; she was asking for pardon for her defiance in riding with Zack. Her *daed* was a gentle man, but he had a temper and little forgiveness. She didn't know how her *mamm* dealt with him, but by the look on his face she was about to find out.

Chapter Twelve

"I don't want you around Zack." *Daed*'s forehead was creased with permanent lines. But this morning was one of the times they seemed even deeper, meaning the discussion was over. He stood and pointed a finger at Lizzy. "Period, end of story. No ifs, ands, or buts."

She thought of a reply, but she knew better than to speak it, as she might have with most other people. Around *Daed* she knew to keep her mouth shut, especially when it came to a character like Zack. She couldn't make sense of what her *daed* wanted her to do. The young men who were interested in her were taken aback by him as much as her lack of interest in them. His sharp eyes and aloof demeanor made the young men regret they'd come to visit—and embarrassed her—so they eventually stopped showing up. They had a large enough community that she could find someone eventually, but what it all came down to was Zack. Ever since they were kids, he'd been right there hounding at her, giving her a hard time, just because he could. Thinking back, she wondered whether there had been more to the attention he gave her.

"It's worrisome enough you're not married with a baby by now." He let the air out of his nose and grunted.

The words stung but weren't unforeseen. She didn't expect anything less. "Well, I'm not going to marry just anyone."

Lizzy heard her *mamm* suck in air as she put a hand to her chest. Lizzy expected her not to say anything against him, but to her surprise *Mamm* spoke one word. "Ray."

Her *daed* narrowed his eyes and met her *mamm*'s. "*Ach*, to heck with it all." He turned and headed for the back door, shaking his head. "I'd just like a grandbaby one of these days." He opened the screen door and walked off.

"*Ach, nee.* Child, I wish you'd settle down and get married off. You waiting just stirs him up. Don't ya know it only makes things more difficult?"

"Zack's sister is in the hospital, and all *Daed* can think about is how it looks for me to be single? That's not right, *Mamm*. You know it just as well as I do." She hated to correct her, but it bothered her that her *mamm* wouldn't stand up for herself. She was able to do more, in Lizzy's eyes. Women were generally expected to be compliant in their way of living, but not so much with Lizzy.

"It's not easy for your *daed* to live with a family of young women. Your sisters bickering and your *bruder* on his own, his wife hardly visiting." *Mamm* paused and looked at the floor, the gesture familiar when she was trying to vent.

"*Mamm*, you wanted no ripples made by your own doing, only peace." She immediately knew she should have kept her thoughts to herself.

She didn't want to see her *mamm*'s face, so she went to the sink to finish the dishes. It always made her feel better to put her hands to work. She found there was quiet time with the Lord as she cleaned, cooked, and...baked. *Jah*, that was what she needed. Thoughts of pies came to mind, then one specifically—pecan pie, with molasses. It was Clara's favorite.

Her mood started to change as she grabbed a mixing

bowl, large spoon, and whisk, and then went to the pantry and gathered the ingredients.

Lizzy had all she needed but didn't like the consistency of the molasses, and that was the most important part. Her *daed* had saved the extra sorghum cane that he surely wouldn't miss. It'd take a chunk of time to make fresh molasses, but what a treat for Clara. It was a demanding chore, but one that gathered people together.

Milking should be over, so her sisters would be along soon, and maybe her brother, she hoped Luke's farm chores weren't demanding too much of him. He would be a big help making the molasses, if he could stay and pitch in.

Lizzy sighed. Sometimes she wished she could do things the way of the English and pick it up at a store. The time saved would make her more productive by leaps and bounds. As she walked out back and into the barn, she saw Katura at one end milking and Adah near the other end, with Luke between them. He stood with hands on his hips watching one and then the other.

"Morning." Kat slowly glanced her way.

Luke smiled at Lizzy. The connection between them couldn't be contained. She being the next oldest sibling, combined with Luke's nurturing nature, created an instant bond between them.

"Hallo, sis." Luke's slim build and tall stature were much like his *daed*'s. "Come to join us?" He grabbed a couple milking stools, handed one to Lizzy, and balanced his weight to keep his three-legged seat stable. Lizzy set her stool up against him, using his weight to keep her from tipping over.

"Actually I was hoping you all would help me when

you're done. I had a hankering for molasses, and you know how Clara loves anything with sorghum, so I thought I'd make a batch." She watched Luke's smile grow. "Why are you grinning?" He brushed the blond hair from his forehead. "You."

Her eyebrows winced. "What about me? I'm talking about Clara."

"Clara's sure going to love this. She brings out the good in you, lil' sis." He draped his strong arm around Lizzy and pulled her close—a safe haven for her. He was the glue that kept their family together, as much as he could. They were an unpredictable brood who loved one another passionately. One had to get to know them to truly understand their ways.

"I talked to *Daed*." He looked down at her.

She snapped her head over before she could stop herself. She and her *daed* hadn't spoken to one another after their confrontation inside, each waiting the other out until one of them broke the ice. Lizzy could hold out as long as it took. It was her *mamm* who would eventually get her to say the first word. She hoped to never marry a man who was so strong headed.

"What did he say?

"That you were as stubborn as a mule." He looked straight ahead. "Is he right?"

"I'm no more stubborn than he is." She crossed her arms.

"I mean about Zack Schrock."

She tightened her arms around her. "What about him?"

He glared at her. "You know what I mean. Did you expect *Daed* to act any other way?"

She grunted. "I didn't expect you to be of the majority who would judge him."

"And you didn't?"

She paused. He always figured a way to catch her off guard. "I knew of his reputation." She wanted to ask Luke but didn't know whether he'd tell her if he knew. "Do you know what happened?"

Luke shook his head. "Bits and pieces, but until you get the whole, it doesn't count for much."

Adah finished milking and started pulling the suction cups off the heifer's teats to clean them, then glanced at Lizzy and she and Luke talked.

"He gave me a lot of money to pay for Clara's bills." Luke was the only one she could trust about matters like this.

Luke shrugged. "He lives in the city, obviously working for someone who has a lot, and so does Zack. It's different there, Lizzy."

Lizzy wondered what it must be like to have money to spend. Her *mamm* and *daed* had just enough to live on and were fortunate to have that much. Land with good crops was bought out by big companies. Some Amish chose to sell and then took jobs making furniture or working horses; others started businesses such as accounting. Most, though, stayed true to their former ways and remained in the community.

Sometimes Lizzy wanted those things. Electricity at the tip of your finger, milk in the refrigerator—much easier than making or working to have things ready to hand. *Jah*, she could see why some left, but for most it wasn't the conveniences they craved. They didn't want to follow the customs of their people. And Lizzy had to admit it was enticing.

"Where in the world are you, Lizzy?"

"Hmm? *Ach*, sorry." She pulled herself back to the farm.

"Let's go help the Kat and Adah." He stood and offered his hand. He smiled when she teasingly pulled her hand away as he grabbed for her, a game they'd played since she was a little one, but she had Zack on her mind and let her hand drop. She wanted to know what her *bruder* truly thought of Zack. He was a sensible man who gave pardon when others might not, so she wanted his opinion.

"So what are you going to do about it?" He chimed in before she could speak.

"What do you mean?"

"How you feel about him." He took slow steps, waiting for an answer.

She scoffed. "He's a good brother to Clara."

Luke shook his head. "That's not what I'm asking." When he turned and stared at her, she realized what he was asking and suddenly felt exposed. "It would make Clara happy if Zack was married to her best friend."

"Our common interest is all in Clara. Don't make it something it's not." She didn't notice the irritation in her words until she stopped and listened to what she said in her head.

She knew he was staring at her but didn't dare look at him. Not only could he read her like a book, he also seemed to know what she was going to say before she said it. She changed the subject. "How's Neva?"

Luke's wife had lost two babies and was pregnant again, so she didn't leave their farm often. It was understandable, but it must be lonely to be there on her own so much of the time. Others would come and see her now and then, but that wasn't enough for Luke. So he'd been spending more time at home than usual.

He grinned. "She's still got a ways to go before we feel

comfortable enough to congregate much." He opened his mouth to start in again, but she stopped him before he had a chance.

"You'd tell me if there was anything I could do to help." She still hadn't gotten used to her brother's wife. She chalked it up to her brother being social and her not, but she sensed there was something more to Neva's standoffish ways. She would be needing the help of her extended family soon enough. But then that could be the reason in and of itself, especially with her own family nearby.

"She's so fragile. I worry about the delivery...and her."

"We're all here to help." She reached out to place her hand on his.

He waved her hand away and scoffed. "She and the baby are both fine."

She shouldn't have brought it up and stuck with her work—Luke had given up taunting her about Zack—but she was sure it wouldn't be long before he would start in again. But why would her *bruder* encourage her toward someone who was shunned?

Chapter Thirteen

THE SNOW-COVERED FIELDS could be seen for miles, glistening in the bright sun.

This was one of the little things Zack missed about country life. The snow stayed white. At least until the thaw, when the fields were tilled to ready the ground for planting, and the white turned to green. Thinking back to those days brought back good memories, but he was realistic enough to know he was being sentimental, remembering more of the good than bad.

Funny, it's usually the other way around.

Clara wanted a few things from home, but he suspected she was just getting him home to see family. Zack went along, but it would take more than a visit with his family to make things right.

This rental car was better than the one he'd driven down from the city, but not by much. The snow persisted with no sign of stopping. He wanted to make sure he could make it back to the hospital before the streets froze after sundown, especially in this car with little traction.

Halfway there he realized he hadn't eaten since breakfast. He'd been occupied talking to the doctor about Clara's treatments and then her request for him to pick up some items at home. In his mind this meant she would be staying there for a while, but she didn't put it that way, and he didn't want to believe she wasn't getting better, so he went along with her request.

As he merged on to the highway toward the Amish community, some childhood memories came back to him. Most of them were good, funny, or dramatic. Nothing was so bad as to give him any reason to think his decision wasn't simply his own. What had started out as a trip to the city on *Rumspringa* had turned into a relationship with a very beautiful young woman that rampaged out of control. And there were the enticing clothes, movies, cars, and fancy food.

A car rushed past. Zack tightened both hands on the steering wheel and paid attention. He was ready for the emotions he'd experienced from the community, but not those from the city. With his focus on Clara, the thoughts that flew through his mind about coming home had been stuffed away, but now that he'd seen her and knew she was in good hands, his mind kept going back to Lizzy and his brothers, his family and friends, all interested in where he'd gone and what he had experienced. He didn't want to share either answer, but especially not his whereabouts in the world.

Thank God for good doctors and the hope that the cancer would leave Clara's tired body.

That cute little nurse was sure hospitable.

He got a kick out of Lizzy's reaction to the attention the brunette gave him. It made him wonder whether there might have been a bit of jealousy. Then he balked at the thought. Lizzy was too ornery to marry, at least not until she got rid of the chip on her dainty shoulder.

As he drove down the road to the community, his thoughts switched gears. He was tired, and it was late, and he didn't want to stay long. He needed to check in at his folks' and at least say hello...although he wanted to do anything but be cordial when he knew he'd be shunned.

The crunch of ice under the tires continued as he drew closer to his family's farm. It was pretty much the same. The silo and red barn were in good shape, and judging by the number of Holsteins in the pasture, their milking business had grown. He'd told his dad for years to buy more heifers, but he was too stubborn, not wanting the idea to be decided until the finances were to his liking.

Zack sat in the car, studying the movements in the barn and the house. He didn't want to go to either, but here he was, and he kept telling himself that his visit didn't have to affect anyone. He'd do what he needed to do and leave. He knew when he saw his brother Eli carrying two buckets of milk that he'd spill some of it and their dad would have a fit. It was a déjà vu, as he took long strides to catch the tipping bucket just before he lost a quarter of the fresh milk.

Eli looked at him in surprise and set down the buckets. "What are you doing here?"

"Hello to you too," Zack said, a bit irritated. His brother wasn't just shocked, he was worried their dad would come out and give them a piece of his mind.

"Don't get things riled up around here. We got enough going on without you to mix things up." Eli's tongue was sharp, and his disrespect was more than Zack would have expected.

"I've just come to get a few of Clara's things, and I'll leave." Nothing even close to the prodigal son return, he was asked to leave before anyone else had even seen him. For his mother's sake he'd walk away. Not that it hadn't been there before...but seeing his home and his brothers moving on with their lives, like Jonas getting married, made the separation more complete.

"What's Clara need?" Eli's eyes were just like their dad's—gray, shifty eyes.

"Wanna see the list?"

Eli shrugged and watched Zack point to his head. "It's all up here. Lotion, glasses, pen and paper, the *Budget* newspaper—"

"You've proved your point. But that doesn't make up for the time you were gone and she was sick."

"You can't blame me for something I didn't know about."

Eli snorted. "You always had a way to get out of things."

Zack shook his head. "There's no way I can get you to understand, so I'm going to stop trying. Show me Clara's things, and I'll be off."

Eli squinted and let out a long breath. "Come on in then."

Zack put his brain on lock mode. He was prepared for anything at this point. He didn't need to hear what they thought or see the disappointment in their eyes.

He noticed the handprints the boys had made in the cement porch in the back of the house. It seemed so familiar, he could picture the whole event as he walked by.

The kitchen was always filled with the same smell of his mom's favorite spice, ginger. She put it on anything she could get away with, saying it had healing properties. But then didn't all spices have something or another? Zack always thought it was a good excuse to make her favorite Christmas caramel corn. But that was then, before he'd broken her heart and left.

"Are you sure you want to do this?" Eli reached for the doorknob and stopped, his eyes pensively studying Zack.

"I wouldn't be here if I didn't." He realized at that moment that he really did want to, even if it meant being chastised. For Clara, yes, but it was just as important to him to see his family, whether they felt the same or not.

"Are you worried about me or *Mamm* and *Daed*?"

"Jonas." Zack answered without hesitation.

Eli's eyebrows drew together. "Why him?"

Zack didn't respond. He didn't want to bad-mouth his brother, but he was sure he'd be the most difficult, especially with him getting married come fall. His girl wouldn't be too friendly, considering she had wanted Zack to court her. Part of him had wanted to, but he couldn't do that to his own brother.

"Just don't get *Mamm* riled up. You know how sensitive she is."

"I'm aware of that, thanks."

What does he think? That I became a heartless jerk because I was in a city instead of on a farm?

At times he thought his community would start to lighten up, but then they say something like this and shows him how far apart they've grown.

Zack wasn't disappointed when the door opened and ginger lingered in the air. His father's disapproving stare wasn't surprising, either. "*Mamm*, *Daed*."

Daed slowly lowered the paper to level his gaze at Zack and then at Eli. His glare was almost enough for Zack to forget the toiletries, turn around, and head back to the hospital.

Daed addressed Eli. "Why did you let him in our home?"

"He said he's here—"

"I came to get some things for Clara." Zack wanted *Daed* to know he wasn't there to grovel.

His mom's eyes were wide with apprehension, shifting from *Daed* to Zack. Jonas wasn't in the room, which was probably good, although Zack did want to see him while he was around.

"How are you, *Mamm*?" It felt right to use the Amish language to address her. Her appreciation was a small nod in return.

"*Mamm* took some things to her just yesterday." Jonas sauntered into the room and leaned against the doorjamb. "She couldn't be needing anything just yet." His brown hair rested on his collar, longer than acceptable.

Mamm looked to his dad as if asking for approval, but his dad hadn't taken his eyes off Zack.

Daed laid the paper on his lap and smoothed it out before speaking. "Clara put you up to this?"

"Or is it some lame excuse to come home?" Jonas piped in, which brought a scowl to his mother's face.

"I'll be at the hospital later and take a few things she might want." *Mamm* paused. "Weather permitting, that is."

"*Danke, Mamm*." Zack turned to his dad, waiting for his reaction.

His dad ran a hand over his face and let out a breath. "It takes something like this for you to come back?"

"Living beyond the community doesn't mean you automatically became a bad person. Of course I'd come. I wish I'd known earlier."

Jonas scoffed. "Sure you would."

Zack had expected the comment, and it was fitting that it came from Jonas.

"If I'd been told, yes. I definitely would, and you know it, Jonas." He was irked enough to make the comment in hopes Jonas would back off a bit. Zack was a gentle man, but when his boiling point got too high, he would defend himself in a very direct way.

The tension created silence in which only the crinkle of his dad's paper could be heard.

Mamm came back in from the kitchen. She stopped, looked around the room, and then took small steps to Zack. "This should be plenty, since I'll be making the trip soon enough." The wrinkles around her face were deeper since he'd last seen her, but the crystal-blue eyes remained the same—his eyes.

She reached up and cupped his cheek with a sad smile.

"And this." His dad held out the *Budget*, the newspaper he held, which Zack readily took from him.

Eli nodded. "*Jah*, she likes to keep track of what's going on since she's been away."

The feel in the room was almost calm as each spoke in their turn. A certain politeness covered the words, with a slight feel of family. When the quiet went on too long, *Mamm* and Zack spoke over each other.

"Thanks for—"

"I'll be going then." Zack needed to embrace her, but it would be awkward and maybe not welcomed, at least not with the other three in the room. The give and take of Clara's basket was the only contact.

He nodded, walked to the door, and let himself out. He remembered to pull twice to get the door to close all the way. A lonely feeling swept through him as he started the engine of the car, almost worried they would be upset to hear the roar of an engine.

He looked back once to see Eli step out on the porch and watch him leave.

Chapter Fourteen

STEAM ROSE TO the roof of the barn, swirling around the beams until it touched the ceiling. Luke brought the last bucket full of cane juice and set it down by the boiling pan. Lizzy fetched the cloths for straining any piece of cane that might not have been large enough to dissolve. Katura and Adah were sanitizing the canning jars and lids.

"Found the skimmers, but only one wooden paddle. That's gonna add some time." Luke held up the skimmer with a tight fist. "I don't know how you talked me into this in the first place. It'll take most of the day already. We'll have to go around asking for at least one more paddle or we'll miss dinner."

Lizzy had set her heart on making the molasses. "Do you always think of your belly?" She grinned, and then quickly looked behind to see Adah walking toward her. She hoped Adah and Katura would focus on their chores and help them get this done quickly.

"How's it going in here?" Adah stepped closer and took in a deep breath. "Smells good and sweet." She eyed the mill outside that was used to squeeze the cane. "This is *wunderbaar!* What a grand idea." She went to the tack room where the horse supplies and saddles were kept and returned with another paddle.

"Where did you find that?" Luke was busy removing the seeds by using a sharp knife to cut them off at a slant.

Adah giggled. "That time Timothy came looking for me in the barn and he gave me a little too much attention? Well, he had another think coming when I took ahold of that paddle. You know, if you get a good grip, even a girl like me can give a fella what-for if he doesn't mind his manners." She grinned with pride.

Luke straightened and stared at her, unamused. "Timothy Hersberger?"

Adah stuck out her lower lip. She'd said too much, at least to her big brother. Lizzy knew there were many more stories, and it worried her. Their *daed* was a stern man and would not take Adah's behavior lightly. Neither would Luke.

"*Jah*, but he doesn't come around so much anymore. Probably scared him off that day."

Luke scoffed and dipped his paddle into the juice with a strong grip. "*Jah*, I'm sure he was scared."

"Who's scared?" Katura took a cloth from Lizzy and started skimming, waiting for an answer from Luke, but he didn't respond.

He stopped cutting and gave her the older-brother scowl he used when hearing things about his sisters he didn't like. "Don't be getting fresh with these young men. You give 'em too much attention. And besides, what were you two doing alone in the barn?"

Adah flushed. "Well, it wasn't like I invited him. He just barged in." She shrugged, keeping her eyes downcast.

Adah was not a good liar, and Lizzy thought sure Luke would have been a policeman if he were English. It was hard to get anything past him. The pause that followed made Lizzy uncomfortable, and there were too many thoughts to miss the opportunity to speak.

"Can we just concentrate on getting this done? I don't want the snow to stop me from giving some molasses pie to Clara." She might as well have been talking to the barn wall, because no one seemed to be listening to her.

Katura chimed in. "It's not Adah's fault. One look and they get the wrong idea." It made Lizzy sad that Katura had a hard time getting a boy's attention. Lizzy on the other hand had become irritated with the attention. But she wouldn't say that to her. She preferred someone who would be drawn to her mind not her looks.

"I can take care of myself, big brother." Adah's good mood was gone.

Lizzy strained the juice through clean, white cloths, wringing as she went. "Between this here and what's in the buckets, we'll have more than enough."

The large boiler pan spit out the juice as they continued to skim the green film from the top of the liquid with a special molasses strainer.

"Get the canning jars. We don't want this setting up." Lizzy wondered whether it would dry out right. It was different when large groups shared the load and spent the day making huge tubs of the molasses. This wasn't even half of what they usually made, but it was the point behind it, the reason they were there.

Anything to make Clara happy, even a little bit. And the thing about her was that no matter how small the effort or gift, she would act as if it was the most wonderful ever given to her.

Adah straightened. "I'm parched. I'll get us something

to drink. Be right back." She turned quickly and made her way to the door.

Lizzy knew it wasn't the heat that was bothering her as much as Luke's chastising her about Timothy. She was glad to have him there.

"Finish up now, there's a meeting at the school *haus*." Lizzy's *mamm* stood by the open barn door. "Don't want to keep your *daed* waiting."

"We can't *all* leave." Lizzy's concern was not about what the bishop had to say; she could find that out later. She was so caught up in this molasses, she couldn't think of anything else.

"It's still not up to a boil; it'll be fine for a while." Luke bumped her to get her to move, and she reluctantly let go of her cloth and wiped her hands on her apron.

He smiled. "Thanks for making it easier on me. *Daed* expects you to mind him, and for your own sake, you should."

She knew he was right, but she wouldn't admit it. He just liked seeing her give in; she didn't for everyone. Then she tried to think of who else besides her brother might induce her to give in, and the first face that popped up was Zack. She scowled. She'd just been around him for the last couple of days, and that was out of the ordinary. She was already being looked badly upon for being with Zack in places she shouldn't be.

It's not as if I was alone with him in a bedroom, for Pete's sake.

"Ready?" He held out an elbow with a crooked smile, knowing she couldn't resist.

"If anything happens to that syrup—"

"Hush, little one." He didn't look at her, just kept walking, but she couldn't let that go unnoticed.

"Don't hurry, don't worry, do your best, leave the rest." She looked up at him. "Do I need to remind you?"

"Oh, I have it memorized, *danke*." His smile broadened until they rounded the barn to see *Daed*'s extra-wide buggy waiting for them.

"Guess we're late."

He gave her a sheepish look. "I could have told you that. You do like to make things hard on yourself."

"*Nee*, others make things difficult. I just try to stay out of their way so I can do my own bidding."

He shook his head. "You sure know how to swing things around." He opened the buggy door. "But somehow it works for you." He winked and slid inside with her. "Mind dropping me off at home after the meeting, *Daed*?"

Daed responded with a nod.

Lizzy snapped her head over to him. "Does Neva need anything?" She knew what the answer would be but thought to ask anyway. Lizzy didn't blame his wife for not wanting to worry about company right now; she was on bed rest and had a family of sisters who kept her company.

"*Nee*, she seems to have what she needs, but thanks for always asking." He patted her knee. "You're a good sister-in-law—and sister, for that matter."

"What do you hear about Clara, Lizzy?" Adah's eyes widened. Her sisters seemed to live on gossip.

"She's making progress, but nothing seems to be swaying one way or another. I guess it just takes time."

"They say it could be caused by pesticides?" Katura said, a little too direct for Lizzy. Nothing was certain yet.

Daed grunted. *Mamm* and he had hardly spoken since

they'd gotten into the buggy. "Need to do things the old way, not this poison they put in the ground. They expect people to eat it and not get sick? I never have, nor ever will use the deadly poison."

Mamm nodded her approval. "The bishop might have something to say. Our community forbids using pesticides."

Luke shook his head. "*Nee*, it's the weather. This has been a pretty cold year, the coldest since 1950."

"If no one uses pesticides, then how did Clara get sick?" Lizzy spoke loud enough to be heard, but she didn't think her *daed* could hear her.

Daed looked at her through the rearview and scowled. "That's for the bishop to figure out, not for us to question."

Some communities allowed pesticides because they could improve the yield of certain crops. And she knew some of the farmers had a string of bad harvests. Lizzy could uphold the rules of her community only to a certain point, and the older she got, the more she could see both ways on a number of things. Her *mamm* had no interest in discussing her questions, and she didn't bother asking her *daed*. Not even Luke would talk with an open mind concerning why things were done certain ways. That left her with no one. She paused. Zack would be a good person to ask; he had seen both Amish and English ways now.

The meeting was already in motion, which irritated her *daed*. The school *haus* was full, so most of the men stood. She and her sisters found seats, and her *mamm* sat with a friend across from them.

"The storm, Frankenstein, has been looming over us and surrounding areas for the last twenty-four hours." The bishop paused until the murmurs settled. "The National Weather Service warns the rain will be turning to ice after nightfall, with snow to follow. Although it's unusual for such a strong storm so early in the year, we need to make ourselves ready."

Different conversations popped up as they left the room. "Don't ya think it's a little early to be worried? Seems extreme to me."

"Do what you feel necessary." The bishop turned to Stephen, who'd made the comment. "And don't be knocking on my door to pull you out from under your *haus*." Some nervous chuckles were heard throughout the room. "With gusts as high as fifty-five miles per hour, I'll be in my cellar with my wife's canned preserves." More chuckles calmed the room.

"No school, obviously, and take in any livestock you happen to see wandering, or they might be somebody's dinner. This is supposed to be a big storm, so prepare yourself to be together for a long while."

"Good thing is we're prepared and don't rely on all that the English do." Lizzy heard her *daed*'s words and knew he was right, and she knew Zack was careful enough not to be out in this weather.

An elder entered and handed the bishop a note. After glancing at the paper for a several long seconds, the bishop raised his hands to silence the crowd. "It seems the storm has intensified. It won't be safe for some of you to return home tonight, so we will make preparations to use the meeting *haus* as a shelter. I must ask the elders and deacons—you know who you are—to fetch the emergency supplies in the storm shelter."

Some of the women had brought food to prepare for those who were homebound. Now it looked like those items would be needed by more than a few. Lizzy and her *mamm* moved quickly to help the women with the cooking.

The preparations for the storm made Lizzy curious about the conveniences enjoyed by those in the city. Just the few things Zack had mentioned made life seem so much more enjoyable, with time to spare for relaxation and activities other than constant chores.

"Lizzy!"

Luke's voice stopped her thoughts. She blinked and stared at him.

"Daed is going to take me to Neva. We'll be safe in the storm shelter. I'll be up to see Clara when this weather calms down." He waved as they rode away, leaving her with lots of questions.

Chapter Fifteen

Zack couldn't make it to the hospital. A buggy would have done better than the rental car. He wasn't even halfway there when he had to turn around because he couldn't see through his windshield. He sat at a light and called Clara's room. The phone rang five times before someone finally answered.

"Heart of Lancaster Hospital." A woman's voice crackled over the phone. Zack glanced at his cell phone and noticed that not only was the reception poor, but also that battery was low.

"Can you connect me with Clara Schrock?" He could barely hear her and hoped she could hear him. He'd communicated with Clara a few times since leaving the hospital and knew her procedures were being done, but he wanted to hear her voice, to tell her about the weather that was coming in and let her know that he couldn't make it.

He continued to drive slowly so as not slide into another car. His eyes moved from his phone to the road and back again. The waiting and heavy weather tensed his shoulder muscles and made his head pound. He didn't want to be away from Clara, and he certainly didn't want to go back to the community. He couldn't imagine groveling to get them to give him a bed for a night. They'd made it clear that he wasn't welcome.

"Hallo." Clara's voice calmed him, and he let out a breath.

"Clara, have you heard about this weather?" He felt helpless, unable to be with her when she needed him.

"*Jah*, they're prepared for anything that might come up. Got the generators ready if needed. Just like us Amish, *jah*?"

Zack almost smiled at her light description of the hospital's backup plans. He would still feel better if he was there to help. "Are you on any machines?"

"*Nee*, just the hydration drip right now. You know better than to worry about me. I know that for sure, Zack Schrock."

She was trying to distract him, but he couldn't let her, not now, no matter how much he wanted to make her feel better too. "What do they say about your treatment?" He offered a quick, silent prayer.

"Nothing for you to worry about at the moment. We have a blizzard to tumble with. Can't believe the timing of it all, but *Gott* wants me here for a reason, and He has a plan for you, as well."

He didn't like the idea of her not sharing the latest bit of news about her condition. "Clara, if you don't want to tell me what the doctor is saying, I'll just have to start walking back to the hospital." He was only half-joking. He'd rather find out when the chemo would begin and what the latest test results showed than deal with all the thoughts in his head, imagining a prognosis worse than it probably was.

"There's nothing that *Gott* can't get us through. You can't carry both of our burdens, Zack. I can imagine how hard it was for you to come back home, but I'm sure glad that you did."

"It was what I expected." He thought of Eli standing on the porch as he drove away, offering a gesture of truce or maybe second chances. Even if it was only with one of his family, he'd take any kind of reconciliation he could find.

"Well, that sounds like a good thing. Am I right? Maybe there isn't as big a wedge between you all as you thought." Her voice cracked, and he knew he was depleting her energy by drawing her out, as she'd done many times with him. Clara was a listener and very good at it; this was unusual.

"I can't imagine that I'd ever be welcomed back, not that I want to be." He knew what he'd done was wrong in their eyes, but they had no idea how much more he had to work through. He decided not to keep her talking or to let her distract him.

Beep. "My phone's out of power. I'll try to find my charger and call you back if I lose you."

"I do like talking on the phone, such a rare thing for me. I know I'm not supposed to, but just think if we couldn't be talking now. That would be a shame, especially with the weather like this. You know I'm safe and sound here at the hospital, so you just think about your driving. I haven't ridden in a car much, but when I did, I enjoyed it."

She was rambling, something she never did, but now it was to keep him company. He listened to her talk while looking back and forth between the road and hunting for his charger.

The tinkling noise from his phone told him he'd just lost contact with Clara.

He slammed on the brakes as the car in front of him honked, giving him just enough time to stop, avoiding an accident. He slapped both hands on the steering wheel, frustrated that he couldn't see or hear his sister. At least she was at a hospital. He wished she could come home, but he felt better knowing she was in good hands.

The rest of the drive, stressful with the frozen roads and drivers going half the speed limit, made him tired. He wasn't sure where he should be at this point. He'd come for Clara and to avoid the community, but here he was, doing just the opposite.

Once he reached the road leading to the schoolhouse, he noticed all the buggies tethered in front of the one-room school. He parked but hesitated before going in.

I don't know where I should be. What do I do?

He paused at the door and then gently turned the knob. The bishop held a hand to his mouth to amplify the sound. "Three to five inches of snow overnight, so we should prepare for ice in the morning until the next few days."

"*Jah*, and those of you returning home should stock up on food and water," one of the deacons offered. "The pumps might freeze. We might be called out as responders, so those of you who are set up for it, be ready." It was clear from the sheepish shake of his head that this deacon had done the job before.

Zack wanted to help but knew how awkward it would be, so he held his tongue. He looked around the room to see his *daed* coming his way. They hadn't met eyes, so Zack didn't know if he was coming over to see him or pass by. He prepared himself for either. Without so much as a hello, his *daed* started in with a question.

"What do you hear from Clara?" His bloodshot eyes and worn demeanor told Zack he was out of touch with his daughter and in need of a connection with her, even if it meant coming to Zack for the answers.

"She's well. I spoke with her on the phone. Couldn't get

to the hospital before the streets iced over, but she was in good spirits."

His *mamm* bobbed her head. "She's better off there until this is over, ain't it so, Jed?" she said, as if she was hoping that was the right answer.

"I suppose." He nodded, perhaps to convince himself his girl was okay, even though she wasn't there with them. "But I'd rather she were home. It's time for her to be here."

Zack understood his concern but hoped he wouldn't push things too far and seriously expect Clara to come home before she should. Zack suddenly felt as if he were competing with his family, each of them individually. Not to mention Lizzy's protectiveness over Clara. He wasn't surprised that she spent extra time with her, but her possessive way sometimes seemed over the top.

"I'll call the hospital when I get cell service and let you know when I make contact." As he was saying the words, Eli nodded from across the room as if to say hello and good-bye at the same time and walked out the door. He seemed to be the only one who might give him a reprieve and talk to him for more than a sentence or two. If it weren't for Clara, they might not be speaking to him at all.

The community set up makeshift beds, drinks were in coolers under ice, food was brought in, and everyone took his or her role for when the storm came. There were already signs in the sky and in the way the wind was blowing. Zack's memory of tornados as a kid came back to him, and he wondered whether he'd run into one again before this was all over.

There was a faint sound of sirens going off from the firehouse a couple miles away. Everyone in action picked up the pace, including Zack. He might be an outcast, but until this event was over, he thought of himself as one of them.

Lizzy gripped his hand. "Help me with the food." Coolers were stacked in the back of the room, filled with enough food and drinks to tide over a family for a week or so. "Let's grab that one." Lizzy pointed to the largest cooler, and he followed after her.

Just as they gripped the handles on opposite ends, a rumble so loud it could have been a train passing by caught Lizzy off guard. She tumbled to the ground, scattering foodstuffs across the floor. She started to put them back in the cooler, but Zack took her hand and pointed to the other handle. It was too heavy for her, but they could at least take it someplace where they could work together to refill it and move it to where it needed to go. "Over there." She pointed to an empty spot by a wall.

"*Danke*, Zack." Lizzy's humility surprised him, and he gave her a nod.

"What's this I hear about you working with the disaster team, Zack?" The deacon threw a hand up in the air to make his point, but also caught the attention of the others around him.

Zack thought about all the ways he could prove himself worthy, but that wouldn't change anything. He'd left the community and broken his baptismal place, so according to all those around him, he wasn't worthy of anything. As the deacon and another drew closer, he couldn't believe they were worried about his place there when a storm was about to hit.

He held up a hand. "Whatever you're going to say, save your breath. I won't so much as lift a finger. Have it your way. I was just trying to help." He turned to leave, hoping his car would start, even though it would just irritate the deacon that much more. The only person missing was the bishop; Zack hoped he was occupied with more important issues.

Lizzy looked over at the group of men, who were now mumbling together. "He's just trying to assist us. We need all the help we can get before this storm hits." Lizzy surprised even herself by speaking so boldly.

The deacon scowled at Zack and then at her. "You see the division it makes when a defector comes back? He's caught your eye is the problem." One of the elders grunted his agreement, and another nodded.

"*Ach*, this is not the time. Can't you see that?" Her flushed face and quick breaths showed her frustration with the situation, and Zack was both shocked and suspicious. Her cause couldn't involve him, only her disagreement with the harsh treatment of those shunned. He remembered the times she'd expressed the feeling that it was between God and the person who faltered to sort things through, not some board of deacons. At this moment he appreciated her philosophy on the matter.

Zack thought it was a good time to discreetly walk away, even though he thought it ridiculous that he couldn't help. These were prideful people, reminding him of at least one of the reasons he'd left.

He got into his car, hoping it would start and get him to where he was going. He turned it over once with some response, tried again, and the engine sang a sound beautiful to his ears. He let out a breath and put his hands on the wheel just as Lizzy opened the door and sat down in the passenger's seat.

"Did you forget something?"

"*Nee*, why?"

"Because you're going to have the whole community hunting me down if you don't let me go."

"Well, go." She looked straight ahead as if waiting for a planned drive. "Besides this nonsense, the storm is upon us."

Zack looked at her and then at the dark sky. Clouds rolled into darkness around them, and the temperature plummeted as they spoke.

Chapter Sixteen

THE CAR COUGHED. Lizzy worried it wasn't going to make it to the hospital. She watched Zack maneuver through the dirt path leaving the school and then looked up at the sky. A dark overcast was moving with the wind. As they reached the highway, the weather only got worse.

"This doesn't look good." She turned to him.

His eyes were fixed on the road. "Look at the traffic." Cars slowed, some weaved in and out of the lanes, and others sat idle on the side of the road. Large flakes were falling thickly, covering the icy pavement.

"I don't know much about driving a car, but it seems to me we're going the wrong way." She flinched when a car rolled into Zack's bumper—not that one more dent would make much difference. At least they weren't riding in a buggy with this kind of weather and getting hit by a sliding automobile.

She sucked in air when Zack swerved to keep from getting hit again. The car straightened as he slowly maneuvered back into the dense traffic. "Zack, what are you doing?"

"I don't know if we're going to make it to the hospital, Lizzy." He held up a hand just long enough to keep her from talking and then gripped the steering wheel. "I already tried earlier. The storm's coming in from that direction. The roads were impossible." He pointed down the way before them and then beyond. The storm seemed to be freezing the streets right behind them, turning the roads instantly into ice.

"What does that mean?" She clenched her hands, waiting for him to tell her what she didn't want to hear, watching as they moved farther away from the city.

He slowed to stop at a light. She pushed back in the seat, as if it would keep the car from sliding. He pumped the brakes and stopped just in time.

He let out a breath. "Can I think for a minute? At least until I get off the highway?"

Lizzy frowned. "That's miles from here."

"Exactly."

Lizzy folded her arms across her chest. She didn't care that he was stressed. She wouldn't accept that sort of response. As she watched the bumper-to-bumper traffic, her head began to bob, and she caught herself almost asleep a couple of times. The warm car made it easy to nod off. Disgusted with herself for not staying awake, she held her eyes open wide.

None of the sights out her window were familiar. "Where are we?"

"We're stuck going this way for a while. The highway is treacherous, but no one can get off. The exits are worse than the highway with less traffic. The few I've seen who took an exit ended up in a ditch or sliding around with no traction. We're all sitting ducks until the first car spins out."

She kept her eyes forward and wanted him to do the same. "We can't keep going like this." Clara's face came to her mind, and anxiety kicked in. "Do something."

It came out much more loudly than she'd intended, but she didn't regret it. She felt like stepping out the door and walking back home or to Clara in the hospital—anywhere but here.

"You have some ideas? There's nowhere to go but forward. We're trapped." He pointed next to him, to the four-lane highway beside them on either side. "Do you realize how long we've been inching along on this road?"

It had been a while. She could see the sun starting to go down slowly—like the cars stuck on the highway. They were all trapped in an endless sit-and-wait situation. It suddenly hit her: they were stranded, and everyone else with them.

"This is awful. Isn't there anything we can do to get out of this?" It was a ridiculous question, and she knew it, but she was starting to panic, which was unusual for her. Her habit was never to act on fear, which would be weak. She wasn't weak.

"If there was somewhere for us to go, to get off this highway, we could make some headway on a side street. We might even get out of the car." He lifted his arm to the back of her headrest and shook his head. "I've never been in this kind of a backup."

"There's an advantage of having a horse. At least you can maneuver the horse around, unlike these cars." Lizzy thought about how she felt the need to defend their ways when she was around him. He knew everything she was saying, so why did she feel she had to explain things to him? Sometimes Lizzy thought that maybe she was a bit interested in the ways of the English and wished she could have a day—just one—to see the way Zack lived. He must think things were boring here compared to life in the city.

Zack made a quick jerk right, landing halfway between two cars. He stayed in the same position and passed by another car that honked in protest.

Lizzy had mixed feelings about his boldness. They should wait their turn, not push their way in. Everyone wanted to move, but with that came the possibility they would cause an accident. No one else had the nerve Zack did.

"Hang on." Zack turned the wheel sharply to the right, and then with a hard left they were on the access road.

Lizzy let out a scream that made Zack frown. She felt silly once he slowed and they were at a snail's pace again. There were others who had made the bold move, but at least now they were able to steadily move forward.

Once they were comfortably on the side street, Zack seemed either exhausted or just relieved they were making progress. She glanced at him. "Are you all right?"

He allowed himself a sigh. "I thought for sure I was going to roll sideways on the cement."

She didn't like how the vulnerable side of her kept popping out, but it was helpful that he also could express his misgivings in this situation.

"It's going to get worse before it gets better. I had to make a move." He leaned back, his muscles relaxing. "It's getting late."

"*Jah*, it will get worse once the sun goes down." She looked over at him, waiting for a solution.

"I've been thinking about the cabin up this way that we used to visit." He pointed to the winding road that led to a hunting cottage the Amish used during deer season.

Lizzy's brows lifted. "You mean the rundown one-room old lodge our *daed*s used to use?"

"It's better than sleeping in the car, which is a good possibility if things don't change real quickly."

Lizzy looked out the window. The snow covered the car, and inch after inch it kept coming down. The motels were sparse and surely all booked up. But they couldn't possibly stay in that cabin. She glanced over at him, trying to figure out whether he was serious about it.

"Why are you shaking your head?" He squinted as if analyzing her.

"I just can't imagine staying in that cabin. You're not serious, are you?"

He shrugged. "Where else can we go?" He darted his eyes over to her. "You don't think I'm trying to get you alone, do you?"

She was insulted, but more so that he seemed to think he would never even be interested in her. She crossed her arms and looked out the window, but that just made her worry about her situation and Clara's.

Zack made a right turn and started down a one-lane highway. Lizzy watched for signs but didn't see any. "Do you know where you're going?"

"If my instincts are right, this is how we get to the cabin. It's a little ways—"

"Isn't there another option?" The thought of being with Zack, alone in a cabin was too much for her to take. What would people think? She prayed for wisdom.

Zack shrugged. "Where else can you and I sleep? In the car?"

"That's chivalrous of you." She made sure the tone was mocking so he might realize how off base he was. "You might spend the night with unmarried women in the city, but we don't do that kind of thing here."

"You don't think the Amish do all of these terrible things you think I do?"

She started thinking of the Amish who were brought before the deacons for breaking the rules of the *Ordnung* for much harsher infractions. All she knew was that Zack had left after being baptized. When she gave it some thought, what he had done wasn't nearly as bad as what the Amish teens had done. She was getting a little tired of her subconscious arguing with her.

"It scares me when you don't talk, even if it is to chastise me."

His response caught her off guard, as he had done so many times since returning to the community. She found herself wondering what he might say next.

Chapter Seventeen

Does she have *to look so pretty even in the worst of situations?*

Zack tried not to notice. He didn't want to go there. He had before, when they were younger, and he'd thought for a short time she might share his feelings, but nothing had ever come of it. He didn't know whether it was him or her hard-to-get ways that separated them, but sometimes Zack wished he had tried harder.

He knew his harsh words had hurt her. He wasn't used to her showing her feelings the way she had on the drive, but it was intense driving in that weather, and he didn't want anything to happen to her.

Almost there. Then what?

She'd made it clear they couldn't be together, but there wasn't anywhere else to go. At least for now. He thought about how differently he thought of things like this. Few in the world outside would think the way Lizzy did about an unmarried man and woman sleeping in the same bed. As he remembered, there were only cots for the adults in one part of the cabin and sleeping bags for the youngsters. But that was a long time ago.

The snow crackled under the tires as he turned up the long drive. He watched as she looked around the place outside. Neither of them had seen it in years. The cabin was large enough to hold at least a couple dozen people.

They used well water and gas, and that was about all they needed to cook and clean.

He pointed up to a tree on one side. "I remember sleeping over here, in a tree house we made. The boys slept out there, rain or shine." He turned to Lizzy, guessing what she was thinking, and thought he'd end the topic with some humor. "But I guess I'm a little big for that now."

She smiled and let out a breath. "This old cabin looks as good as the last time I saw it." She pulled her shawl tight around her and looked up into the tree. "You boys wouldn't let us up there." She frowned.

"There wasn't room. Besides, it wasn't ladylike." He grinned, and then grunted, knowing that wasn't the reason for her.

"No one seems to use this place much, especially this time of year." She paused. "You don't think anyone is here, do you?"

"Not in this weather, but I'm sure they come around to hunt here every now and then." He could see her discomfort, but he didn't know whether it was because of the sleeping arrangements or their isolation.

"So now what?"

The apprehension on her face made him feel even worse; it had nothing to do with him. She was just plain scared.

"We're gonna be fine, Lizzy. Let's go see how things look inside." Anything to get her mind off their situation would benefit them both. Although he had no inappropriate intentions, he well knew that, for an Amish woman, it was still disgraceful for them to be alone together.

He led the way and walked up to the log cabin made of long cuts of spruce trees meshed between cement. The windows on either side and one in the back were all the lighting they had, but the fireplace and stove, if they worked, would give them some heat.

"My, this is a big room." She said as she entered the cabin. When Lizzy rubbed her hands together, Zack responded by going to the door to get some kindling.

"Where are you going?"

"We need to warm this place up. I'll get some wood and see if that fireplace works." He moved toward the door and gave her one last look before he walked out. The old door creaked as he shut it. He turned to see if the structure was in good shape.

Of course it is; it was made by Amish.

He glanced at the window to see Lizzy's dark figure puttering around in the kitchen. She moved closer to the window, and he caught her eye. She smiled and went back to work. They both seemed to be a little more relaxed now that they were off that highway.

He felt a twinge of regret for getting after her when he turned off the highway. But who knew where they would have been if he hadn't?

He scouted around the area to see what they might find useful. Tall trees were dense, standing all around him. The snow was thick and crunched under his boots as he trudged around the area. White rabbits scattered as he walked past the cabin. Soon after, a hawk swooped down and perched in a nearby tree. Zack kept walking in search of kindling and saw a large shed behind the cabin. It was locked, so he tried to look in through the doors. He had an impression of some sort of farm equipment but couldn't make it out.

He snapped off any thin branches he could reach until he couldn't carry any more. They might need to be dried out, and he didn't know how much the fire would help with such a large room, but they'd prepare as best they could.

He saw the area where he remembered a path led to the fishing pond. He couldn't make out the path, though, not under all this snow. He'd like to come back here sometime but knew that wouldn't be acceptable.

He wondered whether the bishop, his own father, would ever accept him back. He doubted it. His dad didn't even pretend to be glad Zack was back, even if it wasn't for a happy reunion.

He headed for the trail area. There might be more kindling around. Noticing a fallen tree made him wonder if there was a good, sharp ax around. He'd have to figure out a way to get into the shed.

He picked up more kindling, balancing it as he walked through the drifts of snow. As he walked by the huge, old, fallen tree, he was almost sure that was where he and his brothers had carved messages on the trees as kids—sort of a mode of communication they'd made up.

He looked up at the sky covered in a gray haze. After the storm, it would be only a matter of time before Lizzy's family would start looking for her. He, on the other hand, had no one to answer to except his boss. But at this rate, he didn't even know whether he wanted to go back. Just before he left Philly, he found out his boss was illegally taking over properties and using them again with a different name. He knew his boss could be ruthless and often took advantage of people, but he wanted no part of his illegal activities.

Does it matter that I didn't know what was happening?

As a young, naive Amish man, he'd trusted his boss and

liked the money. Now he was learning the hard way. He would have to lay low until he figured out what to do next.

"There you are."

Zack tried to hide his surprise as he saw Lizzy lift up her dress to step over the dead tree.

"Looks like you found some wood." She stopped next to him. "Do you think it will be enough?"

"Doubt it. I'm going to get into that shack and see what I can find. Hopefully an ax." His mind was elsewhere, thinking of the times a group of them went swimming together at night when the parents were asleep. Lizzy would jump right in, never worried about how cold the water was or how little they could see in the darkness.

"Zack, I lost you for a minute." She tilted her head, waiting, but he had nothing to share.

"Thinking too much." Which he was, but about all the wrong things. "Let's get this to the cabin before it's too dark to see." Zack thought he was farther away than he had ended up. Lost in memories, especially of her.

"Are you worried?" She took a handful of the sticks. "If it's about food, there's some nonperishable items in one of the cabinets. Not a lot, but it should last a couple days. The well isn't dry. Iced over, but we can fix that once you get into that shed."

"I'll go; it's getting too cold and dark for you to be out here." To his surprise, she listened.

She paused as if unsure of what he'd said. "*Jah*, it's going to be a chilly night if you can't find more wood."

"Exactly. Besides, I'm starving." Which he was, but he wasn't thrilled with what the food might be.

She nodded and then walked away, head down, and didn't stop for as far as he could see. He'd figure out what she was thinking later. It was awkward and scary to be up here alone, but they'd have to make the best of things until the sun rose and they could get back on that highway.

The lock on the shed was sturdy enough that he'd have to break in. He set down the kindling and took out the largest branch. It took only one hit for the glass to break, but the echo into the darkness made him uncomfortable, as if he had announced their presence over a wide area.

Rustling sounds came from underfoot, and he heard flapping of wings overhead. Then it was silent again. He wasted no time looking for helpful supplies. He found kerosene, tools, fishing equipment, charcoal, camping supplies, and more. The biggest find, literally, was an old combustible-engine tractor. Interesting, since most Amish used horses, not machines.

Zack made his way back in a hurry, not wanting to worry Lizzy. When he got there, she put one hand on a counter and let the other drop.

"I heard a noise and thought something awful had happened to you. Are you all right?"

"Had to break through the window to get into the shed. It's good-sized, enough to house a small tractor."

"Where would that have come from?"

"Not sure; it's not something Amish."

"Anything we can use?"

"Several things, but for now I'll check out the fireplace to see if it's working." He walked over and withdrew a lighter. She frowned. He guessed she thought that was cheating, but there was nothing else to use. He took out his pocketknife and cleaned away as much of the snow from the branches as possible, and then lit the sticks. The leftover snow sizzled and steamed.

Lizzy walked over and put her hands up to warm them. "It's nice but won't last long."

"I didn't see an ax, but once it gets light, I'll look around again." He grinned. "Your nose isn't red anymore; you must be thawing out."

"*Jah*, but it's going to be a cold night." She blushed, turning pink again for a different reason.

"Lizzy, don't worry. I'll sleep in the car." It would be mighty cold, but her body language told him how uncomfortable she was. It would be a lot warmer to sleep together, completely clothed, of course. But he hoped it would be only one night. He could do that once.

She shook her head. "I can't let you do that, Zack, you'd freeze."

"You're too innocent to do anything other than this. And I'm the last person anyone wants you around."

Lizzy was as white as milk. Her eyes watered, and she looked at the floor. "I'm not as naive as you think."

Chapter Eighteen

Lizzy turned and walked away. She squeezed her eyes shut and then opened them before taking another step. Memories sifted up into her mind. She wished they hadn't come to the cabin. It was years ago, and she still couldn't fight it off.

Let it go.

"Lizzy. Wait." Zack jogged up behind her as she walked to the door and followed her out. She could feel his eyes on her, waiting for an explanation.

I can't...I shouldn't have said anything.

But then again, it had popped out for a reason. Maybe it was time to confide in someone.

But not Zack. Not now.

"Lizzy." He stepped in front of her.

She moved around him. "Stop, Zack."

She heard the breath come out of his lungs, and he stepped in time with her. She could feel the tension and frustration between the two of them. But there was nowhere to go with the information she held so tightly.

His warm hand rested on her shoulder. "I won't ask you again. But the look on your face tells me there's something you want to get off your chest, and for a split second you wanted to share it."

His hand was too warm and his explanation so right, to a T, as if he knew what she was thinking.

With his wayward ways in the city, who knows what he got into?

She shook her head. She had no place to think that way. Maybe it was easier to blame someone else with their flaws than it was to examine her own. But Lizzy already had and thought it would get better.

Maybe I should go to the bishop, set this burden down, be done with it.

"Lizzy, stay with me." Zack stared into her eyes. "I won't bother you about it." He shrugged. "At least I'll try not to."

She almost smiled. "Why is it that you always remember the good about this place before the bad?" Or maybe it was just her, not seeing the good at all for too long now.

Lizzy looked up at the huge trees reaching for the skies. The air was crisp and the snowfall steady, but she couldn't' deny that it was beautiful, both the land and the snow. *Why did* Gott *bring me back here again?*

He changed the subject. "Why doesn't anyone use this place much anymore? It's so peaceful. Beautiful parcel of land."

Lizzy watched him as he scanned the area. She appreciated his interest, as it seemed he wasn't interested in anything about the people he'd grown up with. But she understood the need to let things go, forget, and move on. She kicked a small stone lodged in the snow. Frustration poured into her as she thought of what she'd gotten herself into. She looked at him out of the corner of her eye. Then she hunkered down, hugging her knees.

"It wasn't safe here for a while." She squeezed her eyes shut, not wanting to explain, but he should know. Maybe her subconscious was pushing her forward, forcing her to release the truth and move on, let it pass.

"Why?" He hunched down beside her but didn't look at her.

"I don't remember." She did, though, now that she was here again. She didn't want to lie, but he wouldn't stop with the questions. She looked up and around. A chill came over her, and she didn't want to be out here any longer. She stood and stepped toward the cabin.

"Where are you running off to?" He stood when she did but didn't come forward, as if he didn't know what to do.

She looked up at the sky with the never-ending flakes of snow showering down on her. She stopped and then felt him beside her. "This place brings up some things I've tried to forget about." How did that happen? She hadn't remembered anything, good or bad. But now that she was here, it was becoming real all over again.

"I don't know what to do here." He paused. "If you're worried about being here with me or for any other reason, just know that the snow has to stop sometime. We'll leave as soon as possible."

Lizzy liked that thought and felt some peace in his words. She let out a breath and forced herself to keep her eyes on the cabin until they were close enough to open the door.

Zack shook the handle of the door and opened it for her. "Better?" He shut the door behind her and waited.

"I'm fine." Lizzy turned her head as she watched Zack's eyes following her. She bent down and looked at the scant food they had. A few canned goods, dried jerky, and a jar of jelly.

"I can't imagine someone leaving even one jar of food, let alone three. It's too un-Amish to be wasteful."

"Maybe they were saving them for something special." Some occasionally wanted to stay an extra night, her family among them. She sighed and sat down. If only she had stayed with the rest of the family.

He picked up a can and examined the mark on it. "Not expired." He shrugged and leaned against the counter. "Could be they were expecting to come back." He sat down beside her. Not too close, not too far. "I must not have come that time."

"*Nee*, you didn't."

His forehead creased. "I'm surprised you noticed."

If he only knew how much I thought about him. And how the girls talked about him after he left.

He was sought after for his handsome face, but also his kind ways.

Her focus was on the fire as he stirred the sticks; they weren't going to last long. "We'll freeze in here if we don't get some more wood."

He stood and rubbed the back of his neck in thought. "I'm going back in the shed to find something that I can use to cut some wood."

He was already walking to the door before he was done talking, and she felt apprehensive at the thought of being by herself. This place unnerved her, and what scared her more was not being able to remember exactly what happened. It made her feel helpless, but she also didn't want to know, sure that what she couldn't remember was something bad.

He stopped and opened the door. "Are you coming?" He smiled and held out a hand for her as she buttoned up her coat. "It'll be dark soon, so let's hurry."

He took long steps, leading them to the shed. Lizzy

tried to keep up but fell behind. When Zack got there, he pulled hard on the door and worked it open. "With this wet, heavy snow, I wouldn't be surprised if the roof fell in."

"Don't even say that, Zack." She felt heavy enough with everything going through her mind. She couldn't handle even one more thing to worry about.

The sun was going down. Time was precious. The last thing she wanted was to be walking outside in the dark. She shivered, not knowing if it was from the cold or the fear pumping through her.

The shed had seen its day. The structure had been there before the cabin was built, and it was old. Her great-great *dawdi* had helped build it.

"I'd say ladies first, but in this case, I'm going in." He put up a hand until he'd had a look around and then motioned for her to come inside. "What do you think of this?"

The shed was packed full. Unable to see through the doors, they couldn't know the amount of paraphernalia that was in the large shed. The tractor was the only thing that stood out due to its size.

"What is all this?" She had started to walk forward when she felt Zack's hand clasp hers.

"Why are you so edgy?" He kept eyeing the shed's contents as he waited for her to reply. When she didn't, he went on, "This is strange. Someone is hoarding food and supplies here." He walked over to a tall shelf filled with nonperishables and put his hands on his hips as he studied the mix—from dried food and powdered drinks to cereals and breads.

"Why would the Amish store so much dried food when we make everything from scratch?" She wiped the dust off of one of the containers and blew it off her finger. "It's been sitting here for a while."

"Strange. But then again, I remember gathering food and delivering it. Does anyone still do that?" He turned to her, looking interested in her answer.

"Whenever there are food drives and what-not. Why are you so interested?"

"I always liked it, I guess." He turned and started digging around again. "You're looking at me like *they* do."

She knew who he meant but asked all the same. "Like who?"

He scoffed. "My dad, for one."

She couldn't imagine how it must feel to be the bishop's son. She knew he could be grim. Her *daed* was sharp and grumpy, but his protective side evened things out. The last time they argued, it had been about Zack. But her *daed* was less upset about Zack than he was at seeing her grow up. She was old enough to know he was worried to death about her. She didn't know if he was believing the stories that went around about Zack or if he even cared.

"What are you looking for?" She started peeking around too, and they found essentials that would come in handy, from toothpaste and other toiletries to beans, lentils, dried fruit, and canned foods.

He pointed at the stocked shelves. "My gosh, this could feed a family for months."

Lizzy leaned back, trying to make sense of it all. "Who would do this and why?"

"The occupant."

She didn't want to have this conversation. That meant dealing with the possibilities that had been swirling in her head.

"You think someone's living here?"

"That or they need some storage space. They're not using the cabin. At least they don't seem to be, anyway." He studied her. She felt as if she knew what he would say. "You know who this is, don't you?"

Chapter Nineteen

He knew she couldn't deny his discovery, although she tried by placing her palms on her scarlet cheeks to hide her exposure.

She stepped outside the shed door. Zack moved to stand beside her but didn't speak. He knew anything he asked her right now would be blocked with an excuse or no response at all. He actually felt sorry for her. Whatever had happened to her here was more than she could handle. He wished they had never come to this place, once a dwelling of good memories, now a place of fear for Lizzy.

She picked at her shawl, avoiding his stare. Her head tilted, and she closed her eyes, letting the flakes of snow melt on her face. Drops of water slid down under her jaw and dripped from her chin. It appeared she was crying. Maybe she was, covering the tears and memories that seemed to torment her.

"I didn't mean to upset you. Let me help. I'll do anything you need if you'll just tell me what's wrong." He wished he could break through, convince her to tell him what she was scared of. But she stood quietly, as if waiting for the snow to stop, frozen as a statue.

He leaned forward, running his fingers through his hair. At this strange moment, he wished he could touch Lizzy's long locks that were sacredly tucked under her *kapp*. He understood what it meant for an Amish woman to let a man touch her in that way—both the beauty and the intimacy of it.

She turned to him, and he quickly looked away, uncomfortable with the thoughts he'd just had. He felt obvious even though there wasn't any way she could know what was on his mind.

Lizzy wiped her face. "I don't want to talk about this. It has to go away, and you're not helping by trying to figure things out." She met his sidelong gaze. "It doesn't matter."

"Whatever's bothering you isn't going away. As a matter of fact, it seems to be getting worse."

Her demeanor changed from cold to hot as she whipped her head over to him. "You don't know, Zack. Don't sit there and tell me what I should or shouldn't do." Her resolve seemed to break. She turned away and then back to him and wrapped her arms around his waist, leaning her head against his chest.

The sensation was so strong, he only lightly placed his arms around her, and kept his distance. All of his senses came alive. The smell of her hair, the touch of her soft hand, her raspy voice, and the blue of her eyes, all brought out a side of him that he thought had left a long while ago. His own memories of this place seeped into every cell of him, so different than what she was experiencing. What was it that drove him into this unexpected passion and her into fear and sadness?

When she started to move away from Zack, he brought her closer, not ready to let the feeling end so quickly. When she pushed again, he slowly let her go. "Sorry, I was enjoying the moment, selfishly, I guess."

She shook her head. "Don't apologize. I shouldn't have—" She paused again. "*Jah*, I'm glad you did. I don't feel safe here." She glanced around, causing her to lean in to him again.

"Lizzy, if there's a possibility of any kind of danger, we need to take some action. No more excuses. This isn't just about you anymore, we're in this together." He was firm yet gentle in order to get the message across. They had no way of getting down from this area any time soon, and if they had to stay here, they had to be ready.

She turned and led him to the cabin, looking from side to side and behind until they got through the front door. Zack noted there was no bolt to lock it or the window at the far end of the cabin. He wondered why they didn't have better locks, something he didn't think about as a kid.

"Are you hungry?" She went to the kitchen and studied the food.

"Starving, but it can wait. Tell me what you know." He sat at the table, which was long enough for two or three large families to sit comfortably. A good-size open kitchen took up part of the room, with a large counter and cooler that ran on gas. Tall cabinets that at one time were stocked full lined the work area.

She turned around and leaned against the water pump that served as a sink. "It's not fair of me not to tell you, but I really don't like reliving it. I let it go a long time ago, at least for the most part."

"Go on." He leaned forward, interested in what she had to say, but now feeling badly that he was bringing back a difficult situation for her. "You don't have to tell me everything, just what I need to know."

She let out a breath and twirled a ringlet of her blonde hair. "Do you remember playing hide-and-seek in the woods here?" She sat down next to him and looked out the window.

"We played all kinds of games, why that one in particular?" He forced himself to go back to that time and try to identify with whatever she was leading to. This place brought up memories for him too, but good ones—a better time before he decided to leave.

"That's the first time I saw him...the man who lived up here. He was an *Englischer* who didn't like us."

Zack held up a hand. "Wait, how did you know that about him?"

She shivered and closed her eyes for a moment. "I wanted to go outside one day and make some snowballs."

He grinned. "We used to have some great snowball fights. Up here the snow was always a few inches deeper..." His grin faded. This wasn't a happy story for her. "Sorry, I got carried away."

"You don't need to apologize. I'm glad you remember this place in a positive way. Maybe I will too someday."

"Go on."

Part of him didn't want her to tell him. They were trapped up here with nowhere to go and her homesick with fear.

"You know the stories about the man who lived in the woods." She held her hands around her waist and rocked slowly.

"Yeah..."

"I saw him one night."

A tingle went down his back, as he remembered all the stories about the mysterious man. The way Lizzy looked at Zack, he worried she might think he didn't believe her. She had probably stuffed it away for many years, and for her to come back around here must have been difficult. On their way she probably hadn't thought they would end up staying the night. She was so adamant about them not going there. Who else would stock food and water but the person she must think was the one she knew of all those years ago?

"Just tell me, Lizzy. What's this all about?"

"We were sleeping in the loft." She pointed to the wooden ladder attached to the loft where most of the boys slept, with the girls on the other side of the cabin. "I was almost asleep when I heard someone walking on the roof above us. I closed my eyes and said a prayer, but the noise only got louder."

"Must have been a cat or raccoon." He didn't mean to blurt out what he was thinking. He was just trying to make her feel better, but it wasn't timely. Judging by the look on her face, his answer wasn't appreciated.

"Then it was silent, but my heart kept racing. It felt too quiet. So I lay there and waited for something to happen. But it didn't, not until I fell asleep."

"What was it?" He spoke calmly, but he was listening to every word.

"I must have fallen asleep, because the next thing I remember was a hand over my mouth."

"What, seriously?" His forehead tightened, and he leaned in closer. "Who was it?"

She shrugged. "He started to lift me up as if he was going to take me away but stopped, letting me drop back down onto my sleeping bag. I only saw him for a second, because when I opened my eyes, he ran off." Her skin looked clammy, and her voice had started to shake. She needed to stop now. It must be too much to continue.

"Did you tell anyone?"

"*Jah*, my *daed*. He'd heard something and checked on us. I told him about what happened, but he didn't believe me." She paused. "Maybe I wouldn't have, either."

"Or maybe he didn't want you to be scared." They both sat quietly for a moment. "What did he think the noises came from?"

"He never did say. I suppose he thought it was one of us kids horsing around. But I wouldn't make up something like this."

"Your dad is a sensible man. He'd need proof about something like this."

She hesitated. "Or maybe he just didn't want it to be true."

Zack frowned and tilted his head. "Well, that's not sensible. And your dad is a sensible person."

"To a fault." She wrapped her arms tighter around her waist again. "We should eat something." She stood and started over to the kitchen.

He frowned. "You're done talking about this?"

"*Jah*, it took a long time for me to stop looking over my shoulder. I don't want to start doing it again." She leaned over the counter and then looked out the nearest window. It was too dark to see much, but there was something that drew them into the only place they could see outside.

"I hate to say it, but I'm going to have to go to the shed and get us some food."

Lizzy's bright-blue eyes opened wide. "We have some for tonight. Can't we wait until morning?"

"That's not a meal, Lizzy." He stood and walked over to her, resting his hands on her shoulders. "You can't let something that happened years ago control you. If you want to come with me, we can stock up and bring everything back here that we need."

"You make it sound like we're going to be here for a while. I can't do that, Zack." She shook her head. "I understand why we had to come. The weather is what brought us here, but it won't make me stay."

"I don't think we have much say in the matter. The snow hasn't stopped since we got on the road." The more he thought about the incident, the more he wondered if the stranger was the man next door. Horrible to consider, he knew, but maybe he'd been here all along. If so, was he dangerous? And what was he doing with Lizzy? One physical connection like that was enough for some people. Maybe it was because Zack had been through much worse in the city that he hadn't taken it as seriously as he should have. Or maybe there was more than she was telling him.

"I'll go with you." She was in motion before he could ask her to join him. This reminded him of how sheltered most of the Amish were, especially someone like Lizzy. She'd been sheltered by Luke, her older brother, and although she looked at her dad as overbearing, Zack saw him as protective. But maybe things had changed since he'd left.

When she opened the door, a blast of frigid air hit them. "This feels like the coldest winter I've ever known. I'd love to find some mittens and a warmer coat."

"I'd take food over clothing. It's gotta let up some time. Wish we had a radio…anything that would tell us when the snow might stop."

"Let's just get this over with." She followed him to the shed, trudging through the deep snow.

Zack studied the gray sky and the endless flakes that

brushed his eyelids and melted on his bare skin. "Did you notice any warm clothing in there?"

"I wasn't paying much attention. Just wanted to get out of there and back to the cabin."

Zack smirked and grunted. He was hungry and tired.

"I understand if you aren't worried about that man, but I am, and I wish you'd give me the benefit of the doubt that what I said happened."

Zack was exhausted. There might be some man using the shed, but there was nothing they could do for the moment. "One thing at a time, Lizzy. That's all I've got right now."

They walked to the end of the shed and put as much food as they could into a crate Zack found. The quicker they got this done, the quicker they could go back into the cabin. Not that it was a safe place either.

Chapter Twenty

HE MUST THINK *I've lost my mind. But I know what I saw.*

"Lizzy." Zack's voice brought her back.

"Sorry, I'll get what we need for some meals." She waded through the endless amounts of food and then started in with the garments. Unless there was running water around, they'd need a change of clothes. She'd never seen so much of...well, everything. Such a stock would last an Amish family for months on end. She wondered what this person was doing with all of it.

"The weather hasn't changed."

Lizzy's couldn't hide her disappointment. "It's got to change sometime soon. I've never known it to snow this long without stopping."

He shook his head. "You have. It's just different when you're out with the farm to tend to. You work in it every day, rain or shine."

"I suppose, but it is different when we have a family who helps and a warm *haus* filled with everything we need." She noticed he was watching her, and she frowned.

"It probably is different for you to be away. You always liked sticking around. You wouldn't even let me take you to singing, saying you had chores to do."

Her frown dissipated.

"You've never liked me much, have you?" He grinned,

making light of it, but she had thought a lot about him—and them.

"Why are you smiling?" he asked, keeping the grin, obviously curious as to what her answer might be. She was too surprised to think of an answer right off, so she turned away to think of something good to say.

"I didn't think you liked me." It was a short response, but she didn't want to appear picked on, even though she felt that way. He seemed to have glossed over her, but now that she was thinking about it, he treated most girls the same way.

He grunted a small laugh. "Quite the opposite."

Scraaatch. The noise came from near the door.

Zack grabbed her hand and held up a finger for her to hush. Neither of them moved as the noise repeated. He looked her in the eyes and slowly stood and looked around the area. He shook his head.

"Coast is clear. The door's just not shut."

"I've got us spooked. Sorry." She let out a sigh. "I feel silly about my childhood fears. It was probably nothing then, and it isn't anything now."

Zack leaned against a shelf and studied her. "You worry too much. I'm glad you told me. If there's anything out of the ordinary, I'll be prepared."

She wondered whether he was just being nice, or he really believed there could be something to it. Lizzy wondered herself. But she could still feel the rough hands against her mouth and smell the stale breath. That couldn't have been just a dream.

Zack raised his arms. "And there is no doubt that there is someone here. I just can't figure out what they're doing."

He dropped his hands to his sides and squinted. "You think maybe they're one and the same?"

Lizzy had thought the same thing, but she didn't want to continue on with her stories. No, they weren't stories; it had really happened to her. She'd just blocked it out for so long, she couldn't separate the past from the present.

"*Jah*, they could be. But all these years later?" She shivered and reached for the food she'd picked out, pondering who this man was and if he could possibly be who was here now.

"I'm so hungry, I could eat a cow." Zack reached around her and opened the door, then shut it behind them.

She looked through the items in the box. "You're going to have to settle for my vegetable stew. Do we have enough wood to cook this over a fire?" She hoped they did, or they would be eating cold mush.

"I got some earlier that should be somewhat dry, but I'll look for more." He made his way to the cabin door and grabbed the doorknob. "I'd feel better if you were with me."

She jumped at the offer. Not that she wanted to go out in the cold again, but she didn't want to be alone, either.

"*Jah*, if you hang this pot above the fireplace, it will speed things up."

"We shouldn't take too long outside, then. We don't want to burn the place down."

He arranged the little bit of wood they had and lit them. The room instantly felt cozier and made her want to stay and curl up around the warm tongues of flame.

"Let's make this quick." He stood and walked her to the door. He went out first, and she was close behind. "The dead limb ends on the trees are best. I also found some lumber we can use if necessary."

"Why not use it now?" She'd like for them to have a decent meal, and she was counting on leaving as soon as it was safe to drive, so why wait to use the better wood?

He looked up at the sky and shook his head. "The sky's still gray, and the snow hasn't let up since this morning. I don't want to take any chances on running out of wood."

"You may be right, but I hate to use damp, flimsy pieces of wood." It was the cook in her as well, not wanting her meal to be spoiled for something as simple as not having a sufficient fire.

As they walked along gathering the driest pieces of wood, Lizzy started thinking of Clara. She wondered about her chemo treatments and when they would be over so she could go home. It was only ten days until Christmas, and she wanted Clara to join in with everyone on Christmas Day.

"Zack."

He jerked back, hearing her voice in the silent winter wonderland they were walking through. "Something wrong?"

"*Nee*...well, *jah* and no. What do you think Clara is doing right now?"

He stopped in his tracks and looked at her. "I've been wondering the same thing. I just don't like to talk about it."

"Well, I think we should. I want to be with her at Christmas and for her to get better so we can have a very merry Christmas."

He smiled. "That's the best thing I've heard all day." He looked up as a hawk flew by.

"Let's say a silent prayer for her." Lizzy smiled and

bowed her head and then looked up to see him watching her. "Why aren't you joining me?"

"I've gotta change some things before I can go before God."

He started to turn away, but she grabbed him by the arm. "You don't think *Gott* will listen if you're flawed?" What could he have possibly done to think *Gott* wouldn't forgive him?

"With the way I feel about myself now, no."

"So that's it. You're giving up on the most important relationship you can ever hope to have?"

"Yeah, until I figure some things out." With that he turned away and started picking up tree limbs as if nothing had been said. This was too important to ignore, but Lizzy could see this wasn't the time to push it.

She'd seen what it did to people who weren't ready to turn their lives over, and in a way she admired them for being honest enough not to commit until they were truly ready.

But he was so compliant when he was a teenager, not abusing the boundaries of Rumspringa *and never causing any trouble...*

At least from what she knew. They were a large community, and church groups were divided on Sunday church, so maybe she'd missed something. There would be a right time to talk with him. But not today.

"Any luck?" She picked up some of the twigs that he'd missed and tucked them into the basket she'd brought from the cabin. It wasn't much, but she hoped it would be enough to make her soup.

"What's wrong?" He stood straight, watching her as she picked through the limbs.

"I can't promise this will be a good meal. But it's better than nothing."

"I'm too hungry to complain."

"I'll have to work with what I have to make dinner." As they returned to the cabin, she was thinking about her recipe. Without any spices such as basil or pepper, and with no meat, the soup would be bland. Then she remembered the beef jerky. "How about some beef?"

Zack was tending to the fire, which was minimal at best. "I was just wondering if there were any rifles in that shed."

"I meant the jerky in the cupboard. It's too dark to go hunting." She stirred the pot of soup over the meager flames. "It's taking a while to heat up."

"That dried food is sounding pretty good about now." He looked down at her. "Not that yours won't be good."

She chuckled. "You don't have to try and make me feel better about our dinner." She took a spoon and dipped it in the soup and handed it to him with a half-grin. He took it and sipped.

"If we're still stuck up here tomorrow, I'll be doing some hunting for dinner."

Lizzy held in the anxiousness in her chest. There would be no need for hunting. They would be going home. Even if she had to walk.

Chapter Twenty-One

ZACK TOOK ANOTHER bite and then another. Lizzy was a good cook, considering what she had to work with. This wasn't exactly his favorite meal, but he was so hungry he couldn't complain. He'd gotten used to the fancy meals and how his associates splurged on clients when they were making a deal, convincing them they were getting a great contract on the property and then turning around to resell at twice the price.

"This is good."

"I never thought of you as a liar." She took a taste and puckered. "This is awful." She stirred her spoon around in the bowl. "You're a good sport."

He grinned. "That's what we say in the city."

"*Jah*, I heard you say it to that in the nurse in the hospital." She dipped her spoon back into the hot soup.

"Sounds like you're jealous."

As soon as he said it, her face turned to stone. "What? I'm not jealous." She stirred her bowl of soup with vigor. "It's none of my business what you do, Zack."

Her tone was brisk, and she hadn't taken another bite. He was tickled at what he was seeing. All this time he'd thought he was the one who was silently interested, but now he could see that she had feelings for him. What else could she be upset about? But then he looked around and decided there was quite a bit to worry about, stuck here in this cabin with little heat and no fresh food. It made him a little depressed when he thought about it.

"I knew you didn't really like our little feast. But how could you?" Her smile returned as she watched him squirm a little.

"I forgot how well you ladies cook. After being away from Amish food, this actually tastes better than a lot of what I ate in the city."

"You just gave me an idea. I've been thinking about what I want to do for Clara this Christmas." She leaned in closer to him, smiling. "I was hoping to start on the seventh day before Christmas, making each day special by doing something with her and making her special dishes"

"She loves Christmas." He choked up a little but didn't think Lizzy noticed. It would be hard to see Clara unable to participate in the festivities. He could remember her and Lizzy as two young girls making up some cookie dough and him and the guys taking chunks of it from the bowl before they got caught. "Those were good times."

"*Jah*, Christmas is one of the best times of year." She frowned. "Have you been praying for her, Zack? I know how you feel about praying for your own circumstances, but you wouldn't let that stop you from praying for your own sister now, would you?"

Lizzy always did say what was on her mind, so he shouldn't be surprised, but he didn't want to go there, even though he knew he should. "I will in my own time." And he wanted that to be the end of it, at least for now. He had thought more about praying since being home again, away from the city where he'd become self-absorbed and greedy.

She let out a long breath. He knew she was frustrated with him, but he wasn't the kind of person to say things just to please. When someone got an answer from him, it was honest.

Lizzy turned away, as if knowing he wouldn't budge. He hoped she'd understand.

She stood and took his bowl. Her boots tip-tapped against the floor as she went to the water pump and washed the bowls in the sink. The clatter was enough to let him know she wasn't happy about his decision. She pushed so hard on the pump handle, he thought it might break.

"Seems like I disappointed you." He walked toward her and started drying a bowl she'd placed on the counter.

"I'll get past it. It's just hard to be around someone as stubborn as I am." She started to slow down a little after getting her thoughts out in the open. This time he didn't have to guess what she was thinking.

After their dishes were clean, she untied her apron and wiped her hands on it. She set it by the fireplace to dry and stared into the bits of orange fire. She sat down on the hearth and took out the blue dress she'd stashed in her purse to work on at the hospital. She ran her hands over the material before folding it and setting it aside. Then she slipped her arms around her legs and yawned.

He came over, feeling awkward about the question he had to ask. "Where would you feel comfortable sleeping tonight?"

He expected her usual pink cheeks to answer for her, but this time she kept her eyes on the flickering, warm fire. "I'm so tired and cold, I don't much care, if you want to know the truth."

He wondered whether she meant it. He knew he'd be sleeping with one eye open due to her story and the mystery in the shed. Between the two of them, he wouldn't get a more than a couple winks. "I don't think either of us will sleep well tonight."

"*Jah.*" She looked around her and stopped at the back window, which was pitch black outside.

"The window is strange, isn't it?" He sat on the hearth next to her.

"There must be a reason the windows are so small. Maybe to keep in the heat?"

"Something we can ask when we get back."

"When do you think that will be, Zack? And tell me the truth."

He glanced out the window again and shrugged. "If the snow stops tonight, we might be able to get out of here by midday tomorrow when some of the snow might melt."

"I feel like a little girl."

"What do you mean?"

"I want to go home." She half-laughed and half-cried.

"Am I that bad?" He grinned to lift her spirits. He didn't know whether he should bring up the man who was somewhere out there.

If we talk about it, maybe she won't worry so much.

"The way I look at it, if this guy wanted to do harm, he would have. Back then and now. From what he has in that shed, he's either found a place to store his goods and probably lives around here..."

"Or?"

"He might not want us here." He didn't want the conversation to go this way, but he wanted her ready for anything.

"*Jah*, I still don't understand what to think about it right now. When I was younger, it seemed more real. Now that I'm older, it's foggy."

His mind went back to the topic of sleeping arrangements as Lizzy told him of her ideas for Clara's Christmas. Making Christmas cards was first on the list, along with reading the story of the three wise men.

"No matter what Christmas brings us, Clara will be there." Her lip trembled.

He put his arm around her, wondering how her positive outlook could change to sadness so quickly. "We'll appreciate every moment with her when we get back. I promise."

"*Jah*, I'll make sure of that." She sat up and let out a breath. "If I was with her right now, I wouldn't feel like this."

"Understandable. I felt that way when I got your letter."

She shook her head. "I should have written more, but I thought your *daed* would be upset with me if I did."

"Why?" That irritated him, and he remembered the controlling ways of his dad and why he'd left.

"The bishop wanted me to ask you to come home."

"He did?" His mind went into overdrive. From the way his father had acted, Zack would never could have guessed he'd wanted him to come back home.

"To repent."

Zack's first thoughts were far from what he expected. He knew his *daed* had washed his hands of him, but after all that had happened, the bishop should be repenting. He scoffed. For a split second he'd actually gotten his hopes up that his dad might really want him home again. He should have known better.

"I'm sorry, Zack. I know you were hoping for something different. But I thought you should know." She placed a hand on his knee and stared into his eyes. It was almost enough to take his mind off what she'd just said.

"I'm all right. I shouldn't expect anything different. I can't count on things changing. His own son did something against what he stands for. I'd probably be the same way."

Lizzy pulled away, shaking her head. "No, you wouldn't, Zack. You're not your *daed*."

That actually brought tears to his eyes. He looked down to gather his composure. "I doubt I'll find out. I wouldn't want to raise a kid where I live."

"You won't have children?" She said it as if he'd committed a crime.

There was no use trying to explain to her that there were a lot of people who didn't have children.

"I figured you'd have a family." She waited intently, her eyes glued to his as he raised his head.

"For a while. Didn't work out." He was heading for deep water, a place he didn't want to go, ever, not with anyone. He prepared himself for the answer Lizzy would be looking for, unsure how much to tell, if anything at all.

"That's too bad." She said it with little empathy, which he found interesting. "What happened?"

"Something that split us up. It was for the best." He paused. "I think, anyway."

"Do you feel comfortable telling me?" She moved closer to the fire, which was almost out, and waited patiently.

"Just a bad situation with someone I met." He didn't know whether he wanted to tell her about it. It would be exactly what his dad would call him out on—why it was so wrong to live outside the community. And in his case his dad would have been right.

"She did the unthinkable, something I couldn't live with. I tried, but I just couldn't feel the same about her." This was about all he could share at this point. Now he wanted it dropped.

"Well, all can be forgiven. Even this, whatever it is."

"Even if God forgives me, I'm not sure I can ever forgive myself."

Chapter Twenty-Two

LIZZY SAT UP and looked around the room. She pushed away the blanket that Zack must have laid on her. The last thing she remembered was sitting on a couch watching Zack stir the fire; then she awoke because her teeth were chattering from the cold.

She sat up quickly and noticed her *kapp* beside her. Looking around the room, she saw no sign of Zack. When she reached for her *kapp*, the pins fell out.

Thoughtful of him to do that for me; I don't remember taking it off.

The idea should have bothered her, but it didn't. If it had been someone other than Zack, maybe, but he didn't strike her as one to take advantage. Suddenly she remembered their conversation from the night before. His holding back so much about his time away made her wonder what he'd done. And she'd never thought she'd hear him say he wouldn't have a family. She remembered how he would pick up the little ones when they fell playing baseball.

There has to be more to it.

She looked around the room. The back window became a focal point in the daylight. It drew her in and actually gave her a nice large view of the area on that side of the cabin. Then Zack came into view. He'd found an ax and was using it to chop wood.

He must have been up before dawn.

His strong arms twisted over his head as his hands clasped the handle of the ax. He stopped, wiped his brow, and took off his jacket. Despite the snow, sweat poured down his chest. Lizzy watched him wipe his forehead and then turned her way. She cast her eyes downward, hoping he hadn't seen her.

She was doing nothing wrong, but it would be embarrassing if he'd seen her gawking at him while he was trying to work. Lizzy had to admit she was downright staring at him and enjoying every second. She busied herself to take her mind off him and found a few things on the counter—a large spoon, spatula, and griddle.

"Morning." He stomped his boots on the scratched, worn wooden floor. "How did you sleep?"

His grin made her pause. "Fine...why?" She pulled the *kapp* over her head and grabbed one of the pins.

"You fell asleep while I was talking." He didn't move forward, so she assumed he must be going back outside. He didn't seem uncomfortable that they'd slept in the same room together, and now that Lizzy thought about it, she wasn't either.

"*Ach*, sorry. I was really tired."

Then their conversation came back to her. As she looked over to him, she saw him in a different light, not as the worldly man she'd first thought when he came back to the community. Perhaps Clara's situation had changed him.

"Did I say something?" Her mind searched their discussions, trying to find out whether she'd said something she shouldn't have or given away her thoughts of him. Oh, what if she'd said it in her sleep! Luke had told her she mumbled while she slept and said a word or two when they were on a family trip visiting relatives. Lizzy wished she hadn't asked.

"Nothing I could understand." He wiped his feet on the hand-spun rug.

"Do you think we'll be able to leave today?"

Lizzy realized she hadn't finished putting on her kapp. She fumbled with the last pin, although he had already seen her with her hair down. All she could do was try to wrap it up and fix it later.

"It's slowing down, but I think it snowed all night, so there would be a lot to maneuver through."

Lizzy sat down, disappointed with the news. She thought sure it would lighten throughout the night. "Well, I'm hungry, so I know you must be starving."

"You've got that right. I'm one step ahead of you. How's this for breakfast?" He pulled out a box of pancake mix. "What do you think?"

Lizzy turned up her nose, but her stomach told her to appreciate what she was given. She was letting her pride get in the way of filling their bellies.

With breakfast decided, Lizzy pumped out some water and went to freshen up in one of the rooms down a hallway. She'd forgotten these small details that made this place seem a little more inviting. As a kid, she probably didn't even mind the outhouse. It would be awful cold here.

Her stomach growled at the thought of having pancakes, but she paused when she thought about how different they would taste made with water and not fresh milk.

When she came back into the kitchen, Zack was nowhere in sight, and his boots were gone. So she went ahead making breakfast. The jam they found would have to serve in place of syrup—she stopped in midstride. They never did have a chance to finish making the molasses for Clara. Things had happened so quickly with the storm. Making the syrup would be one more thing to add to her list of things to do for Clara for Christmas.

When breakfast was ready, Lizzy went to the window to look for Zack. The beautiful white covered the ground for as far as she could see. A bluebird flew past the window and on into the forest of tall, dense trees. She was enjoying the view when Zack came in the cabin door. He shed his boots and walked over to the window.

"It's a beautiful sight to see, isn't it?" He leaned in next to her and watched the wildlife come out of hiding now that he was inside the cabin.

"*Jah*, most of our scenery is crop, not this." They stood in silence enjoying the menagerie until their stomachs brought them back to the kitchen area.

He grinned. "Let's eat."

"Don't expect much." She lifted one eyebrow. "I'm a much better cook than this."

"You might be surprised to know that I am a pretty good cook myself." He nodded.

"Really? What's your specialty?" she teased, but with a sudden realization that he might really be able to cook.

"Cheesecake, Thai noodles."

Lizzy scowled. "Are you serious?"

He shook his head. "No, but it was fun to see your reaction." His expression changed, and he dropped the playful chitchat, thinking of her fears about the stranger. He imagined she tossed most of the night.

"You must be tired." He studied her with sympathetic eyes.

"*Jah*, but not as much as I thought I'd be."

He shrugged. "Well, that's good. What made you feel better?"

She was too embarrassed to tell Zack that it was his presence that made her feel safer. "It was just nice to have company." With that she set down a plate of pancakes. She watched him take a bite and then another.

"Well, how is it?" She took a taste and put her fingers over her mouth.

"That bad?" He chuckled.

"There's no taste to it." She was almost embarrassed, but she'd done the best she—or anyone else—could have under the circumstances.

"I've had much worse. We're lucky to have this." He took another bite as if to prove to her it was fine.

"I should quit being so prideful. We're blessed to have this place and food to eat." Just as she was looking up, a crackling sound came from the other end of the cabin. They both scanned the area where it came from. "What is it?"

Zack was still, waiting for the noise again. He stood and looked up.

Crrrack!

He jogged to the door with Lizzy close behind. He looked up, and she followed to see where he was looking. A chunk of a tree limb had hit the roof. "I hope there's no hole in that roof."

"And it's still snowing." She lifted her hands up and dropped them to her sides. The problems didn't seem to end. The lump in her throat seemed to grow, and she swallowed hard.

"Yeah, you're right. It might not be safe to be in this side of the cabin. We'll have to make do for now, and I'm going to see what we can do about getting out of here." He paused and looked straight at her.

"You don't look too convincing. Should I be worried?" She'd seen the men putting up barns and other buildings and knew he'd grown up learning the trade, but he didn't seem too confident about repairing the roof.

"Can't tell from here. I'll get a ladder from the shed and take a look." He placed a hand on her shoulder. "We'll figure something out."

When he removed his warm palm, the chill at once made her shoulder cold again. It was hard enough to sleep in the cabin in these conditions, let alone with a hole in the roof.

Zack returned with a ladder, climbed up, and scanned the area from above. "It's gorgeous from up here. I can see why they picked this parcel of land."

When Lizzy looked at him, she saw him for what he really was—a strong and courageous man who was misunderstood by his own people. And in watching him now, she wondered what she was going to do with these new feelings she had for him. This was no small flame like she'd had for him as a youngster. Lizzy was falling for the last man she thought would ever satisfy her.

Chapter Twenty-Three

COCK-A-DOODLE-DOO!

Zack jumped back and then leaned forward to stop from slipping off the roof. "What the heck?" He heard the door open and then Lizzy laughing. "How did he get up here?"

"He flew right to you from one of the tree limbs. I thought for sure you were going to fall off the roof." She held a hand over her eyes to block the bright sun shimmering against the snow.

"He'd make for a nice dinner." Zack lifted his brow. The thought of some fried chicken made his mouth water and his stomach tighten.

"If you can catch him, I'll make a pleasant chicken dinner." She grinned. Catching a chicken was one thing, but a rooster was a whole different experience; most males would fight for a hen or for their territory.

With each step Zack stuck his boot down into the snow to keep his leverage. But the bird still had the advantage. Funny thing was, the rooster seemed to like the standoff. He could have just flown off, but he chose to stay and mess with Zack.

"What's going on up there?" Lizzy called to him and took another step back so she could see. "Is he that hard to catch?"

"He has it in him, that's for sure." Zack didn't want to

tell her that the bird was taking him to task. If it was a horse or a stubborn bull, that would be one thing, but this black rooster was holding his ground. "He's quick."

"I take it you're losing the battle." She took another step away from the cabin and laughed out loud as he fell to one knee, jumped up, and went after the conniving bird again.

"Are you all right?"

"Just tired. He's wearing me out." He wasn't about to admit defeat.

The rooster took a sudden leap and landed, running as fast as he could, head bobbing and all. Zack threw up his hands and came down the ladder. Lizzy came up beside him and watched the rooster go. "What's he in a hurry about?"

"You got me. But I think I won." He turned and grinned at her, enjoying the sparkle of her eyes against the snow.

"That was entertaining." She was still watching the rooster with a smile.

"It would have been better if we were plucking him right about now." He realized what a bad sport he was and chuckled a bit.

"Why are you laughing?" She started to the cabin but stopped when he did.

"I'm pitiful, figuring I had the upper hand on that rooster." He shook his head, realizing how much fun it really was, especially having her there with him.

"All this messing around makes me feel guilty." Her smile disappeared, and she looked toward the road where they'd driven in the day before.

"Having fun makes you feel bad?" He lifted his brow in question.

"I bet my family is wondering about me. I've been

thinking about them, knowing they're fretting over the weather and unable to find me."

"There's not a lot we can do until the roads are clear." That might not have been the best thing to say, but that was the reality of it.

"Yeah, we should try and dig the car out of that snowdrift." He knew it wouldn't help but said it for her sake. He'd wondered how long it would take before she started worrying, and he was surprised she hadn't mentioned it earlier. But then they had kept themselves busy, and it didn't help anything to mope.

Lizzy's head snapped over to where they'd had to leave the car because the snow was too deep. "It doesn't look much better, but I guess it's worth a try."

As Zack scanned the area, he thought how nice a place it would be to live. It was peaceful, a feeling he hadn't had in some time now. He'd be close enough to the community that he might be able to make a visit now and then. But it would be lonely up here all alone. The summer might be doable, but the winter months would be nasty to live in for too long at a time.

When they got to the car, Zack knew it would be difficult to dig it out. And even if they did, the drive down would be more dangerous than driving up. Slipping on that ice would land them in a ditch sure enough.

"Sorry, Lizzy, but I don't think it's a good idea. Until the sun melts things, especially the roads, we wouldn't have control driving." He could see the disappointment in her face, but there wasn't much he could do about it.

"I can only imagine how worried my parents are about me." Her voice was shaky, and she didn't meet his eyes.

"I'm sorry, Lizzy. I wish I could get you home to them."

She put back her shoulders and lifted her head. "But there's nothing we can do, so let's get out of the cold."

As they walked through the snow, which was turning to ice, she almost fell a couple of times, and he wished he could carry her. She was sad, cold, and stuck with him for who knew how long. So...was she being nice because he was all she had or because she was scared? She hadn't said anything again about the alleged man who taunted her and seemed to have slept well enough. He knew because he woke up every couple of hours to see if she was okay.

He still wasn't sure what to think of the story. With kids sitting around a campfire telling scary tales, it was easy to make stuff up and embellish an innocuous event. But Lizzy was insistent that this man really existed and had even touched her. She wasn't easily riled up and wasn't one to gossip, so he didn't know what to make of it.

"Lizzy. Do you remember anything else about this person who came to you that night?"

She turned her head away from him and then looked him in the eyes. "You don't believe me, do you?" She started walking back to the cabin.

"I believe you believe it. But that's not saying much, since I wasn't in the same situation. We might want to put something in front of this door so we can both get some sleep." He paused. "We might stay warmer if we conserved body heat."

Her face turned a light shade of pink. "I guess we'll do what we have to." She put her hands on her face and walked down the rows of benches and long table that led to the kitchen area.

He was starting to take it as a compliment that she got embarrassed when he mentioned the sleeping arrangements. He liked that about her, a tenderness unlike many of the women in Philly, especially in certain areas of town. The longer he was home, the less he wanted to go back. But he had made a good living in the city, and he didn't relish the idea of starting over at the bottom.

Zack scratched his head. "I don't know what to do first. I guess I'll make this room smaller, move away from the side of the cabin that has a tree in it."

Lizzy grunted a laugh. "I shouldn't laugh, but it keeps me from crying. It's already cold in here. We'll freeze tonight."

Zack could think of ways to keep her from the cold, but always being the gentleman, he decided to put himself to work. "I'll use the larger pieces to create a barrier to that side of the cabin. That should help keep the warmth on the side of the fireplace." He looked at the ceiling, judging where to separate the two areas.

"I'm going to the shed to see what tools are in there." He was about to turn around, but stopped when there was no response from Lizzy. He was stumped for a second. She looked around and then back to him. "Do you want to go with me?"

"*Jah*, let me get my shawl." She wasted no time and walked straight to the door.

When they got to the shed, Lizzy looked around, ever alert.

"I doubt we'll run into anyone up here, including your family or the mysterious man. So try and relax." Although he didn't want her too far away, both for his own pleasure and for her peace of mind. "If he meant any harm, he would have done something. But he hasn't."

"It's not just that. I keep hoping a forest ranger or someone will show up."

"You have a point. There might be so much going on down on the highways, they haven't had time to make it up here yet." Zack realized he was hoping for the opposite. Even through the hardships since they'd been here, a part of him wanted this private time with her.

Lizzy watched as he opened the shed and then hesitantly followed him in. "What do you think he's saving this for?"

Zack picked up a box of nails and a hammer and then looked over at her. "How do you know it's him?"

"I just have a feeling about it. Don't you ever feel that way about someone or something?"

If you only knew my feelings since I got here... "Yes, as a matter of fact, I do."

"That's all you're going to tell me?" She leaned against a shelf full of boxes that held a variety of paraphernalia, from dried goods to cereal and canned food. He tried to focus on the task at hand but felt her stare. "I'd rather not get into it right at the moment."

He found an old leather bag filled with papers. It stood out in contrast to the basic food and carpentry tools. He brushed it off and opened it.

"What is that?" Lizzy squatted down beside him and pulled out a handful of papers filled with handwriting. She knelt down and picked out one to read.

"A bunch of paper, looks like." He took one and started reading. It was a diary of some sort.

"They were taking turns sending letters to each other." Lizzy actually sighed. "This is so romantic." Then she blushed.

Zack was getting fond of her inability to hide her emotions because her face colored different shades. He couldn't help but think it was because she might be feeling the same way he was.

"These don't have dates on them." She looked up at him. "Can you guess how old they are?"

"Old." He held one up in the faint light coming from the glass doors of the shed and read the first sentence: "'When I was around you, I felt I was in a safe place. One where I would never get hurt. But you did. I never knew the depth of heartache until you left me…'" His voice trailed off.

"What's wrong?"

"I feel like I'm eavesdropping…or something." He read one more entry and put the paper back in the bag.

"Yeah, but this might tell us who the mystery man is."

Chapter Twenty-Four

Zack shook his head as he looked through one of the letters. "I doubt that. These letters are too old."

Lizzy glanced over at the papers he read. "*Jah*, but mine aren't. Listen to this: 'This is the final letter I will ever send you. I hope this letter will touch your heart before it's too late.' He must have changed his mind. There's more in here." Lizzy put a hand on the paper. "I can't stop now. I want to know what happened to these people." She tilted her head. "Don't you?"

How could he say no? It was nice to go into someone else's life for a change. And it was a good diversion from fixing the cabin, looking for food, and chasing chickens. "What else do you know about them?" He didn't want to hear about love and romance. It was too close and yet far away from him. He didn't want to dwell on his feelings, even though he couldn't seem to stop.

"Look! He was in the Vietnam War." She pointed to the sentence she'd just read. That caught his attention more than he wanted it to; they both had chores to take care of.

"Really? What does it say about him?" They were silent for a moment, reading this young man's journey. "His mission was to drive out the North Vietnamese."

"Nineteen years old, so young for such a big task." She moved closer, and he took in the smell of her, the soap he'd seen her washing with that morning, her hair in a ponytail hanging over her shoulder as she cupped the water over her face. He'd left the room before she could see him and he wondered what her reaction would have been if he hadn't left.

Zack looked from her to the cabin roof where they were supposed to be mending a hole. "It would be interesting to find out more, but—"

"*Jah*, we need to fix the roof. I'll help if you..." It was as if she had finished the sentence he was thinking. These letters created a curiosity in Zack, which surprised him, and it seemed she did too.

He suddenly thought of Clara and wondered what she was doing right now. The doctors were optimistic, so he would be as well. He had found a gas-operated saw in the shed that had some fuel in it, but not as much as he'd like. This place had become a gold mine when it came to their basic needs. He headed back to the cabin with what he hoped was enough material for a covering that would at least keep away any snow or sleet that might decide to come their way.

He met Lizzy inside the cabin, staring at the counter. She turned to him and pointed to something he couldn't make out. "We have milk."

"What?" He took quick steps to see for himself. Sure enough there was a sealed glass bottle filled with cold milk. "Where did this come from?"

She shrugged. "Is it from *him*?"

"We don't even know who he is." He was thinking about the letters and wondering whether any of this was related.

"Maybe we can find out more with those letters." Lizzy lifted a brow.

"We're getting distracted. First things first. Let me see if

I can get rid of that branch." He was already in thought on how he would make that work. If it was just the one weak branch, they should be okay.

"And I'll make lunch. More pancakes but this time with real milk." She turned toward the counter and then back to him. "And syrup? Did you find this in the shed?"

Zack frowned and shook his head. "This keeps getting more interesting. Where did you find the syrup?"

"Just now on the counter." She wiped her brow. "I don't know if I should be scared or thankful."

"While you work on lunch, I'm getting rid of this tree limb." Zack went out the door and climbed up the ladder. He set the saw on the roof and then stepped on the last rung. He picked up the saw, and it vibrated in his hand as he sank the blade into the limb. After three cuts the tree limb was clean off the roof, with no other branches around that might be a menace.

As soon as the motor was off, Lizzy called him to come down and eat. Zack didn't need to be told twice. He went quickly to the kitchen. Their situation was becoming something he'd hoped for but didn't think would really happen. They were forced into being alone together, with nowhere to go. "All done. With no other problems in the area, either. We'll have plenty of wood for the fire now."

"You've earned a hearty lunch, then." She set down a plate with three large pancakes and syrup.

He took a bite that made his mouth water. "So the syrup just appeared on the kitchen counter?"

Lizzy held up her hands. "That's all I know." She sat down next to him with a plate. "He must be watching us, which should make me uncomfortable, but you can't be upset when someone brings you syrup."

"And now you have both of us wondering whether this man is the one in the letters."

"I was hoping you'd say that." She took one more bite and then went to the fire and sat with the bag of letters beside her. "Let's see what else he did."

She read: "'Seeing you at the hometown send-off meant a lot to me. I looked for you as I marched up Main Street. When I lost sight of you, I was distracted to see how many of the guys that I knew were going. The cheers from the townsfolk made it seem real, that I was shipping out.'"

"All right, you have my attention." Zack was just as interested in hearing her voice, soft yet clear. He sat down next to her, taking in the warmth from the fire.

She continued reading: "'I am ready to go, but there was a minute when I thought, *What am I doing?* My bunk buddies, Joe, who I've told you about, and another guy, Chris, know it all would be for nothing if we don't follow through. I've seen pictures of Vietnam only on TV when I joined. I am not worried though. God's got a plan.'"

Snap!

The tarp Zack had put over the gaping hole in the roof fluttered in a gust of wind. "I need to tie that down better. The wind is getting stronger."

"Well, be careful. I don't trust anything around here to be in good shape. Everything is old and worn out."

"Count our blessings. At least we have this much to get by. Think about where we'd be by now if we didn't have what's in that shed." He lifted his brow to emphasize what he said. It was only by God's grace they had been given what they had.

"*Jah*, you're right about that. But you can't blame me for

being cautious. I need you too much around here for you to get hurt."

Zack took her concern to heart. He might be misreading her intentions, but it didn't hurt to hope a little.

Lizzy didn't mean to lead Zack into thinking she wanted more from him than friendship. She was sure he had some fancy girl in the city who was waiting for him. He surely thought she was plain and boring, that they all were. That was probably why he left the community. At least that was why most Amish left, but most came home as well. Zack was one of the few who stayed in the city. If it weren't for Clara, he wouldn't be here at all, so Lizzy dismissed any feelings she had for him except that she needed him in this crazy predicament.

Then a thought popped into her head. He hadn't complained about being here with her. She wouldn't have been surprised to see him hiking around the area looking to escape from her and this place. There must be a reason he didn't complain and stay away from her like she'd thought he would. He would go back to the city once things with Clara were better, and they would get better, Lizzy was sure of that. She'd prayed unceasingly, knowing *Gott* heard her. All she wanted for Christmas was Clara well again.

Zeeeep.

The sound of ropes being tied caught her attention. Zack was tightening the zip cords, pulling the tarp in. It would keep the flapping noise at a minimum and trap the warmth from the fire in the room. But it was such a big room, Lizzy was dreading another cold night. She hoped and prayed they would be able to leave the next day.

"You all right in there?" Zack called through a small opening overhead before pulling the last cord.

"*Jah*, I'm *gut*. How's it going up there?"

"Tight as a trampoline. I should have used this the first time around." Soon she heard him climbing down the ladder, and the front door opened.

"That should take care of it. At least for a while." He paused at the door, getting out of his boots and studying her. "Are you all right?"

She didn't like that he could read her so well. She had him on her mind, and she wasn't going to tell him anything that she was thinking of. Except about Clara. "It's getting close to Christmas. I have to be with Clara, Zack."

"I agree, but we don't have much leverage to make that happen at the moment. Unless you know something I don't." He pulled off gloves that she assumed were from the magic shed.

"Actually, we do—pray. As far as I'm concerned, this is the most important Christmas we might ever have. And you should be part of making it happen." She felt her eyes moisten, and she wasn't ready for the emotions to flare up so quickly.

Zack pulled Lizzy close and held her tightly. "Clara is lucky to have you for a friend, Lizzy."

His words brought tears to her eyes, and she let herself sink into his strong arms. She knew he was sharing her sentiments, making the emotions even stronger. "I feel completely helpless up here when we should be with her right now."

He let her go, and she quickly wiped her eyes.

"These letters are pretty interesting. I'll read some to you," He said, trying to get their minds off the sad situation. He flipped to the last page she had read and settled on the couch. She took a seat next to him and sat back, enjoying the sound of his voice.

"'I still haven't received any letters from you, but that won't stop me from sending them to you. You get close to the guys you fight with here. Only one has passed on. Ben always was the quiet one. I hate that he died on enemy soil. When we crossed the Pacific, I wondered again what I'd gotten myself into. Most don't like to talk about it, since we are going where the fighting is. But I know the good Lord above has me under His wing.'"

Lizzy let out a breath at the last words. This man was doing what to the Amish was unthinkable.

Chapter Twenty-Five

"Wonder if I should have done something like that." Zack looked back at his life and realized how much he'd given up when he left. At least being in the army would have been nobler than what he ended up getting involved with.

Lizzy snapped her head over to him. "Why would you say such a thing?"

"Because it's an admirable thing to do. What if the US was attacked? We would need trained men and women to protect our country. That's one thing that bothers me about the Amish. Even though I understand why they don't fight, I think it's necessary at times."

She lifted her chin. "Well I don't agree with that at all. Violence just leads to more violence. I think about our young men and can't stomach the thought of them dying that way. It's inhumane, plain and simple."

"Women go too." He grinned a little, knowing it would get a rise out of her.

She lifted her eyes to meet his. "What happens when they're with child?"

"They try not to be." His smile widened, waiting for her rebuttal. He knew he'd never sway her. He wasn't trying to; he just liked the banter.

She folded her arms. "You're just riling me up on purpose."

"I suppose so."

She smiled and turned back to the fire. Lizzy always seemed to have a love-hate relationship with him, and now he was learning why. They were more alike than even he had known until the past couple of days, and because of that he found he wouldn't even mind if they had to stay here another night. That was good because it was looking more and more likely.

Lizzy asked, "What are you smiling about?"

"You. Didn't you hate me when we were growing up?"

He was curious to hear what she'd say to that. She was direct, savvy with her responses as a young girl, but seemed to have simmered down a little more now. She had changed in the few years he had been gone. He wondered whether she noticed that he had changed too, and in what way. But he wasn't sure he really wanted to know.

"You don't have to answer," he added.

When she didn't respond, he kicked himself for giving her the opportunity to ignore his comment. "It's okay, I can take it."

"Are you sure about that?" She stood and walked into the kitchen area, still not looking at him.

He nodded. "You know I can. You hated me, didn't you?" He asked as he took a seat at the table.

"Quite the opposite." She turned and looked him in the eyes. "Will you tell me what you really did in the city?"

He was still digesting what she'd just said when she changed the subject. Most Amish who knew someone who left the community figured they'd done something bad, which was far from the truth, for the most part. But in his case she would be right if that was what she assumed.

He sat up and leaned forward over the wooden table. "Why do you ask?"

Lizzy set down the noodles she was working on and walked over to him. "Whenever I bring up anything that has to do with your time there, you look sad. I don't mean to pry. I just wish you hadn't had to go through what you did... whatever it was."

An unexpected flood of emotion made him pause and take a couple of breaths. "How do you know so much?" He didn't like the way his voice sounded different and hoped she couldn't tell.

"I know you better than you think." With that she sat down and waited for him to talk, as if she knew he needed a minute or two.

"You think so?" He looked down at the divots in the wooden table and chuckled awkwardly. He could cheat and lie, but he couldn't look her in the eyes when he told her.

"To make it plain, I set up clients for a guy who was basically a con man." He hoped she would understand enough so he wouldn't have to explain. "Does that make sense?"

She nodded. "You helped someone take people's money." She said it matter-of-factly.

He must have looked surprised, because she tapped his hand before she moved her hands together in her lap.

"That's it? All you want to know?"

"What else is there?" she said with no expression, as if she'd known all along.

"Well. It was wrong, and I did it for years. I thought you'd be upset." He frowned, trying to figure out what he was missing, or maybe there was something that he'd left out that would appall her.

"I know." She leaned back in her chair in thought. "Sort of like when the Fiser boys stripped a bushel of the Yoders' corn? Or the Beachy kids running off with the Millers' tobacco." She tipped her head to one side.

"I get the point, but those pranks don't compare to what I did."

"A sin's a sin. And all sin can be forgiven." Lizzy said it as if she was reciting a recipe for her pumpkin pie.

But there was more to his time in Philly, more than he wanted to share. He prayed it would just all go away, that he could come before the Lord and humbly ask for forgiveness. But he didn't yet feel good enough to do that. At some point, when he felt he deserved freedom from his past mistakes...then, maybe.

"I didn't expect this reaction from you. I just wish everyone would have the same response."

"Well, I'm not the same person I was before you left." Her eyes watered. He reached for her hand, but she pulled it away and stood. "I should finish making us something to eat. You must be getting hungry again. I know I am." She immersed herself in her cooking, canned broth and noodles they'd found in the shed, not looking up at him when he spoke, so he decided to give her some space.

"I'd like to see if that shotgun works, and we can eat some meat for a change." She didn't look up. He left without waiting for a response. Maybe they both had secrets too difficult to share now—or ever. Some things were just too hard for words. "Be back in a bit."

She waved but kept her eyes on her cooking.

When he got to the shed, he looked around, fighting the odd sensation that someone was watching him. Anything suspicious that came up brought the mystery man to mind. He was starting to feel the way Lizzy seemed to about it all.

He scanned the area looking for anything different, to tell him if anyone else had been around lately. If this guy was living around here, they might be occupying his space, which Zack found unsettling. But so far the stranger had only shown kindness.

He went straight to the gun, which was more complex than any gun he'd seen. It was an M1 rifle. Zack knew about guns, but not one like this. This must be an old military gun used in the wars. Even if there were bullets around, he didn't know if he should use such an imposing weapon. He paused and wondered whether the mystery guy ever used it. But it was so old, it might not even be in working order.

There's only one way to find out.

If he could find the bullets, he would have to look for a safe place to shoot it off. Lizzy would have a fit.

He took a rag off the workbench and carefully took the gun apart the best he could. With each piece, he wondered what stories this rifle could tell. He laid out each piece of metal on the bench and used an old rag to clean the gun inside and out. When he finished, he looked high and low for bullets but found none. He was still glad he'd spent time on the weapon.

It had to belong to the mystery guy. He was beginning to think there was something going on that he didn't want to deal with. The thought of some guy who was a former soldier with a gun was more than unsettling. But then there was the mystery food that showed up on the counter. The whole thing was bizarre, and he had a feeling he was going to have to face it sooner than he wanted to.

"Zack."

He about jumped out of his boots when he heard his name. "Lizzy?"

She stuck her head around the tractor and put a hand to her chest. "You look like you've seen a ghost."

He could come clean but didn't want to give up his pride. "What are you doing in here?"

"So that's the gun?" She came closer to get a better look. "I've only seen guns like these for hunting and not much of that." She slid a finger down the sleek wood. "You cleaned it."

He shrugged. Although the Amish hunted, some didn't have much interest. He knew she was one of those who not only didn't approve of violence but also had a hard time being around it.

"That was nice of you." She smiled and dropped her hand away from the gun.

"What do you mean?"

"That you'd make it look nice for him." She twined her fingers down in front of her and kept the smile.

"Actually I was intrigued with such a great piece of wood and metal." He looked at it again. "That's all." He reluctantly wrapped up the gun and put it back where he'd found it.

"You're a good man, Zack." Her expression left no doubt of her sincerity. "And don't tell me you're not."

He chuckled. It was quiet for a moment, and then he knew what she'd like to do. "How about reading more of those letters?"

Lizzy smiled. "You read my mind."

Chapter Twenty-Six

I'm writing this by the light of a cigarette lighter, so it might be hard to read, plus a battle with Viet Cong got me knocked out with a concussion.'" They were sitting side by side at the table inside once again, the bag open before them. Zack continued reading: "'I can still see the guy's face who attacked me; he was young like me. Soon as I could stand, I was sent to the line with my rifle in hand. After a week's time, we took the hill. A lot died. We stacked the enemy's bodies to protect us. These are things I'll never forget, but maybe that's not all bad.'"

"The letters seem to get shorter as they go."

"This guy needed someone to talk to." Zack hoped he'd never be in that place again, like he was not long ago.

"He had something to say."

"And he needed someone to tell it to." His eyes shifted to her, wishing he could tell her the burden he carried. He couldn't get it out of this head. Maybe he never would.

She returned his gaze. "What is it? Whatever it is, you should tell someone. I can see it in your eyes when we talk about certain things." She touched his arm.

He jumped slightly, not expecting that from her. "Sorry, I'm thinking too much is all."

She moved away. "I think it's more than that."

He must be more discreet. Dwelling in the past didn't help anyone. He was the only one still stirring up the pot every time something reminded him of things all over again.

"I never thought I'd find someone as stubborn as I am, except for you," she taunted.

He didn't take the bait. "I doubt that."

"How so?"

"Because I'm here, and I shouldn't be."

"Why do you say that?"

He grunted. "It wasn't exactly a warm welcome when I saw my folks. I should have lowered my expectations." The thought of that cold reception almost brought a tear to his eye. The only saving grace had been his brother stepping out on the porch and watching him leave.

Even that could have meant anything, though. Maybe Eli had to feed the chickens and merely glanced back for a split second.

He shook his head as he watched it over again in his mind.

It was quiet for too long, until she broke the silence. "Why don't you try out that gun?"

Zack's eyebrows drew together in hesitation. "I didn't expect you to say that."

"Neither did I." She grinned.

For whatever reason, Zack moved forward, leaned in to Lizzy, and kissed her long and hard until she leaned back. He opened his eyes to see her wide eyes staring at him.

She sat still with a quizzical look on her face, with one side of her face tipped up as if amused. He hoped that was what he saw. If not, it would be a long ride back down the mountain.

Zack took a second to speak, just stared at her. "I don't know where that came from—"

Lizzy pulled away, her back rigid and her half smile gone. She got up and turned toward the door.

"Wait, Lizzy." He rose and quickly caught up to her. "What just happened? I thought you were okay…you were smiling."

Lizzy turned around abruptly to face him. "So you didn't mean anything by it?"

Now he was thoroughly confused. If he said no, that would mean the kiss meant nothing, and if he said yes, it meant something? "No…I mean *yes*…it did mean something."

She crossed her hands over her chest. "Is this how relationships are in the city?"

That made him think. The two lifestyles were too different to even try to compare. "No, not at all. There's no courting like here."

"That's what I've heard." An awkward few seconds passed. Zack was treading water, waiting for Lizzy to speak, because he was sure he'd say the wrong thing. But she didn't say another word; she just turned and continued toward the door.

Zack kept his distance behind her, treading lightly.

"Do you miss her?" Lizzy's tone was so even and steady, she seemed to be emotionless.

"Who?"

"The woman in the city."

Unsure what to say, he decided not to tell her anything. "I don't want to talk about it."

"I understand."

But did she? She changed when he said those seven little words. It wasn't a surprise she would ask about who he spent time with in the city and about his relationships there, but he didn't expect her to ask about the particular woman who brought him pain.

I've done too much and gone too far for too long to ever have a calm, simple life again among the Amish.

He could live with that. But he was beginning to think it wouldn't be so easy to leave Lizzy.

When he'd first come, he hadn't thought little Lizzy would make much of an impression on him. She'd grown into a bright, exciting young woman, and she hadn't married. He guessed that was because she'd probably intimidated the other guys away. But he'd grown up with her like a brother and knew her ways. At the time they annoyed him, but now he embraced them.

He hoped she would soon be in better spirits. If so, he'd like the opportunity to find out what she was thinking about without stumbling all over himself and her.

He decided to start a fire; evening was coming on. When it was warm enough, he sat down on the hearth and waited for her to come over.

Lizzy handed him a cup of soup she'd made out of chicken stock and noodles.

"I sure miss your mincemeat pie." He turned to see if she was receptive to his compliment. She was. He could tell by her meek smile and how she looked at him for another word of approval.

"And your meatloaf. That sounds like heaven about now." His mouth puckered a bit when he took another sip of soup.

"You're just making it worse by talking about real food. I feel helpless; there's nothing here to work with."

He stood abruptly. "I'm gonna get that gun and find us some meat to eat, if it's the last thing I do." He felt like he was going a bit crazy, and he had to do something. Even if he came back with nothing, at least he'd try.

"Well, be careful. And I sure hope you catch something. That, or the car could get us out of here." She rubbed her hands together and moved toward the fire. "Go on and be careful."

He was halfway out the door when he turned back. "And don't read any more of those letters until I get back." He winked.

Her jaw dropped a little, so either she had been thinking about it, or he surprised her with the wink. "It would keep my mind off things."

"I'll hurry back." He shut the door behind him and went back to the shed to find those bullets. Zack went to the back of the shed and worked from the left side of the shelves to the other end. Every time he was about to give up, he'd find some interesting gadget or more dried food, blankets, and woodworking tools. Whoever was stashing all of this away was getting ready for something.

He walked by the workbench. There in the center lay a single bullet. He could have sworn he'd thoroughly looked through the ammo boxes after cleaning the gun, but then again, it seemed to follow the pattern of the mystery man. He loaded the bullet in the gun and said a quick prayer. He had only one shot.

The forest was peaceful and cold. He watched his breath become a foggy mist as he pushed the air from his lungs. He looked up to the pale blue sky, remembering the games, laughter, and fellowship here, and he missed it.

Crack!

Zack jumped and looked behind him. No animal or human was in sight.

He stood tall and scanned the area again.

Could have been just about anything; nothing to worry about in a forest this big—most varmints are probably hibernating.

He saw movement out of the corner of his eye and stood stock-still.

"Anybody there?" The sound of his voice in the silence made him feel more vulnerable than he was already.

No answer. He realized this might be his only chance to see who this person was. The man obviously wanted to remain anonymous. That he could understand. He'd thought of coming back here after he had Lizzy safely at home, but it wasn't his to have. As far as he knew, it was still property of the Amish community.

"Never thought you'd put me here, Lord. Show me Your ways. Where I should be going and what I should be doing…" The emotions got the best of him, and he had to stop to gather himself. "I'll be darned if I have to go back to that city."

Another snap drew his head up to see a squirrel making a run for it. He stood, aimed, and pulled the trigger.

Chapter Twenty-Seven

BOOM!

The peace of the forest shattered instantly when the shot went off.

Lizzy jumped up and ran to the door, startled. Not that she was unfamiliar with the sound of a gun—just not here, right now, with someone always lurking around them.

She couldn't get to the door soon enough. Then she paused.

What if it isn't Zack on the other side?

"Zack, are you out there?"

No answer.

She paced the room and then went to the door and opened it. Seeing no one, she stepped outside and looked around.

She had wrapped her arms around her and stepped out onto the snowy wilderness, wondering how wise it was to be out here alone when someone had shot off a gun. Surely it was Zack, but with all the strange things that had happened since they'd arrived, she thought it best to be cautious.

The wind bent the trees, creating a chill in her bones. Lizzy noticed every movement that surrounded her. Two branches rubbing together, the whistle that went through the valley when the wind picked up. Waiting for someone or something to appear out of the snow or trees. She hadn't grabbed her coat, fool thing to forget, but she was more concerned about Zack.

"Lizzy."

Zack's voice immediately calmed her, and she let out a breath. "Thank *Gott* it's you." The next thing she noticed was the squirrel he held and the rifle resting on his shoulder.

"You shouldn't be out here. You must be freezing."

"I heard the shot and got worried." Her teeth chattered as she spoke.

He started walking her to the cabin with quick steps. "Hurry up. You need to get warmed. Is the fire still going?"

She nodded and tried to keep up with him. "*Jah*, but I should tend to it."

When they reached the cabin, he stopped at the door. "I'll be by the shed if you need me. I'll make it quick. And warm up." He was backing away as he spoke. Then he turned and went to the shed.

When he was out of sight, she turned to the cabin and went straight to the fireplace. She threw another log on the fire and stirred the embers, thinking about making squirrel stew. Not the most desirable meat to eat, but they were too hungry not to take what was given to them.

As she prepared for Zack to come back with their meal, she decided to clean up the place. They had been there long enough for it to bother her when she saw things out of order or dirty. The place didn't seem like it had been used for a while, and she wished they had kept it up.

She used what little she had to clean with and a few rags she found in a cabinet. It was nearly empty, and she grew sad remembering how much all of the families had enjoyed time up here, with the women cooking, the men fishing or hunting, and the kids playing games.

I wonder why we stopped coming here.

She lost herself in time and didn't realize how long until Zack touched her on the shoulder.

His eyebrows lifted. "What did you do to this place?"

"I couldn't stand it anymore. There wasn't a lot to work with, but it's an improvement." Everything was put away or in order, counters and tables scoured, and the floor mopped. The back window was clean on the inside but not the outside. "I'd like to clean that window."

"We have more privacy without them clean." Zack's face twisted, and he took a few steps forward. "There was something about a cave. Remember?"

She shrugged. "I remember us kids making up stories about a cave, but I didn't think it was real."

"There was a path around here that went up a short hill somewhere around the cabin. It must still be here."

"But right now we have to finish making dinner." Lizzy was getting really hungry. This was their second day in the cabin, and with just canned broth, noodles, pancakes and syrup, she felt her stomach was shrinking. The thought of something substantial now made her stomach growl.

"I won't argue with that." Zack helped prepare the meal and then they sat down.

"Does it seem a little lonely in here alone?" She tasted the soup and was grateful to have a decent meal.

He took his time to respond, and she was about to speak again when he looked up at her. "We're not alone; we have each other."

She smiled, appreciating his comment. "You know what I mean. We're used to being here with a roomful of people."

Again he was quiet. But this time she waited, knowing he was thinking on what to say. "I like it here with just you."

Lizzy felt her face heat and wished she could stop it from happening. She was touched by what he'd said and wondered where this was going. They'd never been able to stand each other as kids, and now, forced together, they were finding they had feelings for each other. Or was it just being here, needing each other, and being alone?

The kiss was one Lizzy wouldn't forget. She'd been kissed before, but Zack was tender and sweet in the way his lips touched hers. Thinking through it all, she never knew if boys really liked *her.* She seemed to get more attention than the other girls. She learned why as she got older and liked the attention only until she started to get annoyed with how boys were responding to her.

There's more to me than a pretty face.

"I don't mean to embarrass you when I say these things. But I'm thinking it's a good sign when I make you blush."

She felt her cheeks color more deeply and kept her eyes averted until they cooled down. "I don't know why that happens, but I wish it didn't." She still couldn't meet his gaze. He was kind enough to keep his attention on his meal. "But I'm glad you don't make fun of me like you did when we were kids."

"It was hard to get your attention back then. It's a little easier now. At least I think it is."

"It is." She boldly looked him straight in the eyes and resisted the heat creeping up her neck. "You've gone from making me blush to helping me stop. You're a confusing man, Zack Schrock."

"I'd like to think I've made amends for things, the past

and present. Things I've tucked away and don't want to dwell on anymore. Being with you up here has helped me with that."

"I wish I knew what you were talking about; it might help me understand better what you've gone through. You left here an angry young man." Lizzy hoped that wasn't too personal. Zack had made it obvious how much he disliked growing up in their community, but she'd never known exactly why.

"I don't think you want to know. Things got pretty bad toward the end of my time there. And people don't want to hear it. They'd rather pretend it didn't happen."

Lizzy thought back and remembered some to-do going on with his family. Her *daed* scolded her for asking, so she stopped. "You're safe here, Zack, if you want to share. I'll understand either way."

"No one really knows everything, but it's probably best that way, especially with it being so long ago and because of who it involved. My dad used to come home angry a lot of the time about not getting his way or someone disagreeing with him or confronting him, but it's tough to sort through things when the problem is with the bishop. He used to take it out on us kids, mainly me."

"I understand." Lizzy wanted to listen without interrupting, but she wanted him to know he wasn't alone with his situation.

"He used to smack me around, saying I was the oldest and was to be an example of what they'd get if they made him look bad. I never knew what it was I did any different than my siblings, but eventually he had brainwashed them into thinking that I was a bad kid, not a big brother to look up to. Word got out, and I had some hope maybe it would stop, but it's no easy thing to convince people the leader of their community is doing wrong."

Lizzy's heart sank as she listened to Zack. She'd heard grumbling on one issue or another about the bishop but hadn't known what was going on. "I'm sorry, Zack." She thought about how her *daed* and she butted heads, but he never laid a hand on her or anyone in the family.

He shook his head. "I don't want pity, just the truth. I hated leaving my brothers and hoped he wouldn't do anything to them, but I had to get out of there."

She knew better than to ask about his *mamm*. Most Amish women didn't have much say in a family. "You stayed a lot longer than most people might have. No one could blame you for that." She knew it wasn't that simple, but she wanted to stay positive. This new information about the bishop was too hard for her to know what to do with. "No one ever did anything to help?" She hated the idea of her community not getting involved; she wasn't surprised, but it made her sad. "I'm so sorry, Zack."

He nodded. "I don't want to talk about it anymore."

"*Jah*, I understand." She slipped her hand into his and squeezed. It would be nice about now to be able to change the mood. He didn't want to dwell on it, so they wouldn't.

"There's one more letter, if you want me to read it." She tipped a smile his way and picked up the last of the discolored pieces of paper.

"'It's been a while since I've written. A lot has happened. It rained on our homecoming day, fitting, since there were no welcomes to be had, only protesters. I was okay with it though, thinking more about my new little one on the way. I hope my time in the service won't be forgotten. Even so,

I'll have a child to love and hold. You won't hear from me again. This is my last letter. I'll always love you.'"

She slowly lowered the paper to the table. "That was short and sweet. More sad, I guess. I wish it was something with a happy ending." She should have read it first, but she'd been sure this guy would end up with his girl.

"You look apologetic. Don't start feeling sorry for me, Lizzy. Everything happens for a reason, and I already think I know what God's plan is for me."

"Which is…"

"I'm still working on it." He smiled, which was nice to see. He seemed to be one who grew stronger rather than weaker through crisis. She admired him for that.

Chapter Twenty-Eight

Zack woke, blinked a couple times, and adjusted himself as to his surroundings like he had the previous morning in the cabin. But he felt especially warm. He raised his head and saw Lizzy sound asleep beside him, with one arm draped over his chest. He jumped off the couch, wearing only thermal underwear. That woke her up, increasing his surprise when she didn't seem at all shocked.

Zack raked his fingers through his hair, wondering how they'd gotten into this situation. "What happened?"

Lizzy sat up, absently twirled her hair into a twist, and then looked around her. "What's wrong?"

"The sleeping—our arrangement—"

She waved a hand. "Oh, that. Well…" She paused but only for a second. "I was cold, and you were warm."

He dropped his hand to his side and stared at her. "Now, if I had done that, you'd be throwing a fit."

She shrugged. "Maybe before we came here, I would have, but it's different now."

What does that mean?

She had his full attention, and he'd calmed down a bit, so he could figure out what was going on. If he was reading her right, it was more than just being warm. "So you slept well, I take it."

She smiled. "*Jah*, I bet you did too."

"Yeah. As a matter of fact, I did." He cupped his hands over his face, thinking about how nice it would have been if he'd known and could have enjoyed the feeling of Lizzy's body next to his. He kept his face covered until he could look at her without thinking things about her he shouldn't.

"Are you all right?" She frowned as if concerned.

No, he wasn't. He'd never imagined the two of them together in any way, especially sleeping on the same couch together. This wasn't like what he'd had in the city. One-night stands, living together, and unwanted pregnancies were much more common outside than in the Amish community. After living in Philly, he could understand why. The teenagers here should appreciate their parents, who put up boundaries as the *Ordnung* demanded and for good reason.

If only I'd known then what I know now.

It was quiet—too quiet—but he was still too baffled to know what to say. Who was this girl, who'd become a young woman? And what was happening between them?

"I'm going to wash up." She stood and smiled.

"Yeah, go ahead." They only had one outhouse to use, and for once he was glad to have somewhere to go and think. He'd longed for her to be around him. Even when he was doing chores, Zack wanted her there. He rushed through so he could return to her side, but now it seemed she might reciprocate his feelings.

He looked down and realized he was still in his long johns. He'd waited until she was asleep before he stripped down to them. He wondered how comfortably Lizzy was sleeping. The cold by itself was enough to give anyone the chills through the night.

Zack dressed and went outside to do his business. He

headed toward the shed. He had a good idea that whoever was hanging around here would be glad for them to go. He wasn't sure what this person was doing, but it seemed harmless enough.

He shuffled through the boxes of food, all of it either undesirable or needing certain utensils to cook it, and let his stomach growl.

When he walked out of the shed, he saw something from the corner of his eye. He stopped cold and turned slowly to see a deer, its head down, foraging for food under the snow. Zack picked up a block of wood and started to whittle as he watched. He tried not to make any noises. He wanted to keep the deer close by so he could see how to carve it.

As he chipped away at the cold wood, he started thinking about the deer coming out in the open and searching for food. He lifted his head and took in a breath. It didn't freeze his throat like it did when the snow was below freezing. He stood, hoping against hope this was what he thought it was.

He walked quickly to the cabin, but a few stretches in, he slowed down and was soon standing still. He took in the forest of white with the occasional bird flying overhead or critter running by, scattering to shelter. During the short time they'd been here, he'd been preoccupied with getting them out, but as he looked at the surroundings, he realized he should have appreciated the beauty around them a little more.

"Zack, did you hear that?" Lizzy trudged through the footprints he'd made when he came to the shed. She almost fell, but he reached out to catch her, holding on until they were looking each other in the eyes. He thought of the kiss, wondering if she was thinking of the same thing. She hadn't objected before, so he bent down and pressed his lips against hers. This was the best way he could explain how he felt about her, and he prayed she felt the same. When she opened her eyes, the softness of their blue and her lips slightly open told him she was content.

A humming sound made him pause. He glanced around, looking for the source. A snowplow labored along the road, its blade shoving snow to the shoulder. The noise was piercing after the few days they'd been in the quiet forest. Neither of them said a word, just watching as the truck turned up the hill to where they stood. Soon it backed away again and continued up the road.

Lizzy twined her fingers into his and squeezed. Zack understood why. They'd been together in what turned out to be much more than a place of refuge. It had been a time to be together and—did he dare say it?—fall in love. However things went when they returned home, he would always think of it that way.

"The snow…" She looked around. "It's stopped snowing, completely." She sounded almost disappointed, and he could relate to that. What began as their biggest setback was about to end, along with their time alone together in this forest wonderland.

"Yeah, I guess it's time to go home." He paused.

Where is home for me?

He wasn't welcome in his father's home, and he didn't want to go back to Philly. What was left?

Clara was the only thing that kept him going. He thought about her every waking hour when he wasn't thinking about Lizzy. He felt his priorities were skewed, thinking about her more than his sister who was ill. But even when he became frustrated not being able to be with Clara, he knew God had a hand in this situation. It was more than a coincidence the two of them were up here in this place with so many memories to share.

He grinned. "Now we can get to the hospital!"

At the same time Lizzy bobbed her head and smiled. "We'll get to see Clara."

"She's the one thing that could keep me from leaving."

"Back to the city?" Her eyes bored into his. For the first time he could see how much she cared about him. There was no doubt at that moment that Lizzy cared almost as much for him as he did for her.

"I don't have a lot of options." He hoped she would leave it at that, but he knew she would want answers. He honestly didn't know what to say to her. She knew his standing in the community, but now how it paled compared to his life in Philly.

"The city should be *gut*, *jah*?" It was a frank question, and he didn't know how to tell her that anything between them might have to end. She would go her way, and he would go his.

"How can that be good?" The fact that she could be right frustrated him.

She looked at the cabin and then the white, glistening snow with the same expression he'd had only a minute ago. There was something about this place that was appealing. Not just the beauty of the landscape, but the childhood one can never let go of as an adult.

"Fewer decisions to make." She gave him a stern stare. "What did you run away from, Zack?"

His head shot up, and he took a minute, still unsure he wanted her to know everything.

Do I want to drag out those memories?

"I'd much rather think back to the Christmases we had as kids. That's what this place reminds me of."

She took his hand. "Tell me."

He grunted. "I'm tired of telling you about my time there. Most of it wasn't good. At least, a good portion wasn't."

"Go on." Her gaze was stuck on him like glue. He wondered how he could hold her attention.

"I was in a relationship with a woman for a couple of years." He scrubbed his face with one hand, not wanting to go back to the memory. "I thought we were going somewhere with our relationship. That is, until she got pregnant. I was excited to hear the news, but she didn't feel the same. She had a good job, benefits included, and was making her way up the ladder with no intention of letting a child get in her way. I didn't see her for what she really was until the pregnancy came about."

"I can't imagine. What did you end up doing?"

He appreciated her nonjudgmental attitude, which surprised him a little. Lizzy was adamant about following rules, as were most Amish.

"I talked her into keeping the baby. It surprised me that it was so easy to get her to agree. But she miscarried. I rushed her to the hospital as soon as she started complaining of pain, but there was nothing they could do. After that we seemed to argue all the time. Then I found out she had been seeing someone else, a guy I knew. I was really devastated. Everything happened so fast. One minute I was about to have a family, and the next I'm completely alone. I didn't realize until then how much I actually wanted to be a dad. I already had his name all picked out."

"You hoped it would be a little boy?"

Zack smiled upon hearing the question. He nodded.

"What name did you choose?"

Zack held the tears back. "Benjamin James. Might be overdone, but I wanted him to carry both my dad's and grandfather's names."

Lizzy's face contorted with held-back emotions. "I'm really sorry, Zack."

They were both quiet for what seemed like a long time before Zack spoke.

"That's another reason why I came. Realizing how important family is. But it hasn't worked out very well for me so far."

Lizzy's tight lips and jaw showed her concern. As much as she stayed on the straight and narrow, she understood how frustrating the bishop could be.

Chapter Twenty-Nine

Lizzy shivered as she watched Zack dig his car out of a four-foot snowdrift. He'd been working at it for a while. "Do you think it will start?"

"Cross your fingers." He stuck the shovel in the pile of snow behind the car and reached for the door handle.

"I'll say a prayer instead." She watched for his reaction.

"Just had to slip that in, didn't you?" He said it lightly, the best response she could have hoped for. When he pulled on the door handle, it didn't budge. "Pray harder, will ya?"

So she did, and watched as he put one foot against the back door and dug his other heel into the snow for balance. He pulled on the front door handle and flew backward, landing on his rear in the snow. She bent over with laughter.

Zack sat up, looking like a kid, confused and probably a little wet. "Very funny. But *this* is not." He got to his feet and held up the handle of the car door. "This kind of thing never stopped happening to me when I was driving out here from Philly. Darn handle pops off."

"*Jah*, I remember." And she did, everything about him came back to her mind. His obvious surprise when he saw her again after the years of being gone; the way he cared for Clara; the conversation they'd had while sitting in the elevator, and him remembering her fear of heights.

"Are you gonna help or just stare at me?" He lifted his chin inquiringly and leaned against the shovel.

She was about to answer him when a four-wheel-drive vehicle came chugging around the bend of the road. It had a Forest Department insignia on the door.

"Good timing. Maybe we'll finally get out of here." As soon as she said the words, Lizzy felt sad. What had started out as simply finding refuge had become much more than that. She hated to go.

The ranger parked and got out close to the entrance of the drive and stopped in his tracks when he saw the two of them together. "You folks all right?" His gray hair and slow gait showed his age, and he took his time trudging toward them.

When he got to Zack's rental car and saw that the handle was missing, he grunted. "You shouldn't get angry, especially over a piece of metal. It's not worth your while, son, believe me."

Lizzy didn't quite know why he was so worried about the handle in Zack's hand. It seemed to be Zack's problem and could be taken care of in time.

"Are the roads clear?" She was almost too scared to ask but had to know if they had their freedom. As she turned around and looked at the cabin, she had a sudden feeling of remorse. Through all the cleaning and repairing they'd done to make the place seem somewhat like their own, neither of them had complained about the time they spent there, only about not having the materials needed to do more.

"Oh, yeah. Been meaning to come earlier, but I know Leonard can take care of himself."

"We thought there was someone living up here. It would

have been nice to know." Zack didn't hold back his frustration. It was a bit embarrassing for Lizzy, but she understood his frustration.

"You folks been here for a while?"

"Yeah, it's good to see someone finally made it up the hill," Zack said a bit sharply.

The older man rested a hand on his thigh and bent over a bit. "This place hasn't been used by anyone but Len. Didn't think anyone else would be around."

"Who is Len?" A chill went up Lizzy's back. The mystery man might have been with them the whole time.

"Haven't seen him around?" The ranger frowned and glanced toward the shed. "Hope he's all right." He stood straight and started walking up to the cabin.

"We could have left yesterday." Zack said, only to her. Her wanting to go home was obvious, but it made her feel a bit sad to think about where and what Zack might go back to. After his confessions, she couldn't imagine him returning to the city.

"Len takes care of this place since it was made part of the national parks and recreation division. The government likes to give veterans jobs as they come up for guys like him." He took in her Amish dress and stuck out his bottom lip. "I believe the cabin still belongs to you Amish folk."

Lizzy and Zack looked at each other for a second, digesting the information. "We didn't see this guy, but we did think someone might be around."

"He keeps to himself most of the time." The ranger was winded by the time they got to the cabin, but he kept walking and went past, toward the shed.

"Where are we going?" Lizzy was cold, tired, but she was curious about what was going on with this man.

"To Leonard's." He frowned as if she should know, but she still didn't exactly see where they were going and why.

When they stopped, she peered down to see a man-made cave. From the outside it looked like a mound of dirt, but when you looked closely, you could make out the smooth sides and top with imprints. A moment later she could see the entrance into his underground home. Like a bunker.

She turned to Zack, who seemed to be observing the same thing and slowly looked over to her. "So this is where he sleeps?"

The forest ranger shook his head. "This is where he lives."

Lizzy looked inside and saw how a person could have room to live in a space like this. She wasn't sure what to make of the whole thing. She'd known something was amiss, and now she could put the pieces together. The walls were flush, supported by log beams similar to the cabin. Lizzy remembered very little about this spot, and even less about the cave like the boys did. Part of her felt sorry for him—for *Len*—but maybe he liked his life this way, sort of how the place had grown on them.

"We didn't see him around. I guess this is why." Zack gestured to the bunker, which could easily vanish into the area around it.

"Yeah, well. If he wanted to say hello, he would, so I'll leave this with him and be on my way. That is, unless you need anything."

Lizzy thought it odd to wonder if they needed help, but after all they'd learned about the place, Leonard included, it seemed expected.

"I could use some power from your truck to make sure we're clear to get out of that snowdrift." Zack was already stepping back as he said it.

"Sure thing, follow me." The ranger turned and started down the hill.

Lizzy thought about the letters and couldn't help asking. "It would be interesting to see him, but he obviously doesn't like company."

"Oh, he might surprise you." He winked at her and then bent down and opened what appeared to be a hidden milk box before turning to go back down the hill.

For some reason she hoped the letters they'd found really were Len's. The more she thought about it, the more likely it seemed her episode with him as a child probably resulted from his protecting her from something or other.

"I'm going to clean up things in the cabin," she told Zack and headed up the steps. Walking into the huge room brought back the talks they'd had and their figuring out how to survive the cold and find food to eat. Now looking back, she was thankful for every minute here, good or bad.

She looked at the rags she'd made into socks that were lying by the fireplace. They were to be a present for Zack, to keep him warm when he went out to the shed. Now he wouldn't need them.

As she tidied the room and put things away, she started thinking of what it was going to be like when they got back to the community. There would be a lot of explaining to do. And given the bishop being the way he was when it came to Zack, it would be twice as difficult to explain all that had happened. It wouldn't be easy to explain to her own father, either. But as much as she knew what to expect, a big piece of her didn't care. She had grown close to Zack, and if he felt even partly as much, it would be worth fighting for their relationship.

"Are you ready to go?" Zack paused by the door and seemed to be remembering some of the same things. His eyes paused at the rear window and then moved back to her. "What are those?" He walked over to the fireplace and picked up the rag-socks.

"I found some rags and thought you might need another pair. Yours were getting damp, but they didn't have time to dry before you were out fixing something again. I made them for you." A lump started to grow in her throat. She pushed it away with a couple hard swallows.

Zack walked slowly back to the door and gave her a nod. "We should go."

She slipped her hand into his and didn't look back. She'd had her mind on Clara throughout their time here, but even more now that she'd be seeing her again soon. Then the foreboding came over her that the worst had happened. She wouldn't let those thoughts creep in and make her worry. Clara wouldn't want that either.

They walked down the hill to the road in silence. Lizzy seemed to hear more than she had before. The cries of the birds and skittering of squirrels made her look up and see the critters running around, probably glad to have peace and quiet again.

"Penny for your thoughts," Zack asked, but kept his eyes on the rental car, probably doubting it would start.

"You wouldn't believe me if I told you." She didn't believe it herself.

"Then I'll go first." They reached the car, and he stood next to her. "I sort of liked it here." He shrugged, as if unsure of her response.

"*Jah*. I did, too. Strange, isn't it? I never thought I would—not without a group of us like we used to do."

"Sounds like the place has more visitors this way, including Leonard. I still don't know what to think about him."

"Those letters got him through a hard time. And us while we were here. Speaking for myself, anyway." She watched Zack stop and reassess the door handle situation. He pushed it back on and tugged to make sure it was secure.

He nodded. "Let's pack up and go before this car changes its mind."

Once she gathered what little they had with them, she settled into the car, praying it would get them home. Zack and the ranger hooked up the cables between the two vehicles, and Zack climbed in and cranked the engine. It sputtered but soon came to life. After a pump or two on the gas, the ranger was coiling the cables, and Zack had turned around and was driving down the hill.

Lizzy waved to the ranger and looked back once more at the snow-blanketed area. Then she thought she saw someone dart around one of the large trees and disappear behind the cabin.

Chapter Thirty

ONCE THEY GOT on the road, Zack started thinking about what would happen next. They'd come a long way since first arriving at the cabin, but where things would go wasn't predictable. They lived in two different worlds, but hers was one he was familiar with.

Do I want to go back to what I came from? Will Dad even let me?

He let out a long breath and concentrated on the road.

"Why the sigh?" Lizzy was staring at him, but he didn't know how to answer.

"Just doing some thinking." He thought about what she was going to ask next. They'd spent a lot of time together, shared a lot of their hearts and souls, especially his. Now he was regretting it.

How could I tell her some of the things I did?

"Well, I could see you're thinking. About what?" She turned toward him, and he was glad he had to keep his eyes on the road, because he would have to lie about what he was thinking and feeling.

I must have been out of my mind to think a relationship with Lizzy could go anywhere. Even if it did, our parents would never allow it.

He shook his head even thinking about it.

"Clara…and some other things." Knowing how much to tell her and when would be the key. He found himself thinking of lies and ways to leave without completely ruining their relationship, but he realized there was no way out this time. He'd sometimes schemed and lied to get deals done, and he had to look at this the same way. He disliked how it had to go down, but he didn't see any alternatives. By the time Clara was taken care of, he would be packed up and headed out of town. The disappointment from Lizzy would hurt more than anything else—more than cutting ties with his job and starting over somewhere, and more than leaving Clara.

"You're not very talkative." She tilted her head, the way that made her look like the girl he knew her to be as they grew up—innocent and free—unlike how he'd ended up living his life.

"Do you have any doubt that Clara is still alive?" It was harsh but did change the subject.

Lizzy jolted and drew her eyebrows together. "Why would you say that, Zack?"

"I just want to be prepared. We've been gone awhile." The scenario was almost too much to take, but it was in Lizzy's best interest to create distance. The closer they got to the community, the more he felt he was doing the right thing, even though it was one of the hardest things he'd ever done.

He felt her hand on his arm and tightened. Toward the end of their time at the cabin she'd become more affectionate, which he would miss. But he had to balance the change he was creating, so he let the warmth of her stay with him.

"Do you feel all right? You seem a little warm." She put her hand to his forehead, reminding him of when he was a child and his mother would touch his cheek with the back of her hand to see if he had a fever.

"I'm fine. Just ready to get back."

If she only knew how much I'm not all right.

Would she be angry or sad about his decision? Maybe both, but with the change in their relationship, he guessed the sadness would be the hardest to see her bear, now that the protective side of her had melted away for the most part. His shoulders slumped at the thought of how far they'd come and how much this would push them apart again.

"Where will you stay?"

He knew she was looking at him, but he didn't want to look at her when he told her. "Depending on what's going on with Clara, I'll stay at the hospital." He didn't have the luxury of his parents' place to stay, so what else must she be thinking about?

"That's where I'd like to stay too." She smiled, but he couldn't say what he wanted to.

"You should get a good night's sleep at your parents' place. I'm sure they've been worried sick about you."

She opened her mouth and then shut it, probably wondering what was different about him, about them. "I'm going to close my eyes for a minute."

He smiled. He'd gotten used to her habits and the sayings she used. This was one of his favorites. Her minute turned into a cat nap and then to a full one. He found it endearing.

As they got closer to the hospital, the emotions biting against his gut increased, and he let out a long breath. These would be the two hardest things he'd ever done. Checking on Clara and leaving Lizzy. Once he knew Clara was going to be all right, he would leave, this time for good. Whenever a memory of their time together would spring up, he'd tamp it down. He had to.

Lizzy was unusually quiet as they neared the hospital, only speaking when he asked her something, which wasn't much. They both had Clara in their thoughts, and something else hovering over them.

Zack parked the car in hopes it would start again when he left. The one thing he missed about Philly was his reliable, comfortable car.

When the elevator stopped, Lizzy closed her eyes. Then she stepped inside and opened them.

"I thought you might get over that a bit."

"I wanted to do it on my own. After walking up the stairwell so many times and seeing how much easier it was to use the elevator, I decided to be brave." Her faint smile gave him some hope she wasn't upset with him.

"So you're going to stay in the lounge tonight?"

Lizzy watched the lights above the door, apparently relaxed. "That's probably best. I'm just anxious to see Clara again."

"It seems like such a long time ago. I hope everything went all right."

"We left just before the first round of chemo was to be done."

Zack wished he had been there for that, but they couldn't fight the weather. "Yes, I'm sure it went well."

"It was nice up there." She spoke without looking at him. "I didn't expect that." She turned and stared into his eyes and then jumped when the elevator stopped and the light for their floor flashed.

He wanted to answer her and tell her their time together

was a saving grace for him, not just for the beauty of the place but for being with her. "Should be interesting to see what your family says about us being up there alone."

"Is that why you're acting this way?" She stared straight at him, which made him turn away. He expected her to question him but not this soon.

"I'm the same as I was the last time we were here." Which was true, but a weak way out of telling the truth.

She looked away. "I see."

That was all she said, and then the doors opened and she hurried out, leaving him behind her. He followed and readied himself to put on a happy face for Clara. When he got to the room, Lizzy was there, but Clara wasn't. "Where is she?"

Lizzy calmly walked past him. "I'll get a nurse."

"No, stay in case she comes back. I'll go." His focus changed from worrying about Lizzy to Clara. They had been gone long enough for there to be a good reason Clara was gone, and he would rely on that.

He noticed the nurse who had flirted with him before he left and approached her for help. "Do you remember me?"

She nodded, and then tightened her lips. "Have you seen your family?"

"No, we just got in." A slight tingle rose up his neck. Something wasn't right. "Is everything okay?"

"It would be best if you talked with the doctor or your family." She looked away and quickly left the nurse's station. "I'll find someone for you."

He stepped in front of her, keeping her from passing. He saw the fear in her eyes and realized he was hovering in front of her, forceful enough to be way out of line. "No,

I want to know now." A pounding started in his ears when she paused and took a step as if to edge around him. Her bottom lip trembled. "Tell me!"

She backed away, obviously shaken. "Clara did well with the chemotherapy, but—"

"What? Did something go wrong?" A low beating started in his head as he took in the information.

"She had a stroke." The pretty nurse wasn't good at hiding her emotions. "It's up to the doctor to decide what to do." She turned away and then glanced back to him. "I'm sorry."

"Is she going to be okay?"

"I'll call the doctor in to answer your questions." She walked away before he could stop her.

Spots flashed before his eyes, and he leaned over and put his hands on his thighs. He couldn't breathe. This wasn't right…couldn't be. He'd known in the back of his mind that she could get worse but hadn't thought anything like this would happen.

So much for counting on God. Lizzy was wrong too. The people he cared about the most were the ones he lost.

"Zack…what is it? What's wrong?" The intensity raised Lizzy's voice as she spoke, and he knew she was aware of what was happening. He wanted to hear what she'd heard but couldn't stop the pounding in his brain.

When he didn't answer, she turned and walked away. Each tap of her boots grew louder in his head. He rubbed his temples, trying to take it all in. It wasn't supposed to happen this way. Not yet. They needed to have Christmas together, with all the trimmings that Lizzy had mentioned.

After what seemed like an eternity, he felt Lizzy by his side again. "Let's go."

"Where?" He looked sideways at her. He didn't want to leave. He wanted to see Clara.

Lizzy took his hand and pulled to make him get up. "Follow me." The *click-clack* of her heels annoyed him, and so did the fact he was being taken away from where he felt Clara was. He walked through the door Lizzy opened and then stopped.

The chapel was sparsely lit, with stained-glass windows that left a ray of light across the light blue carpet. There were two people sitting together, praying in whispers. Lizzy took his hand and sat at the far left end of the front pew. As soon as she sat down, she began to cry. He wrapped his hand around hers and held on tightly.

It was like hell on earth not knowing how serious this was. He needed to see Clara; he had seen her so little over the past years. He was angrier at himself than he was about her leaving. He knew her faith was strong and that she was ready to go if it came to that. *When God was ready for her*, although it upset him when she frankly brought it up from time to time.

"Pray with me." Lizzy lowered her head and squeezed his hand.

Lizzy continued to comfort him by reciting the Lord's Prayer, which made him calm down. He pushed away the sadness and held her close. His mind moved forward. Maybe for his sake or to find closure, he decided he'd leave as soon as this was over, and he'd never come back to this godforsaken place ever again.

Chapter Thirty-One

They had come too late. At first Lizzy cursed herself for not being there, but *Gott* had put them together for a reason, and maybe that was to bring them closer. Lizzy scoffed. It was too bad Zack hadn't kept in touch with Clara like he wished he could, but he wouldn't have been accepted, and he knew that. The guilt was justified, but not necessary. Clara, of all people, would forgive.

"I thought you might be in here." The nurse walked up behind them. "Will you come with me, please?" She held a chart in her hand and tried to smile.

Lizzy stood and Zack followed. The way he carried himself and his lack of conversation showed just how difficult this was for him. Although she considered Clara as her confidant and sister in Christ, they weren't related by blood like Clara and Zack were. She couldn't imagine what he must be feeling at this moment.

The nurse stopped at the doctor's office and waved a hand toward his door. "The doctor will see you now." Her long, dark hair flipped to one side as she walked away. Lizzy wanted to follow her and not hear what the doctor had to say. But they needed to know what their options were. There was no way of ignoring the situation.

"Zack, your family just left." The doctor stood and shook

Zack's hand, one pump. He was a former Amish and must assume Zack was Amish like his family.

Zack didn't mince his words. "What happened with Clara while we were gone?"

"I understand you were held up due to the storm. Everything happened quickly after you left."

Lizzy's throat was dry. "Why? I thought we had more time in hopes Clara would be able to go home." Her voice broke on Clara's name. It was too difficult to fathom that Clara had gone through this but still might pull out of it unscathed.

"The chemo treatment progressed well, but then came a mild blood clot—which responded well to quick action, and there was no neurological damage, though I recommend a rehab program for good measure.

"Clara had second thoughts about getting any treatment at all. In the end she knew her body better than any of us. She is responding well to the treatment." He paused. "It's common with this type of chemotherapy to have some symptoms, as is true in Clara's case, but she is doing very well."

"What can we expect in the coming days?" Zack's straightforward approach was needed at the moment, and she was glad to hear him ask that question.

"You know my former life as an Amish man and my decision to leave to practice medicine. What you might not now know is I turned against my faith because of the Amish ways of banishing those who leave the community for what I believed was a good cause. The bishop may not agree with our keeping Clara here if it comes down to that. I'm not saying it is going to happen, but just know it's a possibility."

He was watching Zack's response, and so was Lizzy. She'd never heard it put that way, so bluntly, but he was right about the bishop, and so was Zack.

"I appreciate your honesty, but I'll do whatever it takes to help Clara." Zack's demeanor changed from sadness to anger. "I would never have left her side, had the weather cooperated." The fact that Clara wasn't where they expected had taken them off guard at first, but now he seemed more like himself, ready to fight for his sister no matter what the cost, and she was right there with him.

"That's my thought as well. But what can we do at this point?" Lizzy had felt helpless as soon as she saw the empty bed, but now she was ready for action.

"Will you take us to her?" Zack asked before she had a chance to and stood.

"Of course. She should be ready to see you now, and I'll check her chart to see how she's doing." He paused and tapped his fingers on his desk. "Clara's been through enough. I hope the results of these last tests enable her to go home for Christmas."

Lizzy's stomach twisted at the words. She had such plans for Clara this year at Christmas.

Zack walked too fast for Lizzy to keep up, but she didn't mind, only wished she could walk faster. There was no one she wanted to see more than Clara right there and then, with Zack by her side.

When Clara saw Zack's grin as he stepped into the room, Lizzy watched his face glow as she said his name. Words were never sweeter.

"Oh, Clara!" Lizzy rushed to her and hugged her the minute Zack let go. "It's so good to see you."

Clara smiled slowly, taking them in, and spoke slowly. "We've been worried about you!"

Lizzy let out a breath. "You have no idea what we've been through up in that cabin all this time." Zack sat on the side of the bed, and Lizzy did the same. She put a hand on Clara's cheek and moved her hand up to straighten the kerchief she was wearing over her head. "Your hair."

"*Jah*, it was starting to fall out." Clara tried to smile, but it seemed forced.

Lizzy was too surprised to respond. For an Amish woman to cut her hair was against the *Ordnung*. It was difficult to accept even if it was for good reason. Lizzy didn't want to say more and make Clara uncomfortable about it, but it would take some getting used to.

Clara pulled off the scarf and showed her bald head. "I do miss my hair." Her sad tone and wan smile told Lizzy she was having a difficult time digesting the fact she was almost completely bald at twenty years of age. But her humble attitude kept the moment joyful.

Lizzy rubbed Clara's head. "What's important is that you're healing. The hair will grow back. Doc says the therapy is working."

"*Jah*, at the beginning it was exhausting, but the worst is over for now. At least I hope so." She turned to Zack, who had been quietly observing the conversation, enjoying their reunion. "You disappeared for a while there. What in the world happened to you two?" Her eyes were droopy, but she didn't let on that she was tired.

"We couldn't get through to the hospital and got caught up in traffic until I remembered the old cabin we used to go to." Zack paused when he saw Clara's eyes widen. But there was no way around it, and if Clara knew the truth, she'd probably be tickled to hear their stories.

"We finally settled down and just started living off the land and whatever food we could find." Lizzy paused, not knowing how much to reveal just yet. "Did you remember a man named Leonard who lived up there?"

"*Jah*, I remember him. Sweet man."

"I was scared of him when I was little."

Clara laughed. "Leonard doesn't have a mean bone in his body. He's been through a lot. Took good care of the cabin too."

"We found letters he wrote to some girl when he was in the service."

"*Jah*, that was sad. Especially for such a kind soul like Len. I don't remember seeing him much; he kept to himself." Clara seemed to be reliving the memories, and Lizzy was glad to see her distracted from all that went on in the hospital.

"Are we making you tired?" Lizzy didn't want Clara to even take a nap. Now that they were together again, they would spend a lot of time catching up.

"*Nee*, I'm afraid if I close my eyes, I won't see you again. I know it sounds silly, but that's just how I think about it."

"But we're here. I'll leave you alone. Sleep, and we'll talk more when you wake up." She hugged Clara and then Zack.

Clara fixed him with a pensive gaze. "I still can't believe you're here."

"Yeah, well, a little bird told me to come. I just didn't realize I'd be living in the cabin too, while I was here." Zack turned to Lizzy and smiled.

Clara tilted her head and stared at them. "What are you two hiding?"

Lizzy couldn't hold back the grin, and when she looked over at Zack, he was smiling too. "I sent Zack a letter asking him to come when you got so sick."

"You did?" Clara looked over at Zack, who was shaking his head, knowing he'd been duped into the situation. But he didn't seem to mind. "I'm so very glad that you did. You know what I wanted for Christmas? You two to be together."

Zack lifted his head and stared first at Clara and then at Lizzy. "I never guessed you'd be that sneaky, sis." He shook his head.

Lizzy hadn't seen Zack get embarrassed often. She was sure he had a lot of the same emotions she did. Now they had to figure out what to do with this unexpected union Clara had put together for them. She didn't want to make herself a fool. But even less did she want to be without Zack.

Now they were back to the hospital and soon the community. What would he say to everyone about where they'd been and what had happened with the two of them while they were away? She dreaded that part, especially since it would be his own *daed* addressing them. She couldn't get the stories out of her head that Zack had told her about the bishop. She wondered whether he would ever be called out on it if someone came forward.

A young man came walking in the door and stopped when he saw Zack. He turned to Clara and smiled. "Hello, I'm James. You must be Zack."

Zack's demeanor changed instantly. He stood a little

straighter and lost his smile. "Is there something you need?"

Clara spoke up. "Zack, James is a friend of mine. We've both gone through therapy. He's been a godsend to me. I'd like you to consider that."

Lizzy knew exactly what she meant. Zack was a protector when it came to his sister. "Nice to meet you, James. I'm—"

"Lizzy, I know all about you and your family. Clara and I have had plenty of time to get to know these things. I don't mean to intrude in your reunion, so to speak. I'm just very glad that you're all here together safe and sound." He ran a hand over his bald head.

Lizzy was impressed with James but at the same time didn't want to share her friend. It was a selfish thought, but after all they'd been through, she was selfish when it came to Clara.

The nurse came in and stopped short when she saw all of them in the room. "Visiting time is over, and I need to check in with Clara."

Lizzy wanted more time with James, but that would have to wait. She should be happy for Clara, but there was a lot to take into consideration involving Clara's friendship with him.

"*Ach*, you always have to spoil the party, Pinky." James grinned and made her smile too as she ran her hand over her pink scrubs. The Amish were always giving one another nicknames, and James seemed to be very good at it.

"Now, don't you start with me. You two will have plenty of time after I go over some things with Clara. And she needs more sleep than you." The nurse shooed him away and turned to begin with Clara.

Zack gave Clara a look. "Are you going to explain this to me?" But Lizzy was just glad to know someone at the hospital had been there for Clara when they couldn't get to her.

The nurse went over some of what they would be doing to boost Clara's strength and overcome any side effects she might have. As she walked past them, she smiled wide. "She's a wonderful patient. I'm going to miss her."

Her words gave Lizzy the hope Clara would be home soon, eating the Christmas turkey, but she wouldn't count her chickens until they hatched. And if she couldn't come home, Lizzy would bring Christmas to Clara.

Chapter Thirty-Two

Two days and counting. Zack found that he wanted Clara home for Christmas as much as Lizzy did. In fact, he really didn't care where they were as long as they were together. But he knew how important it was to Lizzy. He'd asked every day how Clara was healing and gotten the same answer. One day at a time, and they would release her when the doctor ordered them to. It was ridiculous to keep asking. The doctor would tell them.

A knock on Clara's hospital door made him freeze. He had avoided seeing the bishop, the name Zack used instead of *father*, and wasn't surprised when he was told the bishop was expecting him. He was waiting for another visit by one of the deacons, and this time, he would have to go.

The tapping of fingers created the same anxiety he'd had as a kid when the bishop was around. He took a deep breath as the curtain moved and his brother Jonas walked in and around the curtain where Clara rested peacefully. It didn't set well with Zack. He didn't want to start up with his brother while Clara was finally resting.

Jonas's six-and-a-half-foot stature was just enough to make Zack look up a notch. He'd always hated that. At least he was taller than Eli. Size, girth, and strength were important in their family. Their *daed* believed in corporal punishment regardless of their ages. Zack wondered who had taken his place once he was gone. No one had been spared but their little sister, Clara.

"If you're staying, I'll leave." Zack hated to act like a coward, but he didn't want to disturb Clara.

Zack took a step forward. Jonas held up a large hand. "We need to have a conversation."

Jonas was a taciturn man. When Zack looked into his eyes, all the years growing up came back. Most he didn't want to remember. A few scattered times were all right. But things had changed, and his brother didn't intimidate him.

"Fine, we'll talk, but not in here." Zack nodded to where Clara was. He walked past Jonas and left the door open for him to follow. "So what is it?"

Jonas let out a breath through his nose and set his eyes on Zack. "Ever since you came to the *haus* that day, I've done a lot of thinking." He paused as if searching for the words. "I want things right for Clara."

Zack scoffed. "So do I." It seemed like a big deal for Jonas to confess his concern about Clara, unlike what Zack did, believing it was obviously the right thing to do. "Where are you going with this?"

"Don't get me wrong. This is about Clara. Not you. *Daed* wants to see you, and I'll make sure he does."

"I'll see him on my own accord if and when I want to. This isn't about us—not you, the bishop, or anything else." Zack brushed past him, bumping into his shoulder. When he sized up how close they were in height, he smiled. Maybe he was catching up to Jonas after all.

"What were you doing up there at the cabin with Lizzy?" Jonas knew what would hit the hardest, but Zack wouldn't take the bait. He expected it. Why would he think anything had changed?

"Nothing I shouldn't, except keeping us alive in a snowstorm. Any other questions?" He glared at Jonas and then turned again to get away from him. There was nothing left to say.

"That's not what's been said around the community. You should know better than to be alone with her. *Daed*'s gonna have a heyday with that." He grinned.

It was all Zack could do not to smack him one. And if Jonas said anything else, especially about Lizzy, he would. Zack was about to open the curtain when Jonas spoke again. "She's my sister too, Zack."

Zack looked over his shoulder, waiting for Jonas to talk or remember what he was trying to say. "Then act like it."

With that, he opened the curtain and shut it behind him. When he returned a while later, his brother was gone.

"Visiting time is over." The nurse stepped in, closed the curtain behind her, and bent over Clara, straightening her blankets.

"I guess I'll be on my way." Zack didn't want to leave just yet, so he started in with the pleasantries. "Is it still freezing outside?"

"Not as bad. But don't hurry. I told your brother he should come a little earlier. Clara seems to sleep better when you're around."

Zack knew it was just a nice comment. Ellen had become a little more professional since their first meeting. "Thanks, but I think it's the medicine. Will she be out of here for Christmas?"

"I would sure like to think so, with so many people praying for her. She must really like Christmas."

"Nobody likes it as much as her. Ever since she was a kid, she kicked it up a notch around Christmas."

"I hope it works out for all of you." She turned to leave but then stopped. "She's the closest to an angel I've ever known."

He grinned. "That's a good description. Thanks for taking care of her."

"It's been my pleasure. Get some sleep."

He watched her leave and thought about how many days Clara had been there. He couldn't keep track, but he honestly felt she would heal and beat this poison, whatever it was.

Now it was time to go see the bishop. He wouldn't relent until he gave Zack what-for, so they might as well get it over with. It would show courage if he initiated it instead of his brother dragging him.

He watched Clara sleep peacefully, more so than he'd seen her do for a while. He listened to her breath and watched her eyelids flutter, wondering what she was dreaming about.

Then he heard Lizzy's boots clipping along. He knew her gait, and most people in the hospital wore soft-soled shoes. When she came around the corner into the room, he was smiling.

She stopped and stared. "Why the grin?" She laid her cape on an empty chair and glanced at Clara.

"It's just good to see you. My brother paid a visit."

Lizzy sucked in a breath.

"I'm going to see the bishop."

She pressed her hand against her chest.

"It's fine. I have a few things to say to him." He kissed her on the forehead.

"What was that for?" She didn't seem to know if she should smile or frown.

"I love you, Lizzy Ryder." He was ready to face his father, but he needed something to make this less stressful, and kissing Lizzy did exactly that.

"Let me come with you." Lizzy took her cape and started wrapping it around her shoulders.

"But you just got here." Zack liked the idea of having Lizzy with him, but he had his doubts about letting her tag along. He had no idea what the bishop might say.

"I won't take no for an answer." And with that Lizzy headed out to the hallway.

They walked silently through the hospital corridors. Every step he took brought Zack closer to the bishop. Unlike when he was a kid, he wasn't scared. The prayer that circled around in his head pushed the negative thoughts away so he could commune with God.

When he got to the rental car, he noticed the handle was gone. "No…" He didn't want his family to think he was too cowardly for this meeting. He had to find it. Lizzy watched as he used his bare hands to search for it through the freezing snow and found it under the driver's door area. He let out a sigh of relief, said a quick praise, and opened the door for Lizzy before jumping into the car.

The drive seemed longer than usual, but the streets were still full of snow, and large drifts were scooped to the road-sides, leaving narrow passageways. The closer he got to the farm he grew up on, the faster his heart pumped. He let out a breath and prepared himself for whatever came of this, and then walked up to the house.

"Say a prayer for me, will you?" He squeezed Lizzy's hand as he stepped out of the car.

He was about to knock on the door when his *mamm* came to the door. "Oh, Zack, it's good to see you, son." She patted his cheek and let him inside. "How are you? You look well." She studied him as if she'd never seen him before, until he heard the clomping of the bishop's boots in the distance.

"I'm well. The city's given me a lot of opportunities." He didn't want to burden her with the difficulties he'd had there. As he looked around the room, Zack realized this place was probably worse than his time in the city, just in very different ways.

"So you like it there. That's good, if that's where your heart is."

"It's an interesting place to live but not to grow a family."

And that was it, in a nutshell. The Amish community wouldn't work for him, and neither did the city. Something in between would be a good fit. Strange that talking with his mother had brought him to that realization.

The sound of the bishop's boots brought out the same anxiety he'd had as a boy, but not near what it used to. He wasn't scared of him like he was then.

"Zack, your *daed* isn't himself. Be patient." *Mamm* turned quickly when the bishop entered the room.

Looking at him now, Zack wondered what he'd been so scared of. This was the closure he needed.

"Zack, I didn't know if you'd come, and so soon." The bishop tugged on his long white beard and studied him. He motioned for him to come to his office with a wave of his hand.

Zack took his time following, rebelling against the way he used to run in to see him when he was young. This man didn't have the same power over him as the man he'd grown up with. Zack was an adult, able to stand alone for himself. He was prepared for anything.

The bishop sat in the tall chair, one a king might use, with the high back and velvet seat cushion. "Do you know why you're here, Zack?"

"Do you want an honest answer or what you want to hear?" That was the way it went when he was a kid. Say what he wanted you to and take responsibility, even if you hadn't done anything wrong. Someone had to take the blame, and being the oldest, it was usually him. He just never knew for sure if that was why.

"I left the community and live in sin. Is that about right?" Zack tried not to be flippant; it wouldn't get him anywhere, but he wouldn't hold back the truth like he used to.

"Tell me, what are you here for?" The bishop's eyes flickered, as if he'd had a shock.

"You just asked me that. Maybe you didn't like the answer. I'm just trying to give you what you want so I can leave here without any ramifications following me. I have no intention of living here, only to see Clara through."

The bishop blinked rapidly. "You did something you shouldn't."

"What are you talking about? Lizzy and the cabin?" Zack was honestly confused. The bishop wasn't anything like he used to be. But Zack didn't trust him enough to empathize.

The bishop leaned back, and his hand twitched as he moved it down. He wiped the perspiration on his forehead and moved forward. "*Gott* hates haughty eyes, lying tongues, shedding innocent blood, and a heart that schemes."

Zack remembered the passages when his father labeled

them according to what sin he believed one of the children had done.

"Feet quick to run into evil, false witness stirs up dissension. You reap what you sow." Sweat trickled down the bishop's cheeks as he went on. It was right out of one of his sermons, without any words of his own. There was something very wrong.

"I don't know what else to say. Maybe I should go."

When he'd come back not long ago, the bishop had seemed pretty much the same as he remembered. But this man was not like his father.

The bishop stopped momentarily and looked at him, and for a moment Zack thought maybe he had come back to his senses. But his eyes glazed over and he began again.

"Fear of the Lord is the beginning of wisdom." His voice was scratchy, and his eyelids drooped. He'd lost his power in Zack's eyes, and to his surprise, the hate went out of him. His dad was too far gone to let Zack fear or hate him anymore.

Chapter Thirty-Three

Lizzy watched Zack walk to his car, where she sat waiting for him. She wrung her hands with apprehension. She knew how the bishop could be, especially since Zack had told her about his childhood with him. Her own *daed* was protective, but aside from being a little grumpy, he was a good *daed* and husband. After being away from them, she appreciated her family even more.

He sat and unzipped his jacket. "Is it hot in here?"

"*Nee*, it's cold." She'd told him to turn the car off, thinking it would be a long visit, but apparently not. He couldn't have spent more than half an hour. This wasn't a good sign. "How did it go?"

He shook his head and stared sadly at the *haus* where he'd grown up. His lower lip shook a little, and he turned away. "Anyway, it's done. That's all I can do at this point. He's not in a good place. Something's wrong."

She pinched her brows together. "What do you mean? I'm curious because people have been talking about him. Not in a bad way so much as he just doesn't seem himself."

Zack had been gone long enough not to notice. "I put the bishop out of my mind as much as possible. My family had no way of reaching me, and I didn't want to come home, and that's the only thing they would talk to me about if I did contact them."

He started the engine and headed out the gravel roundabout driveway. "Do you want me to take you home?"

"*Jah*. You're welcome to come in. It's been a long day." Lizzy sincerely hoped he would, and she wouldn't let him get away easily if he said no. Besides that, she wanted to be with him. They'd learned a lot about each other during their time in the cabin, and she didn't want it to end. Neither of them had said anything about what was next, except for the kiss.

"I should talk to your parents to explain what happened and why we were gone so long. I'm sure they were worried."

Lizzy felt for him but hoped her *daed* would understand Zack's situation and make him comfortable. His protective side usually popped up when boys tried to court her. Her brother, Luke, was the opposite, wanting her to settle down and start a family so their kids could grow up together.

"What will you do from here?" Her mind was turning with ideas. She didn't want to speak without asking her parents first, but she wanted to open their *haus* to him, at least for the night.

"Go back to the hospital. I'm hoping they'll give us some good news if I'm there to bother them enough." He smiled in the way that told her he was feeling okay. It was just one of the many idiosyncrasies she'd learned about him and had come to like.

"What do you think about James, this young man that Clara has been spending time with?"

"I'm not sure. He seems to be a likable guy, but I haven't had a chance to talk to him alone. I'd like to see how he is without Clara around." He shook his head.

"Hmmm, I don't know if I should be happy or skeptical. Maybe a little of both?"

"It's nice she has someone who can share what they're going through together. That could be all it's about between them."

He chuckled. "I suppose you're right. Just because two people spend time together doesn't mean they're a couple."

Lizzy froze. How should she take that? Was he insinuating the same thing about them? Maybe she should be prepared either way. Her stomach soured, unsettling with each thought that went through her head.

Zack parked the car and turned it off. "I should go back to the hospital."

Lizzy could smell her mother's cooking, making her stomach growl. "Are you sure? My *mamm* and *daed* will want to thank you for helping me find shelter during the storm."

"I've taken enough of your time that you should be spending with your parents." It had started snowing again, and the flakes were falling faster, almost as if a huge bucket had thrown them down from heaven.

"It's no bother. They realize we had no other option but to stay together in that cabin. They'll be glad to hear how you took care of me while we were gone."

"You did a good job of keeping us fed, considering what you had to work with."

"I guess we're a pretty good team." She paused and waited for his answer, hoping it leaned toward what she wanted it to be. The more she thought about it, the more anxious she got.

He smiled. "I don't want to intrude. Your parents will want you alone."

"Are you feeling bad because you left the community, or is that just an excuse?"

He looked out the windshield, watching the flakes increasing in number. "Probably a little of both. You can do better than me."

She frowned. "That's for me to decide, isn't it?"

He shrugged. "You tell me."

Lizzy didn't like his placid way of deciding what she thought was an important question. Then she thought about what it would be like to walk into the crowd of Amish at singing with Zack by her side. The girls would sigh, and the boys would scoff, knowing all the girls' eyes were on him. It would be a nice way to let others know she was taken, which was what she wanted to be.

"Come to singing with me, and we'll see."

Zack shook his head and was about to respond, but she beat him to it.

"You don't have to stay long. It would be nice to have you to go, though." She tilted her head just enough to get his attention and saw him smile a little.

"You really want me to go, don't you? Why?"

Lizzy didn't know how much to say. Her first thought was to show everyone that Zack was alive and well. That he had made a life for himself outside the community. Even though it wasn't as clean-cut as most Amish were, he'd left and prospered while he was gone. Another reason was for him to see he could live outside the city and the community and be successful with what he did. But what was the in-between? That would be something he'd have to figure out.

"If it's that important to you, I will go." He grinned and watched her climb out of the car.

"It's good to have you back, Zack. Whether you want to be here or not." It was quiet for a minute. "You know, Clara's in good hands at the hospital, and hopefully we'll be taking her home tomorrow. You could stay here tonight."

Zack pursed his lips. "Well, I wasn't going to tell you this, but she's going to be released tomorrow, if all goes right. Just in time for Christmas." He was beaming as he said it.

He held up a hand. "No, don't tell anyone, and I don't want you to get too excited; things could change. But that's what I dragged out of the nurse."

Lizzy rolled her eyes. "The one who flirts with you?"

"I think she's gotten over me. Let's not lose the moment here. Your job is to get things ready before word gets out. Due to her condition, they could call it off, and she'd stay at the hospital. But I wanted you to be prepared just in case."

She was starting to get cold standing outside the car. "Come in and get warm before you go."

Her pleading eyes told him he had to say yes.

"Looks like my *bruder* is here," she commented as they walked by Luke's buggy on the way to the house. From what she could remember, Zack and Luke got along well.

"How is Luke these days?"

"His wife is expecting. She has had some hardships now and then, but all is well." She knew Zack would understand what that meant. Mental issues were difficult to diagnose, and natural remedies didn't always work, so some of the Amish had a difficult time in social situations.

"He's a good man, and probably a good husband as well." Zack said it with a straight face, almost solemn. "I wonder if that would be where I was at if I'd taken a different path." He kept his head down, and she wondered if he was regretting his past.

"There's always new beginnings." She glanced at him, smiling his way, and took the last step to her *haus*.

When she stepped on the wood porch, her *mamm* opened the door and then hugged her tight. "*Ach*, Lizzy! Now that you're back, I never like to see you go."

Her *daed* walked in from the kitchen holding a plate full of apple pie. He set down his goodies and hugged her for good measure, even though she'd returned home days ago.

Luke stood in the doorway with his arms crossed. "You had us worried, you know." He grabbed Lizzy and nodded to Zack. She hadn't seen Luke since she and Zack got back.

"I know, I'm sorry. We were stuck at the old cabin."

Zack jumped in to fill Luke in and to clarify what had gone on. "We were on our way to see Clara and couldn't get around the traffic. We ended up in the hills where the streets were gravel and less congested."

"*Jah*, there were a lot of accidents. We were lucky to make it there and back unscathed."

"But that's not to say that the cabin did so well. A fallen branch punched a hole in the roof." Zack shook his head.

"And then there were the letters that we found. We think they were from Leonard to his girl." Lizzy had liked that part of their time there.

"Is he still around? Great guy, but you couldn't get a peep out of him." Luke half-smiled, half-laughed. Lizzy couldn't understand why everyone knew about him but her.

"Tell us everything." Luke's wife, Neva, came in from the kitchen and sat next to Luke. Her tummy had grown quite a bit since Lizzy had seen her last. They both had the same bright-blue eyes. "I liked that place. What ever happened to it?"

"It wasn't in good shape, but we were lucky to have it. Anyone who uses that place had better love the old ways. It doesn't have the luxuries we do now. We about froze ourselves."

The more they talked, the better Lizzy felt about the decisions they'd made. She'd already answered questions from her *mamm* and *daed,* and it seemed everyone was just glad they were back safe.

"How is Clara?" Lizzy's *mamm* asked Zack.

"Better, Mrs. Ryder, much better." He grinned at Lizzy, who was fervently hoping Clara would be out in time for Christmas. "I saw her just before I went to the bishop's."

The room was quiet until Zack spoke. "I sense there is more going on than I found out at the bishop's when I visited him today."

"*Jah*, the community's elders will be meeting about it, if you want to go." That was something Luke would do, and Zack might have at one time, but not with his current standing.

"I haven't earned the privilege, but I would like to know what's decided. I have my mother and brothers to think of."

"I'm sorry, son. That's not a good homecoming for you." Ray had definitely made a turnaround about Zack. He had good reason not to when they took off in Zack's rental car.

"You're welcome to stay here, Zack." Lizzy offered because no one else had. Even though she knew the answer.

He looked at the clock on the mantel and stood. "Thanks for the offer, but I'll make do."

He shook Ray's hand, and Mrs. Ryder gave him a piece of pie wrapped in a hand towel.

"*Danke*." He walked to the door and nodded to all of them, with a wink at Lizzy. A warm sensation came over her, and she wondered what *Gott* wanted for their relationship together.

Maybe this Christmas she'd find out.

Chapter Thirty-Four

After fighting with the traffic as the streets started to freeze, Zack stopped in at the singing. The heat of the gas lamps flickered as youth aged sixteen and up poured into the room. Zack wasn't sure he was ready for this, remembering back to when he was part of the singles group of Amish who would find others to fit in with and then eat and sing for hours. He watched as Lizzy commanded the room, greeting everyone she passed. When he was their age, it seemed silly to find your "fit" with certain groups and to find someone to marry this way. But then he thought back to his relationship in Philly and rethought the situations.

Lizzy took his hand and addressed a young brunette with a question. She was very good at small talk and get-togethers like this. She mingled with the "higher" group that was less conservative, which he appreciated. "You do remember Zack, don't you?" She would ask as if they knew him, and most did, surprisingly enough without judgment. He appreciated that; it kept the situation from becoming awkward.

Luke bumped into him with a grin. "Having fun yet?"

"Thank God you're here. Aren't we too old for this?" They scanned the room together, and Zack actually found a few close to their age.

"For the most part. Lots of the in-between help with food and drinks for the younger set. Come with me."

Zack nudged Lizzy and pointed to Luke. He couldn't tell whether she approved of him not mingling more, but he wasn't one for small talk.

Luke took him to the table where the drinks were and looked over the variety that was available. One thing the Amish always did well was food and drinks.

"Zack...Zack Schrock." Sam, an old friend, held out his hand to Zack.

"Sam, it's good to see you, my friend. How have you been?" Zack realized he couldn't use his smooth talking with the Amish. They were down-to-earth, honest people, for the most part. Conversations were of more simple things like the weather and what crop brought in the most revenue. Again, Zack wondered what it would be like to have the best of both worlds.

"You back visiting from the city?" Sam grabbed a couple of oatmeal cookies and waited comfortably for Zack's reply.

Zack looked around the room to see the teens laughing—the guys one-upping each other to impress the girls, and the girls giggling as they sat on a table letting their legs swing. He decided he didn't want to talk about his job in the city. He just wanted to talk.

"I've been at the hospital most of the time. We got caught up in the storm and were stuck up at the old cabin for a few days."

"I heard you were in town but didn't know about the cabin. Had to be awful cold. We took the worst of it down here too. Couldn't even get outside the *haus* for a couple days. But it was kinda nice for the family to be together without any chores to be done. Just a lot of eating, talking, and playing some games together as a family."

And there it was, what Zack wanted: to live with the Amish traditions and beliefs but not in a community to answer to.

But is that even possible? What would that look like, and where could I go to get that kind of life?

He listened to Sam and watched the teens playing games, remembering their summer volleyball and baseball games—all good thoughts, if not for the bishop's temper and parenting, if it could be called that.

The games were picked up and put away, and then supper was served. Macaroni salad, meat loaf, and casserole were served along with plenty of other sides. Homemade bread, coleslaw, and pickled eggs were some of the many dishes passed around the tables full of homemade goods.

Zack remembered participating in all these events, but his favorite was the singing itself, when such a large group would sing long and loud, their voices in the German dialect filling the room. The adults took seats on opposite ends of the room. The barrier was removed, and the residents split the farmhouse, making a large, open area the length of the kitchen, which seated around a hundred. The young men came in and sat on one side, and the girls sat on the other.

Zack sat next to the men, and Lizzy sat with the women. Sam's youngest came over, looked at his dad, and then at Zack. Then he hopped on Zack's lap and leaned against his chest. He was all of about three years old but definitely didn't have any of the stranger-danger issues the kids in the city had, and he entertained himself with Zack's car keys until he nodded off. Zack glanced over to Lizzy, who was smiling at him.

Once everyone was seated, the leader stood and led them with the first notes of a song. Their voices all but shook the walls as young and old joined together in song. The girls took turns leading from the songbook, and the young men switched to other lively tunes during the remaining hour. The songs in German brought back the words Zack had sung so many times in his first language.

The heat of the lamps made him sweat, and he gingerly handed the sleeping young boy on his lap to Sam. "I need some air."

"*Jah*, he's a warm little guy." Sam took over, and Zack stood to take a quick break outside. The cold wind was harsh but felt good after two hours of singing with so many people in one room together. He'd forgotten all this, maybe on purpose, because he remembered how much he'd enjoyed it back when.

He watched Lizzy through a window as she laughed and handed out trays of cookies, popcorn, and chips, with drinks all around. The hot cocoa looked good, but he saw her make herself some hot tea. She was used to all of this, whereas he'd lost sight of it and wasn't sure he wanted it again. A visit now and then would be nice, but probably not doable as long as his father was the bishop.

Lizzy popped outside and stood in the dark, snowy night with him. "It feels good out here, but you're missing the best part."

"What's that?"

"Remember the Slow Moving Vehicle sign on the buggies?" She slowly walked over to where some of the buggies were and pointed. There were all different ones with pictures of bucks or hunting club logos on them.

He grinned and took his time looking at them, appreciating their creativity. "I don't remember anything like this."

"It's different now." She folded her arms over her chest and shivered.

"Let's get you inside. This has worn me out."

"You should get some rest, but I'll be at home in the kitchen." She smiled widely, and he knew exactly why.

"You're going to start baking, aren't you?"

"*Jah*, I went through *Mamm*'s pantry and picked up a couple things I needed. I want to have a nice basket of goodies for Clara when we pick her up tomorrow." Her cheeks turned a shade of pink, showing her excitement. This was what she loved, to be here in the community. As much as he wanted to be with her, he didn't know if that would ever happen.

"Did you have much time to talk to her this afternoon?" Lizzy seemed to get more information out of Clara than he did. But that didn't surprise him. They had always been close.

"*Jah*, until her new friend popped in." Lizzy smiled her approval, but he wasn't as convinced he liked this guy.

"Do you know anything about him? I heard the nurse say he's a cancer survivor and has spent a lot of time with Clara."

"Well, that was quick. Did all of this happen just while we were gone?"

"Sounds like they've spent a lot of time together since she was admitted. It's probably kept her mind off things."

Zack paused and stared straight ahead. "I'm not sure I like that. We don't even know this guy."

"I wasn't sure at first, either, but when I heard about it...Clara's a grown woman. We need to give him a chance. He was there when we couldn't be." She shrugged.

"So you're okay with this?" Zack stopped and saw that her shawl wasn't keeping her warm. He brought her close to him.

Lizzy didn't answer right away, but then she did in a whisper. "*Jah*, I am."

He felt her shiver. "Let's go back inside and get you warmed up."

As they made their way back to the house, some of the young men and women were pairing off. Some went to the barn for privacy to talk, and others stayed in the house to chat a little longer. It all took him back to the way things used to be. He had mixed feelings, some good but most bad. As he opened the door for Lizzy, he decided he wouldn't let the past control him anymore. God had given him a second chance. Clara's journey had brought out some good things as well. He never would have come if she hadn't needed him. And as far as things went with Lizzy, he didn't know. Only time would tell.

Chapter Thirty-Five

"MAMM, DAED!" LUKE's shrill voice brought Lizzy running to the family room. He met her halfway down the stairs and wiped the sweat from his brow. "Where is everyone?"

"*Daed* took *Mamm* to town. What's wrong?" Lizzy could honestly say she'd never seen him so rattled. It just wasn't his demeanor to get riled up. Then it clicked. "The baby!"

"*Jah*, you know how Neva is, so weak and all. I need the doc and for you to stay with her for me." He was walking fast and furiously, making her worry even more. "Lloyd is there with her, but I wanted *Mamm* to see if she's really in labor."

"Calm down, Luke. You're not doing her any good if you're upset." The only two times she saw him really upset was with Neva, so this was expected.

"Can you watch her for me, Liz?" He looked into her eyes for a moment and jogged out the door and to his buggy. He hadn't called her "Liz" since she was a girl and the last time Neva went to the hospital and lost their baby. She could see why he was so worried now.

Lizzy grabbed her jacket and ran after him, but his long strides left her behind. "I'm coming. I'm here." She trudged through the snow as quickly as she could without falling, but the mounds *Daed* shoveled off the driveway made it hard to move around with the way Luke parked.

Once in the buggy she shut the door and held on for what she knew would be a wild ride. Luke was already a fast driver, but with his wife and baby at stake she would have to hang on.

He stayed on the wheel tracks to keep from getting stuck, but it kept him from going faster.

"Why didn't you use the Fisers' phone in their barn? You could have gotten ahold of the doc by now."

"All I could think about was getting here to find someone to stay with Neva." He took a corner that had her tightening her grip on the door handle.

"You're not doing us any good with your driving like this. Slow down, Luke. You'll get there." She let out a breath when he slowed but started up again almost as fast as he was going before. "How long has she been in labor?"

"I don't know…it might be something else. And what gets my goat more than anything is that she doesn't tell me." He hit the dashboard once, hard.

"Lucas Jordan! If you don't calm down, I'm gonna push you out of this buggy and drive to Neva without you."

He pursed his lips, angry at first, and then leaned back but didn't slow down very much. "It just feels like I'm living it all over again. Like I was in that godforsaken hospital that I hate and with the English, doing things their way." He ran a hand over his blond hair and put his hat back on.

"If you don't want the hospital, go to Doc. What happened last time doesn't mean it will happen again, Luke."

"I know, you're right. It's just hard to get out of my head. What makes it harder is that she didn't tell me about this earlier. We might have been able to something sooner if the doc knew."

"Luke, you can't blame her for that. Most here still go with the old ways. Doc hasn't lost many babies." She couldn't believe they were even talking about this; it was only making him more upset.

"We're almost there." She said it as much as to slow him down as to get into the *haus* and see Neva. "You go and do what you need to, and I'll check on her."

"I'm going to the Fisers to use the phone and be right back." He'd hardly stopped the buggy before he was off again.

Lizzy walked quickly to the door and made her way to their bedroom. It was a homey color of light blue, not a common color, but Lizzy liked the change.

"Lizzy, thank *Gott* you're here. I need your help." Neva's long dark hair was messed, and she looked distraught. "Help me to the bathroom, please."

Lizzy shrugged off her coat and moved quickly to help Neva slowly find the strength to push herself up.

"How long have you been having contractions, Neva?" The walk was so slow it was all Lizzy could do not to carry her.

"A couple days. It wasn't much the first day, and I didn't want to worry Luke. It got worse real quick this morning."

Lizzy wanted to tell her she needed to let people help her, more than just Luke, but now was not the time.

"Anything else bothering you?"

"I don't eat much or go to the bathroom. Tired a lot too, but that's probably the baby." She stumbled, then steadied herself with Lizzy's help.

"Doc will figure it out. Can you manage in the bathroom?"

Lizzy would be there either way. It was more a comment than a question.

While Lizzy waited, she put new sheets on the bed and then stood by the bathroom. Then she heard noise out front, sure it was the doc and Luke at the least. Once their families knew what was going on, the *haus* would be full.

The bathroom door opened as slowly as Neva walked. Lizzy hated to put Neva back in that bed, but at least the sheets were clean and fresh. "Do you feel a little better?"

"A little." She sighed. "Really, I don't feel good at all." Her eyes teared up, and she looked away. "What's wrong with my baby?"

"Oh, Neva, you don't know that anything is wrong. It's just been a hard time for you. But that doesn't mean something's wrong."

"I don't feel that way. It seems it wasn't meant to be. You hear about women like that, you know. Something's wrong with them, like me." Her shiny eyes held back the tears. "I feel like I'm letting Luke down."

Lizzy patted the bed, and Neva took slow steps to one side of the bed and let out a long breath. Lizzy picked up a brush on the bedside table.

"Luke thinks the world of you, Neva. No matter what happens, he'll be there for you." She squeezed her hand just as they heard footsteps coming up the steps. She tied Neva's hair up in a bun and set the brush aside.

"*Danke*, Lizzy." Her face was drained of color; she must be exhausted.

"I hear Luke. Get comfortable." Before Neva could finish getting settled, Luke walked through the door.

"Doc's here. And everybody else." He paused and looked

at her. "You and the baby are going to be fine." It was a bold statement, but that was the attitude they had to have.

Luke rushed over to touch Neva's cheek. "It's gonna be all right."

"Well, how are you, Neva?" Doc set his bag on the bed and took out a stethoscope.

"Is the baby going to be all right?" She kept her eyes on Doc and waited.

Doc moved the scope around her chest and stomach and then turned to her. "The pulse rate is *gut*. Now we need to see what the bleeding is about."

"I feel like I'm gonna faint. I'm not hungry. I worry for my baby, Doc."

"Because of your history, I want to take every precaution. Let's get you to the hospital." As stubborn as Doc was, he must have seen something about her that he knew was beyond his skills.

Luke leaned over and whispered, then lifted her up. "You going with us, Lizzy? While I was at the Fisers' I called a Mennonite neighbor to drive us. I was worried we'd end up at the hospital again."

"*Jah*, sure." Lizzy suddenly wished Zack was there. They'd spent so much time in the hospital, it would seem lonely without him.

Neva and Luke went down and gathered the essentials. Two cars drove up at the same time.

Zack stepped out of his car and stared at Lizzy. "Anybody need a ride in my car?"

Lizzy clapped her hands and ran to him. "*Danke*, it would seem out of place for you not to be there."

"When I saw your brother driving all over creation, I figured something big was going on."

"*Jah*, it's the baby. And maybe Neva too. We're not sure. Just praying."

"Tell me about it." They got in his car, and Lizzy told him what she knew, glad he was there to listen.

"I wish we weren't going to the hospital again."

"I'd advise going to the one closest one."

"Lead the way, and they'll follow." Lizzy went numb; it was the only way to keep from breaking down. There were just too many health problems, and she felt vulnerable. The only good part of it was spending time with Zack.

As soon as they pulled into the emergency room, Neva was whisked away. Luke paced in the waiting area with her and Zack, and Doc tried to gather some information.

Lizzy's prayer was one of frustration, asking *Gott* why there was so much illness in her family, and why now.

When the doctor came over, Lizzy could hardly stand listening to another diagnosis or procedure. There had to be some good news this time.

"Neva is doing fine. If I didn't know better, I'd think it was good old stress. Keep her occupied until this baby decides to come."

"What about the baby?" Luke was pale, with dark rings under his eyes. Too much had happened to this family, and they were running out of steam.

"We'll take good care of both of them. We want your wife to be here to raise the child."

The doctor caught Luke's eye. "You can do this, be the encouraging husband I know you are."

"So it sounds worse than is it?" Luke didn't have his usual energy and quickness with words.

The doctor paused and looked Luke in the eyes. "Possibly

the worst that could happen is that we'll have to administer oxytocin to induce labor."

Luke nodded reluctantly and went in to Neva's room. She let out a breath, and Luke went to her side and held her tight. "It's all right. You and the baby are going to be just fine."

Chapter Thirty-Six

LIZZY YAWNED AND stretched. She blinked twice before she realized there were just a few days until Christmas. She sat straight up in bed, pulled off her quilt, and set her feet on the cold wood floor. Her handmade robe warmed her as she got ready for one of her favorite days of the year. Preparing meals that her family loved to eat was a passion of hers. There was nothing better than creating something just a little bit different each time so as to keep the dish from being too predictable. Making the exact same thing was boring.

When she was washed and dressed, she started toward the kitchen. At the top of the stairway, she inhaled many different aromas, including syrup and bacon. Lizzy and her *mamm* each had their own portions of the meal to make, and that didn't start until the cows were milked and every family member was present.

As she walked through the family room, she checked the grandfather clock her *daed* had made. Then she saw her *mamm* cooking away. *Mamm* was so focused on her work, she hadn't even noticed that Lizzy was in the kitchen.

"What's all the fuss?" Lizzy walked up behind her, and *Mamm* jumped, putting a hand over her heart.

"Oh, Lizzy. We have so much to do. And since when did you get up after the rooster crows?" She wiped her salt-and-pepper hair across her forehead and flipped the bacon.

She turned to see Lizzy in the dress she'd made and had been waiting to wear today.

"The dark blue looks good on you." *Mamm* stood back and nodded her approval. "Zack will be sure to like it."

"*Ach, Mamm.*" Lizzy scanned the room to avoid the comment, but her *mamm* was probably right. Lizzy found a single egg in the icebox. "I'll go fetch some eggs. Although I thought we had plenty." She had her baking recipes and considered she might not have enough for tomorrow.

"I set some aside to give to Luke. His chicken coop was ransacked by some coyotes."

A thought went through her head. After she got some baking done, she would have a reason to go to Zack's after taking the eggs to Luke. But that wasn't the only reason. She wanted to see Neva, who was doing much better since coming home from the hospital.

After Lizzy returned from the chicken coop with some eggs, she gathered her baking ingredients and got everything in order on the counter. She had a special way of keeping everything she needed at her fingertips to make the process go smoothly. After breakfast she'd be making pecan pie, lemon snowflake cookies, Pennsylvania Dutch butterscotch pudding, caramel corn, and popcorn, with cherry triangles to top things off. With company coming, this would be a good assortment for both children and adults.

Mamm came over to see what she'd chosen to make and nodded. "You should open your own shop one day."

Lizzy grunted. "Spoken like a true *mamm*. There are better bakers than me, that's for sure."

"*Hmmm*, but you always find something different to

make your recipes stand out." She folded her arms over her chest. "Ingredients you won't ever tell your *mamm*."

Lizzy chuckled. "It just comes to me, and I experiment with it until it tastes the way I want it to. Most of the time, I don't write it down. But then neither do you."

Lizzy grinned. There was no better way to bond with family than in the kitchen. As she and her mamm worked on breakfast, Lizzy was thinking about too many other life events, and she had a hard time concentrating. She'd never guessed that Zack being back would affect her so strongly.

When Lizzy had heard about Clara's condition, she thought it her responsibility to tell him. The bishop's breakdown told her she'd done the right thing. She had noticed there was something wrong with him earlier, but it was hard to present the information to anyone. He was the most important person in the body of their community. And no one had come forth to say anything about his condition, at least that she knew of. No one spoke of it until Zack came. He validated what she'd been thinking all along.

"Now then, tell me about Zack." Her *mamm* said.

"What about Zack?" She didn't want to give more information than necessary, so her words would be few. She wasn't being rude; she just didn't have any answers. She could only hope she and Zack might end up together.

"You seem to be more than friends nursing Clara along."

Mamm's direct comment didn't give her a good way to redirect the conversation, so she took a moment to think of the right words. "Why do you say that?" She kept her eyes on the pancake batter she was mixing.

"*Ach*, the way you look at him and touch his arm and

smile a little more." *Mamm* didn't look up, just kept frying the bacon and then moved it to the plate on the counter.

"I guess I didn't notice."

Mamm laid the tongs in the sink, washed her hands, and gazed at Lizzy. "It seems strange that I would notice these things before you. Are you serious about Zack or are you just taking in the time you have before he leaves again?" Her eyes never moved, and her stare was unwavering. She wanted an answer.

But then so did Lizzy. "I honestly don't know. And I can't tell you anything that I don't understand myself." She broke eye contact and looked at her black boots, which needed tending. "I'm not trying to be difficult."

"I can see that. And that's why I'm a bit scared." *Mamm* began to stir a pot boiling on the stove. "And if I am, you must be too."

Her *mamm*'s sweet smile helped Lizzy let out a deep breath. "*Jah*, I guess I am. I didn't want this to happen."

"It's a serious concern. Marrying in the community is one thing. Marrying an *Englischer* would have many obstacles. Are you prepared for that?" *Mamm* tilted her head and waited patiently for Lizzy to reply.

"I don't know how to answer that. But when I do, you'll be the first to know."

It was quiet for a long moment, and Lizzy began pouring batter onto the griddle.

Mamm continued stirring the pot. Then she pensively rested the spoon against the side. "Unless he decides to come back to the community."

Lizzy shook her head. "I don't see that happening. Not as long as the bishop is in charge."

"*Ach*, *jah*, there are many questions. Pray and wait for

Gott to do what's right by our community." Her *mamm* leaned against the counter.

Lizzy frowned. There was nothing anyone could do except the elders. And she couldn't see them acting anytime soon.

"It's not for us to worry over. It's *Gott*'s timing." *Mamm* chucked Lizzy under the chin like she had when Lizzy was a child and went back to her work.

Daed stomped into the kitchen. "*Gut* morning, ladies." He looked around the room. "Where's your *bruder*?" He stuck out his bottom lip as if disappointed Luke wasn't there already.

"It's early yet. The sun's just above the horizon. Can't you see, old man?" *Mamm* teased. If it were up to *Daed*, the whole family would live together for as long as he could keep them there.

"*Ach*, I suppose you're right as usual." He stuck up his nose and guessed what they were making. "Pancakes and bacon with eggs." He frowned theatrically. "What, no lemon cookies? But maybe they don't go together so well." He feinted with one hand over the plate of bacon, wiggling his brows. "How about one for the road?"

"Just go," Mamm told him. "The cows are overdue, and the milk truck will be waiting."

"Ach, he's always late these days. But just in case he's already here, I'll please my wife and set out the milk cans."

He pecked his wife on the cheek and turned to Lizzy. "And you, my daughter. I'd like to know what's going on with Zack Schrock."

His ways always took her off guard. He would soften her and then bring up something he was wanting to know. Lizzy had thought she was clear of having a conversation with her *daed* but should have known better. He was usually loud and talkative, so she hoped he would take over the conversation like he did so well. It was *Mamm* she went to when she needed someone to listen.

"What do you want to know, *Daed*?" It was best to get it over with. She wished he had been there just a few moments ago.

"Being stuck in the dead of winter in a cabin is not what a father wants to hear. But the way things were, I suppose you did the best you could. What I'm concerned about is how you proceed from here."

They were fancy words for her *daed* to use, showing that he was serious about this.

"We were lucky to have the cabin, considering where the storm took us. It was a last-ditch effort to find shelter." She watched his face tighten. "Zack was a perfect gentleman, *Daed*."

He lifted his head, as if hearing what he needed to know. "*Jah*, well, I should hope so. You had us worried. But in this case, I suppose we should be glad things ended well." He scratched the back of his head. "This was one of the times I wish we had telephones."

"*Jah*, but Zack's lost any signal before we even got up there. So they can fail you too."

"I guess I'll have to thank him then. I wasn't sure which way to go with him."

"He's not as bad as people think. He's had a hard life." She stopped herself, wondering whether she'd shared too much. She didn't know who was aware of what Zack had been through. And she wasn't the one to share the information.

"It's no secret the bishop has a lot to atone for when his time is done."

Lizzy wanted to know more, but gossip would only make things worse. The fact that some people knew caused mixed emotions. She felt a little better, but then she felt angry that something hadn't been done.

Daed turned to his wife with a wink. "I'll bring you some fresh milk if you let me take a piece of that bacon." He snatched a piece and munched happily as he walked out to fetch the milk cans.

As Lizzy watched him go, she was all the more grateful to be home again.

Chapter Thirty-Seven

Zack sat in the hospital lounge, waiting for the doctor to approve Clara's discharge. There was no doubt in his mind that she would be coming home. It was Christmas, after all.

Zack's brother sat down right next to him. "Any news yet?"

"No, but it sounds promising." After the words he and his dad had exchanged, Zack wasn't sure what to make of Jonas's hospitable way with him. He supposed when it came to their sister, the barriers were taken down.

"He's a real good doctor. Best around, they say."

"Not much for small talk, but he gets the job done."

"*Jah*, he makes things right by his patients."

"Well, that's what counts."

Although the conversation was awkward, Zack was just glad they were communicating. That made him wonder if Eli might be the same when their dad wasn't around.

"You know Lizzy was promised to another." Jonas stared as Zack lifted his head and turned mechanically to face him.

"No, can't say that I did." A dozen different names came to him as he tried to narrow them down to two or three possibilities. "How long did that last?"

"Not long with the first one." Jonas shook his head. "Her *daed* didn't like him much."

"That doesn't surprise me. I probably wouldn't either."

"*Jah*, I think she always wanted to be with you." He slowly nodded at his own words.

Zack held his emotions inside, hiding the warm feeling that flowed through him when he heard those words. "Why do you say that?"

Jonas shrugged. "She gave you the hardest time."

"That sounds about right." They both chuckled.

"You seem to understand her. Better than I ever could. She's always had a mind of her own, but when I've seen her around you, she's seemed a little softer, if you know what I mean."

Zack knew exactly what Jonas meant. In the community she followed the rules and expected the same from others. At the cabin she didn't have to answer to anyone or be any certain way. She was just herself, the Lizzy he remembered as a young girl, who always knew what she wanted and how to get it.

"And about *Daed*. Just know he's not himself. Hasn't been. The elders try to hide it, but it's so obvious now, it seems silly to keep him going."

"What do you mean? A new bishop?"

"Well, *jah*. The man doesn't have his mind about him." Jonas tugged at his beard. "Sounds harsh, but the community has to think of what's best for all, not just one."

Zack was surprised, even shocked, to hear the words. They hadn't had a relationship for a while now, so Jonas was taking a risk. But then Jonas was always the level-headed one of the bunch.

The nurse walked over to them with a smile. "You can go in now."

"Don't make us wait for an answer...Can she go home?" Jonas pleaded, and Zack let out a long sigh.

She nodded. "Clara is going home for Christmas!"

Jonas offered his hand to Zack and they pumped once. "This is going to be a good holiday after all."

Zack shook his head. "I was as worried about Lizzy as I was for Clara."

"*Jah*, I know what you mean."

"One other thing. What do you think of this guy Clara's gotten to know?"

"He's been a *Gott* send. She made a point not to have her family around when he was there. I wasn't too happy about that, until I found out he was praying and reading the Bible with her."

"Can't argue with that." Zack stood and Jonas followed suit.

They were quiet as they walked down the hall. Maybe there was too much said or not enough, but whatever it was gave them some peace. They stopped at Clara's room. "*Ach*, I sure am glad she can come home."

"Lizzy would be pretty disappointed if she didn't." Zack couldn't even fathom what that would be like, but he had had another plan in the wings if she would have had to stay. "Everything's packed up?" He gave Clara a kiss on the cheek and turned to see what else they might have missed in the room.

"*Ach, jah*. I hope we don't have to come back." Jonas turned as James came in.

He walked up to Clara and tilted his head to see her face better. "I'm going to miss you, Miss Clara." He pursed his lips and looked at her a bit too long for Zack's liking. This man's intentions were most likely right, but it was difficult for an outsider to know the Amish ways and follow their customs.

He moved away from her bed and laid a knitted head covering on the wheelchair. "I want Clara to have this. It will keep her head warm and remind her of me." If nothing else, he knew how to treat a lady. No matter what their friendship entailed, that was what she needed at the moment. They'd worry about this guy after she was comfortably at home.

"Just the thought of her being home again in her own bed will make me happy."

Her cheeks were sallow but had a little pink to them—a good sign, Zack thought. "She won't be needing that head warmer much longer." There was a light at the end of this tunnel, and Zack praised *Gott* for it. He had left *Gott* behind many times in his life, but this was the strongest and hardest faith path he'd ever taken. None had been so fulfilling.

James turned to Zack. "Thanks for sharing your sister with me."

Jonas stuck his hands in his pockets and shrugged. Zack had a good idea they were thinking the same thing.

"You going anywhere for Christmas?" Zack wondered what the rest of the family would say if he invited him to have Christmas with his family. He didn't know how much his family even wanted him there, let alone a stranger.

"If ya got nowhere to go, you can come to Clara's place." Jonas making the offer felt better to Zack than if he had done so himself. He had mixed feelings as to whether that can should have been opened at all. But he wouldn't worry about that now. Clara was finally coming home.

Chapter Thirty-Eight

"A LITTLE MORE GINGER should do it." Lizzy rubbed her nose with the back of her hand and sneezed.

"*Ach*, are you coming down with something?" Her *mamm* was across the room making the Christmas ham.

"So, is Zack coming for Christmas dinner?" Her *mamm* didn't bat an eye, just kept mixing the glaze to cover the large ham.

Lizzy froze, filled with surprise that she would even consider including him in their celebration. She had planned to ask her *daed* if it would be all right to invite him if he didn't have anywhere to go. Lizzy had more feelings for him than her family knew. Zack didn't feel he fit in there, and she understood why.

But no one should be alone on such a joyful day.

"I'd like to invite him." She wasn't really asking. It was more like telling with permission.

"I think he's a nice guy. At least when he was growing up here. I don't think it was Zack's idea to leave."

Mamm had Lizzy's attention, but she didn't want her *mamm* to feel she was telling too much and clam up. She'd had questions about his entire family, but no one ever talked about it.

"Maybe someone should have said something." She thought back to what he'd told her and decided she would tell someone, even if was just Luke or her *daed*. She had to get it off her chest.

"How is the shoofly pie shaping up?" That was *Mamm*'s favorite, and she always asked if it was baked well. She didn't like a hard crust. She came over, took a piece and nodded. "It's *gut*."

"What's *gut*?" Her *daed* walked into the kitchen and looked around the countertops for his favorite treats. Katura and Adah followed him and searched for their favorites too.

"Your applesauce cake is by the sink." *Mamm* pointed him to a half-dozen different kinds of desserts.

Daed held her close. "*Gott* love ya. This is why I married you. You are the best cook around."

"Better than even your *mamm*?" She lifted one brow and got back to work when he didn't answer.

Lizzy was too busy to listen to their chatter, wanting more than ever to make the caramel pie just right. She had to amend her plan to give Clara a gift every day. Instead she'd make the dishes she loved the most. She wanted it all to be just right. Even though she knew it would please Clara, she might not feel up to eating, if she came at all. Lizzy set her eyes on the positive and realized she hadn't finished with the spreads.

"*Ach*, darn it all. Luke doesn't think they can make it. Neva's not feeling well."

Just then Zack walked, pushing Clara in a wheelchair. Everything and everyone slowed down just a little at Clara's presence.

"*Ach*, *frehlicher Grischtdaag*, everyone!" Clara's eyes glistened as they shifted around the room. She patted her woven head covering.

Lizzy hoped Clara would be home for Christmas, but she didn't expect to her to come by. She should have known Zack would know how much she'd want to see her.

"After the hospital released her, Jonas and I took her home. But mom gave me her blessing to bring Clara here." Zack looked down at his sister, thankful that she was out of the hospital and with him and Lizzy on Christmas Day.

Then it was Lizzy's moment to show Clara she was not alone through this time. She slipped the *kapp* off her own bald head and bent down for Clara to see. She'd cut it that morning, and everyone had been too distracted to notice. It wasn't the best job, but considering no one cut hair much, she'd done a pretty good job.

Gasps sounded throughout the room. Clara's hands covered her mouth, and tears stained her cheeks. "I don't know what to say," she whispered, taking it all in.

"You don't need to do or say anything. It's just something I wanted to do. We'll let our hair grow back together."

"*Danke*, sister." When they embraced, Lizzy felt Clara shake. Why, she wasn't sure, but it didn't matter. Clara was home, and because of that it would be the most meaningful Christmas of all.

Zack was standing still and then nodded to Lizzy. She thought he might have meant it for Clara, but she hadn't met eyes with him. She blushed when he continued to stare, and she reached for her *kapp*.

He took two steps toward her and took the *kapp*, then placed it gingerly on her head, but not before he tipped her head up. "You wear that proudly. It doesn't matter what's under it."

Her *daed* wiped his nose and nodded to Zack. Lizzy

had expected their Christmas to be different this year, but she'd had no idea just how different.

"*Ach*! My ham!" *Mamm* ran as fast as her short legs would take her and took out the main dishes—ham, Dutch noodles, green beans, sausage, and dumplings.

"Better every year." *Daed* pecked *Mamm* on the forehead. "Let's pray and bless this food."

As they sat and ate together, Lizzy looked around the room to see and hear the conversations. They were all there except her *bruder* and his wife. The two empty chairs made her miss them even more. But having her cousins and their children there would help make up for it.

Everyone took their time eating; they wanted these hours together to last without everyone rushing off. Even Zack seemed to relax and told stories with the rest of them. As soon as the meal was over, their cousins' children were out the door and playing on the frozen pond or in the snowdrifts from the storm that seemed so long ago. Sleigh rides around the pond kept the children close by but not underfoot so the adults could clean up.

Lizzy found herself hurrying cleanup so she could join the youngsters. When the last dish was squeaky clean, she tapped on Zack's shoulder, and they both went outside. She started in making a snowman. Zack, always the perfectionist, made his snowman look as if it could come to life. The children walked past and stared or reached out to touch it.

Lizzy plopped down on the snow and shivered. Without hair to keep her head warm, she would need someone to make her a hat like Clara's.

"Let me put this on you and don't protest." He put his hat over her *kapp* and smiled. "Looks good on you."

Lizzy looked toward the pond at the children playing, wondering how things had gotten this far and in ways she never dreamed. When she had time alone with Zack, she would tell him about her dreams.

Chapter Thirty-Nine

Luke and Neva finally made it a bit later in the day. With Neva resting at the house, Zack trudged through the snow with Luke and Ray. He had finally gotten around to letting Zack call him by his first name, which suited Zack just fine. Maybe Ray didn't think he was a two-headed monster after all.

"That tree there looks *gut*. Lots of logs for the fire." Luke seemed to just want to get back to the house and check on his wife. She had been doing well since leaving the hospital, but Luke never left her for long.

Ray nodded. "Sure enough, the women will want lot of wood for all that cooking they're doing."

"Timber!" Luke cupped his hands as the eight-foot tree toppled to the ground. Ray looked a little too late and got sideswiped.

"Give a man some warning, would ya?" He sounded fine, but his cheeks were red with annoyance.

"Sorry, *Daed*. I did yell though." Luke knew enough to take the tree and give Ray a rest. He tried to keep up, but his age was showing.

Zack took hold of the trunk, enjoying the smell of fresh cut pine. "This is bigger than I thought." He eyed the width of it and wondered how long it would take to chop it up for firewood. The smell of pine in the fireplace would fill the house.

"*Mamm*'s not gonna like this. It might be too much tree." Luke stirred the waters a little to get Ray going. Ray ignored him and starting humming again. Zack liked Luke's spirit and wished he had some sort of relationship with his own dad. Zack tried to let it go, knowing it was the illness that was making him so difficult these days. It was healthier to think of the bishop in a better light.

Lizzy's *mamm* came out and put a hand over her mouth when she saw the tree. "Oh, my."

"*Jah*, it's a bit much, but it won't last long, with the children coming in from the cold. *Jah*?" Ray was good at persuading people, which came in handy in situations like this.

Lizzy came out and looked from the tree to her *daed*. "*Daed*, what did you do?" She pumped Luke. "And why did you let him?"

Luke shrugged and smiled, not letting on that he'd chosen the tree. "I always do what *Daed* tells me to." There were moans and groans after that comment, considering he'd been quite the troublemaker. Zack had almost forgotten all the mischief Luke used to get in. Somehow, remembering Luke's antics made him feel better about his own behavior as a child.

The men worked on cutting the tree and were about finished when their neighbors showed up. Each person brought a present to give to charity, a custom Zack had forgotten about, and he was sorry for not bringing something. They didn't have ornaments or much Christmas paraphernalia, other than the Christmas candles and the cards the children made. The center was their faith and the birth of a king.

Mrs. Ryder called to everyone, "Come and eat some

of these leftovers. I don't want anything to go to waste." This gave him a reason to find Lizzy in the large, food-filled kitchen that he remembered from his younger years. Lots of desserts were passed around and coffee poured. The chatter went on long after the sweets were gone. The lemon snowflakes on the tree had disappeared, and the children were busy playing.

Zack watched Lizzy walk over to Clara on the couch.

Her stamina must be spent after a full day of people, food, and talking.

He watched them talk, but he couldn't figure out what they were saying. He got up, curious as to what they had started smiling about.

"You need a trim," Clara told her with a grin, referring to Lizzy's head.

Lizzy chuckled. "*Jah*, the nurses probably do a better job than I did."

"You didn't have to do that, Lizzy." Clara's eyes misted, so Zack paused to give her a moment.

"*Jah*, you may be right, but I'm not worried about it.

"The bishop might not see it that way." She touched Lizzy's arm. "I just don't want anything to happen."

"I don't think he'll bother me about it."

Zack knew Lizzy probably wanted to expose the bishop's true condition, but the repercussions might go against Zack if she did. He had always been his dad's scapegoat. Nothing had changed.

"Zack." Clara called him over, her eyes on every step he made. She always made him feel like he was the most important person she knew. Little did she know he felt the same way about her.

"What are you two up to?" He put a hand on each of

their heads and felt the warmth through their *kapps*. It was strange not to see the bun or wisp of hair that usually slipped out of the *kapp*. But the meaning of it, especially at Lizzy's expense, made this Christmas meaningful in many ways.

"I was just going to tell Lizzy that there is a place that took my hair to give to cancer survivors so they can make wigs. The nurses told me about it." Although Clara was tired, her enthusiasm shone through.

Lizzy smiled. "I know. They're making a wig for you with my hair."

"*Ach*, Lizzy..." A tear slid down her cheek. Then Lizzy started in.

"Okay, no more, or I might start crying too." Zack kissed Clara on her head and then leaned over and kissed Lizzy on the mouth.

Clara's brows rose as she watched him walk away. "What was that?" he heard Clara ask Lizzy.

"I don't know," Lizzy said. "But I'm going to find out."

Zack grinned. That was exactly what he wanted her to do. With all that time in the cabin he'd had her to himself; now he wanted to be with her alone for at least a little while. He knew Clara was always tended to well.

He opened the front door, letting the crisp air dry his lungs, and sat on a porch swing watching the boys making snowballs and the girls playing house. He could see how this might become a problem, but it was nothing he hadn't done as a kid.

Lizzy walked out and wrapped her arms around her. "You've started kissing me," she stated, as if he didn't know.

"Yeah, I like it. So I'll keep doing it, if you don't mind."

"I've counted them." She turned toward the little ones making snow angels and smiled.

"Then I should be able to do the same."

She looked at him straight on, taking him in as if studying him for the first time. "That's fair."

He grinned, enjoying their banter but not knowing where they would go from here. As much as he liked this place, it wouldn't ever feel like home to him again. He didn't think Lizzy would leave her family, and he couldn't blame her.

She gazed into Zack's eyes. "You have the strangest look on your face. What are you thinking about?"

"How to make this work—you and me—if it will work at all."

"You went downhill fast. I didn't take you as a quitter... at least not so soon."

"I don't want to, but we might have to." He didn't know if he was making sense, and she wasn't one to tolerate hesitancy. But then, neither was he.

"What does that mean? Are you backing out before we've even started?"

"I think we've been doing *that* since the cabin. By the way, that's where I would be if I had a choice. That time with you, being there alone together, that's what I want."

There. I said it.

He had no idea how she would respond, but she did the worst thing possible. She sat there and stared out at the children having a snowball fight as the twinkling flakes of snow started to come down. She didn't say a word.

"If you have to think about it this long, I'm guessing you're not interested." He stood, embarrassed, vulnerable. He started to walk away, but in a flash of anger he added,

"That was heartless." And he walked away, around the side of the house, and to his car. He just hoped the handle was still attached to the door.

It wasn't, and there he was, without his pride and now on his knees searching for the stupid handle.

Can't wait until I get my nice, expensive car back... Lizzy is embarrassing me just like she did when we were kids... She always teased the guys...

"Are you looking for this?"

Great, she heard that last one. I must have said it out loud.

He reached for it, and she dropped it in his hand. He couldn't get in the car fast enough. His ego was bruised, and she had only made things worse.

Chapter Forty

Lizzy came into the *haus* and decided to get busy. She set down the snacks on the large table. Friendship bread, peach and plum jam with Church Spread should be enough, with maybe some buttermilk biscuits.

Stomping feet from the mudroom filled the kitchen. The younger ones gathered together on the floor. "Gifts! We want to give our presents," said one little guy.

"Just like the wise men did for Jesus." Another popped in, holding up a box from the few that were gathered together in the great room.

Mamm stepped in and stopped when she saw the array of breads and spreads. She scratched her head and then noted Lizzy's mood. "Are you extra hungry this Christmas?"

Lizzy knew Mama was just trying to cheer her up, but she was in no mood to cooperate. She thought of what Christmas would be like with Zack. It would have been so nice to spend the evening with him. She wanted to surprise him with mistletoe. Her *daed* wouldn't like it, but he didn't need to know. She smiled thinking about it, and then frowned. "*Nee*, as a matter of fact, I'm not at all hungry."

"Where did Zack go off to?" *Mamm* took out some napkins and cups for eggnog and cider.

"I'm not sure." Which wasn't a lie. She didn't know where he'd gone. Lizzy didn't want to talk about Zack. The two of them was a ridiculous idea, and thinking about it frustrated her all the more. He'd left the community long ago, and she would never move away, so what was he thinking?

"What are you grumbling about?" Clara stood in the doorway. She looked small and frail when she was standing, especially with no hair to fill out her *kapp*. But then Lizzy's probably looked that way too. "And where is Zack?" She looked around the room, and that made Lizzy feel even worse. She'd taken time away from Zack being with Clara.

"He left." She nodded to Clara and helped her out of the room.

"Is he coming back?" Clara frowned, increasing the line in her forehead.

Lizzy waited to answer until they had gone far enough not to be overheard. "Do you want some fresh air or is it too cold?" They continued slowly out the door and sat on the swing.

"We need privacy, and you've got me worried. What in the world is going on?" Clara stared at Lizzy, waiting for an answer.

"He started talking nonsense. About us being together." She lifted her head. "You know that won't work. Why would he tease me by even talking about it?" We live in two different worlds."

Clara frowned, confused or angry. Lizzy didn't know which.

"Don't misunderstand me. I do like Zack—"

"And he cares for you." Clara's voice was stronger, her stare intense.

Lizzy's head jerked up. She didn't expect such a direct response. "How do you know that?"

"I'm pretty sure everyone suspects you have feelings for each other. Not to mention those nights at the cabin." She tried to hide a smile but couldn't.

Lizzy sucked in air. "Clara, nothing went on up there. You know that, don't you?"

"Jah, I know Zack...and I know you." She grinned, and Lizzy playfully slapped her arm as she went on, "You always were rather prudish."

"Clara!" Lizzy didn't know whether to laugh or cry. This was so not like the Clara she knew. Maybe this experience had loosened her up, changed her priorities. She couldn't help but ask, "Where did this come from?"

"You know James, the *Englischer* I met at the hospital?" Clara's eyes glistened. "We decided that if we both survive this cancer we'll 'go out,' as the English say."

"He's going to court you?" Lizzy could hardly say the words. She'd always known everything about Clara. She wasn't sure she liked this plan of hers. "Whose idea was this?" She thought it must be his and wanted Clara to rethink it. She wanted her to be happy, but this seemed a little extreme.

"He's going to talk to *Mamm* and *Daed* tomorrow. After Christmas, when there won't be so many distractions." She paused and lost her smile. "And you should talk to your parents about Zack."

"There's nothing to say. Why doesn't anyone get that? Can you seriously see me in Philadelphia?" Lizzy scoffed, but her mind was buzzing with ideas of how it could possibly work. She had certainty thought about it. She just didn't think anyone else had. "I'm picturing the sight of my *daed* and yours, with both of us telling them about James and Zack. We might give them heart attacks."

"Hardly." Clara seemed confident. "It might take them by surprise, but I believe they will come around. They love us and want what's best for us."

Lizzy wasn't so sure. They were each considering an *Englischer* to court them. *I don't think that would go well for either of us.* "I wish I had your enthusiasm. I've been pushing it away for so long, I can't get my head around it." She shook her head, thinking that was exactly what her *daed* would do when she asked him.

"Go, find Zack. You look miserable."

"Just thinking. But even if we work things out, I might have pushed Zack too far. You didn't see him when he left."

Clara waved her hand. "Go, no more excuses."

Lizzy kissed her forehead and turned toward the front door. She wasn't sure where Zack might be. The sleigh was still out of the barn, ready for a ride. The evening sun would disappear and make for a cold ride home, but Lizzy decided it was her only choice. She hitched the horse and was ready to hop in when Luke walked up.

"Need a driver?" He climbed in and took the reins, not waiting for an answer.

"Even though you don't know where I'm going?"

"*Jah.*" Luke held out a hand to help her up. "Hang on."

Chapter Forty-One

"I'M GUESSING WE'RE going to see Zack."

The freezing cold forced Lizzy to keep her head down through the fierce wind. She'd never realized how much her hair helped keep her warm.

Gott had a reason for everything—even hair.

"*Jah*, if he'll let me. He left out of sorts." Lizzy wished she could take it all back, stop him from leaving. It had never occurred to her that they could really make things work between them. Maybe that's why he could live in a big city and she couldn't. She wasn't used to taking chances. Things in her world were simple and predictable, for the most part.

Luke slowed the horses when he got close to Zack's family home. "Do you see his car?"

"I don't think he's here, Luke. His *daed* didn't accept him well the last time we came. But I don't know where to go from here."

"*Jah*, I heard something about that. Gossip gets around. I hope Zack didn't take it personal. Although the bishop always did have it in for him."

"I wonder why," she asked herself more than Luke.

"He had his shares of scrapping. Never quite knew why. He seemed pretty even tempered most of the time."

Lizzy looked over at the house and decided she would ask whether Zack had been there. She didn't know where else he would be. "I want to talk to his family to see if he's been here."

Luke hesitated. "I'll go with you." He urged the horses up the small hill to the black-and-white house.

Luke tethered the horses, and they started for the door. "You ready for this?" He didn't seem amused in the least. He was a fixer, kept people and things together. He didn't like drama.

"*Jah*. I hate to bother them on a day like today." Lizzy blew on her cold hands, gathering the nerve to ask about Zack. Shunning meant they ignored the one who left unless they came back to repent. And Zack didn't have any intentions to do that.

"It's just a quick look, and we'll be on our way." He rapped on the door, and Lizzy heard heels hitting the wood floor. It sounded like Zack's mother, for which she was grateful. She hoped she could bypass the bishop altogether.

The door opened, and Zack's *mamm* was silent for a second. "*Ach*, come in. It's nasty cold out there tonight." Once they were all in, she asked very bluntly, "You looking for Zack?" She glanced at each of them in turn.

Lizzy swallowed. "*Jah*, has he been here?"

"Briefly. He was ready to go. Seems like he's always been leaving, independent as he is." Her face flushed as she turned away. "I have some coffee that's still hot."

"*Nee*, *danke*. Do you know where he was going?" She looked tired, worn out, maybe from the Christmas festivities, but she seemed to have aged more than most. Being the bishop's wife had to be stressful at times.

Lizzy turned when she heard boots. One leg dragged a little, and she knew it was the bishop. "Who's there? That Ray's boy?" He squinted and his eyes dropped to Lizzy's.

"And Ray's daughter," Luke offered. "We're looking for Zack. Have you seen him?"

"He stopped by, and we had a meeting."

"*Nee*, *Daed*, the meeting wasn't today. That was a different visit." Zack's *mamm* said it like she was used to setting things right for him.

"Today too. He's leaving again."

"How long ago did he leave?" Lizzy might have spoken too soon, as the bishop gave her a stare.

Luke cleared his throat. "Must not have been too long ago. I saw some car tire tracks when we drove up."

"Do you know where he went?" She knew. He was going back to the city. He had a life there.

"Going to that cabin he likes. Don't blame him. Nice place, that cabin." The bishop mumbled something more and strolled back to his office down the hall.

His wife sighed and seemed to relax a little as her shoulders drooped. "If we see him around, we'll let you know."

If Lizzy didn't know better, she'd think his brother Jonas was the only one in Zack's family who cared about him. Or maybe they just didn't know how to anymore, with the bishop the way he was. She was just glad they hadn't come to blows over the years.

"Evening." Luke nodded to the bishop's wife, let Lizzy out, and then followed her. When they got to the sleigh, they saw the shadow of someone sitting in it.

She couldn't make out who it was at first, but as much as she wanted it to be Zack, she knew it wasn't. She knew him well enough to tell even in just the moonlight.

"Jonas," Luke called out. "What are you doing out here in the cold?"

"Waiting for you. It's freezing in here. It's about time." He patted the bench, urging them to get on.

"What's this all about?" Luke wasn't amused. He seemed to want to find Zack as much as Lizzy did.

"Lizzy, I got a letter for you. Zack said you like letters." He tried to smile, but it was so cold, he didn't bother.

Jonas hopped off and Luke took the reins. "I hope this goes pretty fast." Jonas said, taking a step back.

"We're about to find out." And off they went, despite the freezing cold.

Lizzy reached for the letter and ripped it open with cold, shaking hands.

> Lizzy, I'm at the cabin. I need to think, and my time here with you was one I'll never forget. I was in a bad place when I got here, but time with you changed my anger and frustration into peace and acceptance. I felt God here, where I left Him when I decided to leave and go to Philly. But I realize you can't run from your past or God. You helped me see that. No matter what happens, I'll never forget the cabin and certainly not you.
>
> Completely yours,
>
> Zack

"Completely," she whispered. Luke gave her a stare and frowned. It was a perfect word for what Zack needed.

Not just a part of God, only in hard times. Gott *all the time.*

Chapter Forty-Two

IT WILL TAKE TOO LONG to get to the cabin." Lizzy turned to Luke, waiting for his reply. Luke narrowed his eyes in thought. "Abe might help us out. Let's stop at his place on the way."

Lizzy didn't want to waste any more time but knew it would go better if they made the ride with a Mennonite than an *Englischer*. She watched the two men talk, and when she saw Abe's nod relief went through her.

Abe was quiet for the drive to the cabin, which gave Luke and Lizzy a chance to talk. Abe slowed the car as they got closer.

"It still looks the same as I remember it," Luke said.

"It needs a lot of work, but it's a wonderful place,"Lizzy said.

Luke nodded. "I can see that." He stared at her.

"Don't look at me like that. You're as nosy as Clara."

"We were worried about you."

"Why? Because I was with Zack?" She was looking around for signs of Zack. *What if he's not here after all? What if I came here for nothing?*

"Because you were MIA. I knew you'd be all right with Zack close by." Luke directed Abe to stop before they got too close to a snowdrift.

"*Danke, bruder.* No words of wisdom before I go?" She

desperately wanted some, but she thought she knew what he would say.

"I think Zack's had some hard knocks for the same reasons that some other Amish do. And I don't think leaving was all his idea. There's something there between his *daed* and him. Whatever it was that made Zack do things, I don't think he would have done them otherwise."

"Looks like he's sprucing up the place."

The driveway was covered with salt, and the sidewalk by the door was cleared. A carpenter's belt full of tools was next to it, and smoke billowed from the chimney.

"*Ach*, he doesn't waste any time." Luke turned to her. "I'll wait here with Abe."

"You don't want to come in?" In a way she wanted him to. She didn't know how she would be received after her cold response to what she realized now was an offer of compromise between their two worlds.

He nodded for her to go.

Lizzy hugged him. "That's for sticking your neck out for me. I know *Daed* will get on you for this." She opened the door with a click of the lock and looked back at him with a frown.

He winked and motioned with his hand for her to go. "When you hear the horn, give me the nod if you're coming home with me or ignore me if Zack will bring you back."

Lizzy didn't know whether it would be that easy. The note from Zack was sweet and kind, but he still had things to figure out, and she didn't know how she fit into that process.

She took slow steps to the cabin, not wanting to surprise him, especially since she knew he had a gun around. And she wondered where Leonard was. She looked back once to see Luke watching her. He'd given her *gut* advice during the drive. She didn't know what direction she was going, but whatever it was, she hoped Zack was somehow involved in it.

She walked around the corner of the cabin to see Zack measuring one wall of it. "What are you working on?"

Zack flinched and dropped the measuring tape to his side. "I didn't think you'd come."

"I didn't know I was invited."

"You're always welcome." He shook his head. "I was ridiculous. I knew what I wanted but didn't go about it the right way to get it."

"What was *it*?"

"You." He stared at her and then motioned to the cabin. "And this place. I've never felt closer to God than I did right here, with you, in this dilapidated pile of lumber."

She realized what he had been measuring for. "You're adding windows." She smiled. It had always bothered her that it wasn't lighter in such a big, open place.

"I thought you'd like that."

"So you knew I'd come."

"Yeah, I guess I did." His stare was intense, and his handsome face was strong, with a touch of sun.

"You can't stay here forever."

"You might be wrong about that." He grinned as she eyed him, turning her head to one side. He was a salesman of sorts, making her guard go up.

"Leonard informed me that a Mennonite group actually owns this cabin. There was a disagreement between our Amish and their Mennonite group. I guess some things don't change. Anyway, they don't use the place much and agreed to rent it out." He looked around the place and then back to her. "I thought you might join me."

She grinned. "Zack Schrock, I'm not that kind of girl."

"I beg to differ, after spending time here with you."

She turned a light shade of pink, thinking of the two of them on the couch that morning. "I guess I'd forgotten about that."

He chuckled. "I'm sure you did."

"So is this a proposal?"

"If you want it to be." He took a step closer.

Lizzy thought about her life in the community and then of being with Zack. "What about the community?"

Zack thought about the community, all the pain he'd felt there. There was still a lot of healing to do, but he knew what he wanted to do, what he needed to do.

"I'm going to take my vows with the community. I want to be with you…and with Clara. The bishop may never change his mind about me, but I don't have the strength to stay bitter toward him. I hope to one day be a better dad to my own children. And I know this time will be different."

"It will be different this time. You're going back to your roots, committing to *Gott* when you repeat your vows, not to your *daed*. Everything will hold more meaning this time. No matter what your *daed* says or does, unforgiveness can't keep you apart from us anymore."

Zack smiled down at Lizzy and kissed her until they heard a car horn honk.

"That's Luke. I'm supposed to ignore him if you'll take me back home."

"You never answered. Will you marry me?"

Lizzy laughed up at him. "Yes!"

"I was expecting a *jah*."

"*Jah*, I thought we'd say it both ways."

He put his arms around her and kissed her again. He didn't stop until they heard the sound of a car pulling away. She stepped back and looked up at him and smiled. She knew she had all she needed right here.

AMISH-INSPIRED RECIPES

Amish-style Shoofly Pie Serves 8

This is a take on the sweet gooey pie is a classic Amish dessert.

1 refrigerated pie crust
1 cup all-purpose flour
1 cup packed light brown sugar
¼ tsp. cinnamon
1 Tbsp. butter
¼ tsp. salt
1 egg
1 cup molasses
¾ cup cold water
¼ cup hot water
1 tsp. baking soda
¼ cup chopped pecans (optional)

Preheat oven to 350 degrees. Place pie crust in a 9-inch pie plate and flute the edges.

In a large bowl combine flour, brown sugar, cinnamon, butter, and salt; mix well and reserve 1 cup of mixture.

In a medium bowl combine egg, molasses, and cold water; mix gently and set aside.

In a small bowl mix hot water and baking soda and stir into molasses mixture.

Stir molasses mixture into flour mixture, add pecans and pour into pie shell. Top with reserved flour mixture.

Bake 35–40 minutes. Pie will firm as it cools. Cool completely before cutting.

Amish Sausage Balls Yields roughly 24

1 pound Italian sausage, casing removed
½ cup plain bread crumbs
¼ cup finely chopped onion
⅛ tsp. oregano
½ tsp. basil
1 egg, beaten
2 tsp. vegetable oil
1½ cups ketchup
¼ cup white vinegar
2 Tbsp. soy sauce
½ cup light brown sugar

In a large bowl combine sausage, bread crumbs, onion, oregano, basil, and egg; mix well then form into ½-inch sausage balls.

In a large skillet over medium-high heat, heat oil; brown sausage balls for 5 minutes, stirring occasionally.

Meanwhile in a medium bowl combine remaining ingredients; mix well. Pour over sausage balls, cover, reduce heat to low, and simmer 20–25 minutes, or until no longer pink in the center. Serve immediately.

Note: These are traditionally served over rice or curly noodles. However, these are perfect as an appetizer served on toothpicks.

Church Spread Yields 2 cups

This sweet peanut butter spread can be served on anything from breads to cakes.

½ cup brown sugar
¼ cup water
1 Tbsp. butter
2 Tbsp. corn syrup
¾ cup peanut butter
½ cup marshmallow crème
½ tsp. vanilla or almond extract

In a medium saucepan over high heat, combine brown sugar, water, and butter and bring to a boil.

Stir in corn syrup, reduce heat to low, and simmer 1–2 minutes; remove from heat.

Add peanut butter, marshmallow crème, and vanilla or almond extract and stir until blended. Store in a container in the refrigerator.

Pennsylvania Dutch Green Beans Serves 6

6 bacon slices, chopped
1 medium onion, chopped
1 pound fresh green beans, cleaned, cut in half, and blanched (see Note)
2 large tomatoes, chopped
¼ cup sliced black olives
1 tsp. chopped garlic
½ tsp. salt
¼ tsp. black pepper

In a large skillet over medium-high heat, cook bacon and onion 6–8 minutes, or until bacon is crisp. Add the remaining ingredients and cook 8–10 minutes, or until beans are tender. Serve immediately.

Note: To blanch, cook green beans in boiling water for 3–5 minutes. Drain, then plunge into cold water. Drain again.

Dutch Noodles Serves 6

These buttery noodles are comfort food at its best.

1 8-oz. package medium egg noodles (see Note)
¼ cup (½ stick) butter
2 tsp. caraway seeds
Juice of 1 lemon
2 tsp. chopped fresh parsley
1 Tbsp. chopped chives
1 tsp. salt
¼ tsp. black pepper

Cook noodles according to package directions. Drain and place in a large serving bowl; keep warm.

Meanwhile in a medium saucepan melt butter over medium heat. Add caraway seeds and sauté for 2 minutes. Stir in lemon juice, parsley, chives, salt, and pepper. Pour sauce over cooked noodles, and serve immediately.

Note: Use medium noodles (the ones with curly edges work best) to give the dish an elegant look.

Applesauce Cake Serves 12

1 cup sugar
½ cup vegetable shortening
2 eggs
2 cups all-purpose flour
1 tsp. ground cinnamon
1 tsp. baking soda
½ tsp. salt
1½ cups applesauce
1 tsp. vanilla extract
½ cup chopped walnuts or pecans

Preheat oven to 350 degrees. Coat a 9- x 13-inch baking dish with cooking spray.

In a large bowl cream sugar and shortening with an electric beater on low speed. Beat in the eggs, one at a time. Add flour, cinnamon, baking soda, and salt; beat until well mixed. Add applesauce and vanilla; mix well then stir in the nuts and pour batter into prepared baking dish.

Bake 30–35 minutes or until wooden toothpick inserted in center comes out clean. Let cool.

Note: For a fancier treat, drizzle with a glaze that's made by mixing ½ cup confectioners' sugar and 1–2 teaspoons water or milk for desired consistency Drizzle while cake is still slightly warm.

Amish Friendship Bread Yields 2 loaves

This take on Amish Friendship Bread doesn't require you to pass around the ingredients and wait. Just follow the recipe and enjoy.

2¾ cups flour
1¾ cups sugar
2 tsp. cinnamon
1½ tsp. baking powder
½ tsp. baking soda
½ tsp. salt
1 (4-serving size) box instant vanilla pudding
1¼ cups milk
1 cup vegetable oil
3 eggs
1 tsp. vanilla extract
1 tsp. lemon zest

Preheat the oven to 325 degrees. Coat two 9- x 5-inch loaf pans with cooking spray.

In a large bowl mix flour, sugar, cinnamon, baking powder, baking soda, salt, and pudding mix; set aside.

In a medium bowl whisk milk, oil, eggs, vanilla, and lemon zest. Stir the liquid mixture into the flour mixture and combine well. Evenly divide mixture into prepared pans.

Bake for 55–60 minutes or until toothpick inserted comes out dry. Let cool 15 minutes then invert and finish cooling on wire rack.

Lemon Snowflake Cookies Yields 4 dozen

Here's a simple take on Amish lemon snowflake cookies.

1 box lemon cake mix
2¼ cups whipped cream (approx. 8 oz.)
1 egg
1½ to 2 cups confectioner's sugar (See Note)

Mix cake mix, whipped topping, and egg until well blended. Batter will be sticky. Drop teaspoonfuls of the batter into confectioner's sugar and roll them around to coat. Place on ungreased cookie sheet and bake at 350 degrees 8–10 minutes until golden brown and tops are slightly cracked. Cool and enjoy.

Note: For extra lemony cookies, make a glaze with 1 cup confectioner's sugar and 1½–2 tablespoons lemon juice and drizzle over the cookies before they cool.

Mixed Berry Jam Yields about 16 ounces

This simple jam makes a great gift. Just spoon into small mason jars and decorate with ribbon. Lovely and delicious.

1 cup blueberries
1 cup blackberries
1 cup raspberries
¾ cup honey
2 Tbsp. lemon juice
1 Tbsp. lemon rind

Place blueberries, blackberries, and raspberries in a medium saucepan. Mash with the back of a fork. Add honey, lemon juice, and lemon rind, and bring to a boil. Boil for 15–20 minutes. You will be able to tell it is done by putting a spoonful in the freezer. If after 5 minutes the jam does not slide off the spoon easily, it is done. Store in small mason jars or glass container.

Recipe courtesy of Candace Ziegler

Caramel Corn Yields about 15 cups

Make this fun snack with the kids, or if you can manage not to eat it all, give this as gifts. It keeps for weeks in a tin with a well-sealed lid. You can also package it in cellophane bags and tie with ribbon for individual treats. Always cool completely before packaging.

15 cups of popped corn (plain)
¼ cup light corn syrup
1 cup brown sugar (packed)
½ tsp. salt
½ cup butter
½ tsp. baking soda

Heat oven to 200 degrees. Divide popped corn between two ungreased 9- x 13-inch baking pans.

In saucepan, heat sugar, butter, corn syrup and salt, stirring occasionally, until bubbly around the edges. Continue cooking over medium for 5 minutes.

Remove from heat; stir in baking soda until foamy. Pour onto popped corn, stirring until popcorn is well coated. Bake 1 hour, stirring every 15 minutes. Let cool and enjoy.

Recipe courtesy of Donna Schrader

Pumpkin Bread Yields 3 loaves

Loaves of bread are wonderful gifts. Just wrap them up tight, decorate with a bow, and *voila!* Whether making it for home or for friends, this pumpkin bread is sure to please.

3 cups sugar
1 cup canola oil
1 16-oz. can of pumpkin
⅔ cup water
4 eggs (beaten)
3½ cups flour
2 tsp. baking soda
2 tsp. salt
1 tsp. cinnamon
1 tsp. baking powder
1 tsp. ginger
½ tsp. ground cloves

Preheat oven to 350 degrees. Cream sugar and oil. Add pumpkin and water. Add beaten eggs. Then add all dry ingredients. Grease and flour pans and bake according to directions below.

3 medium loaves: 1–1½ hours
4 small loaves: 40–45 minutes
25 muffins: 25–35 minutes
Recipe courtesy of Rebecca Stokes

Coming From Beth Shriver Winter 2015

The Spirit of the Amish Book Two

Love's Abundant Harvest

Chapter One

THE HORSES STOMPED their impatience as Lucy Wagner scooped a pail full of oats. The dust lifted into the early morning sunlight as she dumped the feed into the bin. Lucy filled a large container with cane for the cows, gentle creatures waiting for their due.

"You're slow today." Her husband, Sam, didn't stop walking, even though he catered to his right hip, a sure sign the cold was causing an ache in his bones.

"The babe's kicking." She put a protective hand on her belly as he glanced down at the bulge in her stomach. The familiar silence swelled with each step.

"It's hot." She wished she had a handkerchief to wipe off her sweaty brow and envied the one Sam had around his neck.

"You're always complaining about the heat." He checked her work to make sure the teat cups were clean.

"*Nee*, you're just cold-blooded," she mumbled, and dropped her shoulders as if to hide from the knowledge that his was the coldest of hearts she'd ever known. The sweat trickled down her face, seeping over the scar on her left cheek that served as a constant reminder of what happened one fateful night. She would never think the same about her appearance again.

She brushed the thoughts to a faraway place.

He grunted and looked up over her head. Being a good

five inches taller than she, it was customary for him to look around but not at her.

Lucy couldn't get used to the Pennsylvania weather. It was plenty cold for about three months every winter, and then it started to warm up again.

Sam handed her a bottle of milk from the cooler and turned toward the *haus*.

Her mind wandered to musing over what her sisters were doing about now down in Tennessee. Being the youngest of six girls had left her lonely and discontented when two of them moved to Colorado to join the new community there. Her heart wrenched to see her sisters go, so much so her *mammi*, Frieda, had come for a visit and ended up staying when she found out Lucy was in a family way. Now that she was pregnant, visiting Tennessee was out of the question, which meant family would have to come to her, namely her *mamm*.

She worried about her *daed*'s health, but her *mamm* was well. Lucy shook her head when reading the letters her sisters sent subtly mentioning a hurtful word or action. Her *mamm* Hochstetler was an uncompromising woman who expected strong daughters. Lucy would honor her *mamm* as God commanded, but she found it necessary to hold fast to Christ's commandment to love Him with all her heart, soul, and mind in order to gain strength for the challenge.

"Lucy, pay attention." Sam's stern voice broke into her thoughts as she looked up in time to keep from running into him from behind.

"Sorry, Sam." Lucy looked past him and walked to the barn door. As she cracked open the heavy door, the wind slapped her cheeks. She paused to wait for it to die down as she scanned Sam's farm. A tall silo filled with grain and corn along with other harvested crops, the largest in the community, was a beacon on the plains.

Sam shut the gate to the back pasture, then walked through the barn. "What are ya waiting for? The wind's not gonna stop blowing today."

"I wanted to go through the barn instead of going around to let the dogs out." She waited. He didn't respond, a rarity for him; he usually wanted the last word.

He frowned. "You go ahead. I'll let 'em out and catch up with you at the *haus*."

When the swirl of dirt and leaves slowly disappeared, she opened the barn door just wide enough to fit through and shut it tight behind her. Pulling down her *kapp*, she walked quickly to the *haus*. It was much larger than she felt they needed, but Sam wanted to have room to grow a family.

Their border collie ran to her and bounded straight up in the air with excitement. "Skip, stay down." She looked around to see what had him stirred up. A buggy rumbled down the lane, a surprise, considering how rare it was to have unexpected visitors here, in contrast to Lucy's Tennessee experience. There she had enjoyed the large community where she spent time with her sisters and made new friends. At Sam's place she was forced to make herself invisible.

Abner Umble pulled the horses to a stop. His place was just behind them to the south, behind the Ecks. He was a bit crotchety but always kind enough to bring them the mail. "Gall darn, its hot today."

His gravelly voice made Lucy want to clear her throat.

"Would you like to come in for coffee?" She kept walking, feeling a bit rude, but it was too hot to stand still.

When he didn't answer right away, Lucy wasn't offended; Abner knew she was not the best cook. Uncommon for an Amish wife, but with five older sisters, she spent more time helping her father than her sisters, whom her *mamm* had taught to do the domestic work. Some had done the cooking; others had taken care of the mending and laundry while she and her sister Fannie, the next youngest, learned how to best help *Daed* work the land and tend the livestock.

"I might need a little coffee this morning." Abner climbed the steps carefully and took out a hanky to wipe his stubbly nose. "Got a letter for ya. Looks like somebody back home." He flipped the letter over and read the return address again. "One of your sisters."

If he were anyone else, Lucy might have taken offense at his prying, but the fussy old man had grown on her after his wife became ill. "Thanks for saving us the trip to the mail box, Abner. I know we should check it more often, but sometimes that community mailbox seems so far away." The community mailbox was located next to the store by the frontage road. Considering she and Sam were at the other end of the community, they didn't check all that often.

Abner shut the door behind him and sat at one of the eight chairs in the kitchen. The table was large, but the room was big enough to hold it, with plenty of space to work around. Lucy had tried to add some color with the rugs she'd hooked, and she had made the quilt that was draped over the rocking chair.

Lucy started the coffee and stirred up some eggs,

sausage, and grits with gravy. Her *mammi* had taught her how to make a few more dishes, but she mainly cooked breakfast food. It was easier, and she always had the ingredients needed.

She handed Abner a cup of coffee and poured one for herself. "How are you and Grace, Abner?" Even though they were neighbors, they both had big farms so they didn't see one another often, and she knew how the weather made his knees ache.

"Me and the missus are getting along. She complains of ailments, but I figure it's just old age." He slurped the coffee and winced. Lucy did too. "She's finally catching up with her old husband." He grinned with affection, something Lucy wished and prayed for from Sam.

"Would you like some cream?" Her hands were still sweaty from doing the morning chores, so she handed the creamer cup to him to pour.

"And sugar, if you'd be so kind." He handed her the mail. "Just so I don't forget."

She'd walked back to the kitchen cabinet to get another mug when she heard Sam enter the mudroom. The gravel under his boots crunched against the floor, annoying her that he didn't take a moment to wipe his feet.

The three-page letter was written in fine penmanship. Abner talked about the weather as if she wasn't preoccupied, but she couldn't pull away. The more she read, the faster her heart beat and her breathing sped up. By the end of the last sentence she felt her face flush with anxiety.

"Abner." Sam glanced at him, but his eyes stopped on Lucy. "What's wrong with you?" He grabbed the letter and glanced at it just long enough to understand.

Abner looked at one, then the other, thoroughly confused. "Did someone die?"

Lucy's shoulders slumped, and she closed her eyes. "*Nee*, *Mamm* is coming. My sister had her baby not long ago, so she must be ready for her *mamm* to move on up here."

Lucy had hoped she wouldn't be with her *mamm* alone, without her sisters by her side.

The one time Sam had met Lucy's family, he'd said he'd never forget it. They were independent women, and so many. And then there was *Mamm*, a beautiful woman with sharp eyes and a sleek build who ran her house like a business more than a place to call home.

Abner studied her as he set his cup on the table. "Who's her *mamm*?"

"My *mamm*…" A sigh lifted from her chest as she said the word. Given her *mamm*'s strict parenting, the title *Mamm* never quite fit in Lucy's mind. The name automatically came in her internal thoughts, but she was respectful enough to refer to her as her *mamm* out loud.

"Maybe she doesn't need to come just yet," Abner counseled.

"*Nee*, it'll be fine." Lucy looked at Sam.

"*Jah*, sure"

Nee, it wouldn't. But he wouldn't tell her that with company in the room, and there wasn't any way to tell her *mamm* no. Lucy was in her third trimester, which was probably the reason for her visit.

"How many of them?" Sam sat and waited for Lucy to bring his coffee.

"Just *Mamm*, as far as I know." That kicked the wheels turning. If she could get Fannie to come stay for a while, it might be manageable. The second youngest, with some fire in her, was just what Lucy would need to get through the visit. Sam was not a hospitable man; he barely spent time with his own family, let alone hers.

"Though maybe a sister or two, as well." Saying two were coming might make him agree to just one. Guilt sank through her chest. She disliked manipulating Sam, but she'd learned it was a matter of survival living with him. She was sure if she didn't find a reprieve in some small way, she would lose her mind. Her loveless marriage and difficulty conceiving, along with a miscarriage, gave her little hope she could please her husband.

The thought made her stop and pray for her unborn child's strength and growth.

Sam's lips turned white as he pressed them together. "Your *mamm* might want some time alone with you."

When his nose lifted after taking a sip of his coffee, she quickly handed him some milk, but bumped the table and spilled the contents of the pitcher. A trail of the cream crawled off the table onto Sam's lap. He slapped the wooden table and stood, wiping his pants with a cloth napkin.

Lucy couldn't get there fast enough. She stopped the trail of milk and righted the creamer cup, avoiding his eyes. "I'm sorry." She took the napkin to the sink, listening to his work boots hitting the wood floor as he left the room.

Awkward silence radiated in the room in which Lucy was never comfortable and couldn't do anything right—not even make a cup of coffee or clean up a simple mess without making it worse.

"I'm sorry, Abner." Not wanting to face him, she continued squeezing the napkin, watching the white turn clear. She could hear his lopsided gait as he walked closer to her.

"A *mamm*-to-be shouldn't be so upset about such things." Abner tapped Lucy's arm. "Whether you're with child or not, for that matter."

All she could do was nod, unable to turn and look at him with the tears threatening to spring.

"Maybe I should go. You let me know if you need me, ya hear?" He slipped out the door and was gone, leaving her alone to receive her husband's wrath.